Untold Truths

A Talia and Dozer Novel

Stacie Ann Leininger

Published by:
Leininger Company
Albany, N.Y.

ISBN: 9798879411270
Copyright 2023 ©Stacie Ann Leininger
This literary piece is an original by Stacie Ann Leininger
copyright first draft © 2019.

Front cover by: Stacie Ann Leininger

DEDICATION

To The College of Saint Rose English Department.
Members of your department taught me many things.
These two have been the most helpful as I struggled to pull my life
back together after a serious mental breakdown:
1. Always strive to be a better writer
and
2. "Hope is only lost when you choose to let go.
The key is to never let go."

ACKNOWLEDGMENTS

A special thank you to the volunteers of the Guilderland Fire Department for being patient with me as I pulled together this series. You are my family.

Thank you to all of the beta readers and proofreaders who helped me through the nine re-writes of this novel.

PROLOGUE

Contempt seeped into my voice, "I swear he's Fabio's love child."

"Next month, your unemployment runs out." Mom's voice came through my car's speakers, and I felt her glare. "I don't care if he has a face like Popeye."

Mom wasn't listening to me. Throughout the pandemic, I had remained unemployed, and I was returning home from another bad interview. Out of complete frustration, I slammed a fist on the steering wheel. An armadillo-shaped, leather-scented air freshener swayed from the rearview mirror.

To push my point further that this was a bad fit, I retorted, "His chest hair shown through a sheer silver shirt."

"Talia Anne Morgan."

The use of my full name in the angry Mom voice stunned me. I attempted to collect my composure as I rounded a corner. The mid-day sun flashed off the hood of my car blinding me.

A muffled female scream mingled with my mother's gasp.

Vision returned; I saw a corgi trot into the road.

"Mom," I swerved to miss the dog.

A horn blared. I overcorrected back into my lane and skidded across the road's edge.

My mother's distant voice was hoarse, "Help me, Talia."

"Mom!" I wailed as my foot slipped onto the gas.

CHAPTER 1

"Talia Anne Morgan." Mom's voice echoed in my mind.

How is it that even when you're in your forties, the use of your full name polarizes you? This time, the emotional slap was as harsh as the airbag's deployment.

My cell phone rang.

I wasn't in the right frame of mind to take the call. I reached into the pockets of my sagging pants and hit the ignore button. The distracted driving ticket and the cost of a new telephone pole had made it impossible for me to buy new clothes. Since the 2020 lockdown hadn't been kind to my waist, I was forced to borrow a polyester suit that was two sizes too large and made me itch.

A chirp let me know that the person left a voicemail.

This wasn't the time for conversations. I had been thrown into a life I didn't want, and my breakfast pumpkin spice latte wasn't sitting right.

Most likely, the call was another person sending me their condolences. I'd appreciate the calls better if they offered to help me pay for a new car. As it was, my ride to bury my seventy-six-year-old mother was running late.

The last time we talked, all Mom wanted to do was discuss her internet dating adventures while I steered the conversation to me. I flicked on the galley kitchen's overhead lights.

Stacks of aluminum foil-covered containers lined the counters. I checked my reflection in the toaster. The blurry image reminded me of a pale Picasso painting. I whimpered. I was, making mom's services about me.

Guilt, my arch nemesis, tugged at my emotions. I tried to push her aside as I threaded my light-brown hair into a ponytail.

The 1970s olive green refrigerator hummed like a helicopter approaching a landing pad. Anger flashed through me. I tore the pictures off of Mom's beloved appliance and tossed them in the junk drawer; it didn't help.

My cell phone rang. This time, I checked the caller ID. It was Dozer. Seeing his name melted away all my trepidations.

His real name is Stuart Wemple. This man has a perpetually tanned muscular body that stands five feet five inches tall. He has a heart of gold and is my best friend.

Nothing is known about Dozer's birth family as he was

adopted by a B-list actress when he was a few months old. That actress had expected him to attend an Ivy League law college to make great changes in the world. Instead, Dozer forged his own path as a world-class pastry chef.

Dozer and I met a few days after he opened his first bakery, and I was an undergraduate at The College of Saint Rose daydreaming of being a successful author.

I answered the phone. "When did we descend to Hell?"

"When that vicious attack dog bit my ass."

A few months back, an intruder woke Dozer around midnight. He grabbed his pistol, dialed 911, and barreled after a dark-clothed masked man. A full moon lit Dozer's way as he raced through vegetable gardens, across patios, and hopped a fence which landed him next to an occupied doghouse. Ninety-nine stiches later, the doctors had Dozer doped up on painkillers that had him signing Country Western songs. He prefers classical music.

"It was a Chihuahua!"

"Hey!" Dozer voice deepened to threatening rumble. "There's no humor in butt stitches."

I snorted. It's difficult to remain serious when someone says, "butt stitches."

"It's better than that college job of yours."

Irritated, I opened the refrigerator in search of milk. "Did you say getting bit by a rat-sized dog was better than bartending?"

"I call it like I see it."

He didn't know the full story behind that awful job. For our twenty-first birthdays, my cousin Franky and I made a bet as to who could get the worst possible job. I tended bar in walking distance of my college while Franky was hired at a sewage processing plant. It's clear who won that bottle of gold label tequila.

My first week as a bartender was a disaster. In addition to mixing up most of the drinks I was assaulted by an aspiring male supermodel, in front of everyone at that establishment.

While the vast majority stood in stunned silence, a person streaked past me. Moments later, my assailant lay in a crumbled bloody mess, insisting he'd been hit by a bulldozer.

My savior sat on a bar stool glowering at my assailant. Once it dawned on me what had happed, I poured the gorgeous stranger a complimentary drink, and called him "Dozer."

That gesture earned me my first glimpse of his dangerous,

deep-dimpled grin. Twenty years and a divorce later, our friendship was stronger than a refrigerator's hinges.

I struggled against the wobbling door. "This house needs new appliances." I kicked aside a plastic bag of kale. "And food."

I allowed myself to relax when the door clicked closed.

"As long as the new food isn't your aunt's herbal brownies."

"Is it a sin if I leave her brownies for the others to eat?" I asked.

"Yeah."

I lifted a corner of aluminum foil to peek inside a plastic serving bowl. "What sick person puts chopped up maraschino cherries in oatmeal cookies?"

"If you'd like to see worse, I know a private investigator who's hiring."

"No." I sealed the covering on the dish and slid it next to a dented chrome espresso machine. "Whatever happened to real comfort food? Like those rainbow cookies from the Italian bakery."

"Tomorrow's breakfast: nut-free marzipan cookies." Dozer's soothing voice was a warm hug. His ex-wife was oblivious to what she threw away.

"Thanks."

I opened the liquor cabinet door. There sat a Chardonnay bottle. My parents had received it as a wedding gift in 1979. A faded tag read: "To be enjoyed on your 50th Anniversary. Cory Jackson, Sr."

"This is overwhelming." I checked the microwave's clock. "Crap. It's quarter to two. Mom's interment is in fifteen minutes. Franky's late again."

"What?" Dozer's deep voice went up half an octave. "No need for Franky to help. My sons and I will transport the food to the VFW while you're at the cemetery."

"Um." I sucked in air.

This wasn't a conversation I wanted to have. I didn't want to impose on either of Dozer's sons, and the only reliable thing about my cousin Franky is that he's unreliable.

"Talia, what aren't you telling me?"

I picked up the letter from Mom's attorney and set it on the counter next to the sugar bowl. I needed answers from Franky and that mean one thing, "He's driving me to the cemetery."

"Don't funeral parlors provide limos for transporting the bereaved?"

"That's an extra cost."

"Whatever the cost, I'd have paid it. Heck, I'd have hired a biker to drive you. That'd be safer than your cousin's driving."

I cringed at the image he conjured. Instead of morning attire, I was in riding leathers, balanced on the back of a motorcycle, clutching my messenger bag.

"How's George?" I changed the topic.

George, Dozer's youngest son, is a college freshman. His major is yet to be decided. Since they hadn't been able to spend any time together, during the pandemic, Dozer and both of his sons went on a month-long cross-country adventure in a rented RV. They were in Montana when Mom passed. The three Wemple men returned to New York as fast as the gas guzzler traveled.

Dozer disconnected.

I tossed the phone on to the counter next to the six-inch-high rectangular box that contained my Mother's ashes and hurried down the hall. I passed the three bedrooms and paused at the threshold of the bathroom. A thump followed by a scratching noise overhead caught my attention.

"Not another squirrel family." I shook a fist at a cluster of cobwebs clutching to the corner of the ceiling. Rodents loved to nestle into the attic's cotton-candy insulation.

I crept to the bathroom to check myself out in the mirror. The neat light-brown ponytail rested at the nape of my neck. Barely noticeable creases sat at the corners of my bloodshot, blue eyes and a long gray hair poked out of my thin eyebrows.

"Dang it." I opened the medicine cabinet for tweezers. A bottle of pills fell into the sink. I plucked them up and stared at the label. "ADHD meds?"

CHAPTER 2

A musical muffled horn broke the silence. It was *Shave and a Hair Cut*: Franky's way of announcing his arrival.

I shoved the bottle of ADHD medication back on the shelf and closed the cabinet door. My sneakers slapped against the hard floor as I rushed to living room. I yanked my messenger bag off a cushioned recliner, snagged the box containing Mom's ashes from the kitchen counter, and ran out of the house, slamming the metal door behind me.

Franky sat behind the wheel of a beat-up 1992 half-ton pickup truck. My cousin is six months younger than me, a couple inches taller, and still has the gangling physique of a twelve-year-old. I wrenched open the door.

"Get in. I ain't your paid limo driver," Franky's high-pitched voice yelled at me. "Fashionably late is one thing. If you take any longer, my mom will lock me in the crypt alongside your parents."

I leaned into the truck. Franky's slicked-back dark hair and black suit made him look like a character from *The Godfather*. His Sicilian father wouldn't approve.

"Are you wearing bargain cologne?" I pulled a face mask out of my messenger bag and covered up. By the smell of it, I guessed he paid a dollar a gallon. "Even three layers of cotton doesn't help."

"Stop overreacting. We ain't got all day."

"When are you going to upgrade your truck?"

Franky knocked empty beer cans off a Betty White seat cover. "I'll upgrade when the government stops tracking us through G.P.S. locators."

An argument was unnecessary. Franky's stubbornness was inherited from his mother. I tossed a dozen cans onto the front lawn. "Haven't you learned from the last DWI?"

"If you ever need an attorney my guy is good. Plus, the amount of business I bring, he'll give you the family discount."

"No doubt." I slid onto the passenger seat, struggled to pull the door shut and clicked my seatbelt into place.

Franky backed alongside the garage. "You'll get through this. I wish I had better advice. Your life sucks."

"Heaven help us if you have children. They'll have the comforting abilities of a rock."

The truck lurched forward past a 1960s brick house; its yard was a sea of colors. A pink angel rested on the top of a birdbath that peeked over the heads of a gaggle of lawn gnomes.

Franky whistled. "And people say I have issues."

"Dude. You're driving me to my mother's funeral that starts in ten minutes and the cemetery is a half an hour away."

"That ain't got nothing to do with lawn gnomes worshiping Catholic Saint statues."

Spinning in my seat, I strained to see a red pointed hat touching the chin of a three-foot-high statue. "St. Nicholas, the patron Saint of reformed thieves?"

"I didn't know gnomes were Saints."

"St. Nicholas," I corrected.

"Santa Claus?"

"Forget I spoke."

Franky turned onto Carman Road and jabbed a thumb to the side. "Nice telephone pole you got there. You think the town would move it a few feet in, make it harder to hit when you've had a few."

"I wasn't drinking. I swerved to miss a dog."

"Right." He winked at me.

I gave him a playful shove. "Jerk."

"Back at 'cha." That was Franky speak for 'I love you.'

Yup, us Morgans are great at subtext translations when it comes to immediate family. "I got a letter from Mom's attorney about the reading of her will. Are you going?"

"So far, no letter to me. And why did your ma need a will? You're her only child." He made the left onto Western Avenue the main strip of road in the town of Guilderland. "She didn't have anything of value. Unless..." He gasped. "Aunt Gladys was the mystery Powerball winner who stashed away the five hundred-million-dollar ticket."

"First off: Mom didn't play the numbers. Second: It was a five hundred-thousand-dollar lotto ticket." I shouted. He pretended to be deaf. I continued. "If you go on a conspiracy theory tangent, I'll tell your mother about that time you and your buddies stole the Greulich's cow to use it for a bar-b-que."

Franky faced me. "That was low."

"Watch the road!"

"You'll never let me live that down." Head forward, Franky growled.

"You tried to cut the head off a cow made of fiberglass."

The truck sped up. "Anyone could have made that mistake."

"The cow was bolted on top of a grocery store!"

I contemplated jumping out of the truck.

"Such a stickler for details."

I redirected the conversation back to where I started. "My mother's siblings and nephews can lay claim to anything of Mom's."

"Her family don't count. They abandoned Aunt Gladys when she married Uncle Jonathan because our side of the family is dominantly Dutch not Polish."

"We can discuss this another time. Just drive."

We bounced as the truck hit a pothole. Franky whined, "Those are going to ruin the suspension."

"Slow down and you won't have to worry about that."

Franky skimmed by a yellow Corvette, a white Guilderland police cruiser, and a couple of downtrodden hand-cuffed teenagers sitting on the side of the road.

"You should've stopped to give those kids your attorney's information," I said.

"I only refer people I know." He ran a red light. "I've had Pickles on retainer since he started his law career. Man, those were the days. His first office was by the Mohawk River, out of the trunk of his car."

The irony didn't sneak by me. I regrated having to ask for Pickle's help. Sadly, he was the only attorney in my budget.

"Anyways." Franky cut off a public transit. "I got that empty bar below Dozer's apartment."

That was an unexpected change. In June, while Dozer was recovering from the dog attack, his bakery had been destroyed by rodents. It was too much to handle.

Once he was able to work again, he was offered a maintenance job at a downtown Albany Victorian rowhouse apartment complex. In exchange, he lived there rent-free. I didn't even know he owned a hammer, let alone knew how to sweat solder a pipe. This maintenance job was a way to help Dozer restart his life except a week after he moved in, Raphael, the owner of the bar on the first floor, vanished.

Since the pandemic, the crime rate on that strip of road skyrocketed. During the bar's second renovation, construction workers called Albany police as they hadn't been able to enter the building for three days. On the postage stamp–sized dance floor a young detective found a letter of complete indignation.

Franky shrugged. "I hear the Feds found the last maintenance guy sneakers up in Arizona, congestive heart failure. Left his worldly possessions to a guy in Ohio."

We came up to the hairpin turn. The truck leaned as if it was going to tip over. I pressed my foot hard against the imaginary brake on the passenger side and said a prayer requesting that I arrive at the cemetery alive.

The road straightened out, so did the truck. Franky glanced down at the dashboard. "Your boyfriend pulled a favor for me and got the landlord to let me rent the place at a fraction of what the other guy paid. He called it the 'pandemic discount.' I think he feels sorry for me after that serial killer used my identity and all."

"He isn't my boyfriend, and he doesn't pull favors."

That was one of Dozer's quirks from having grown up in a wealthy well-connected family.

The dashboard clock flickered 2:05. The screen went dark. I glanced at the speedometer: 70. I clenched my jaw.

Franky's arms shook as his truck rattled. "The best part, I get to keep everything Raphael left behind. All I gotta do is finish sprucing her up."

"That doesn't sound right."

"Nah, it's made that noise since March. I did a few upgrades. You can learn to do anything from those Internet videos."

The thought of my cousin working on anything mechanical was enough to give me heart palpitations. "You should leave truck repairs to trained professionals."

"You worry too much. Now, back to my bar. The decor isn't quite my style and I have a plan to fix it up nice. Tomorrow, I'm hitting up the Schenectady Police auction for items."

Raphael is a minimalist who had taken painful measures to create a warm welcoming place where people stayed a while to enjoy themselves. I was afraid about the new ambiance.

I thumped my palm against my forehead. "This is your worst idea yet!"

"When 'The Bar' opens up, you'll take that back."

"You're opening a bar named 'The Bar'?"

"It'll put me high up on the search engines."

He almost made sense. I didn't want to encourage him. Once

he has an idea in his mind, there's no reasoning. You let it play out and hope you don't get caught up in the smoldering aftermath.

"Since you're unemployed and tended bar for a few years in college this will help you out too."

"No."

"It's not like you got anything going on."

He had to add that last jab. My stagnant life needed a resuscitation not an exorcism.

Mom's sudden death had me thinking about where I was going. I had gone to college to be a professional writer. In my senior year, I discovered that career path paid less than working a slushie machine.

That last part was what led Franky and me to wager a college bet. It still disturbed me the lengths he went to win.

A smudge on the front windshield almost made me miss a state trooper parked in the median. His head picked up as we passed.

"The auction will be fun." Franky tapped the brake. Nothing happened. "There's plenty of crap acquired in raids that can cheer up the place." He tapped the brake again. "Who needs brakes anyways?"

Light flashed behind us.

I glanced at Franky's speedometer. "The speed limit's fifty-five. You're going to make me miss my Mom's funeral." I held up the wooden box. "And I'm the one who has her!"

"Not a big deal. I'm doing three over the limit."

The half-ton pickup lurched forward.

"Thirteen!" I shouted over a loud bang.

"What?"

"You're going thirteen miles over the speed limit." I tried to be heard over a deafening rattling noise.

"Nah, that speedometer broke last month." Franky's head reminded me of a fishing bobber in the ripples of lake water. I guess if I had gotten pulled over once a week, I'd have his attitude too.

The trooper pulled alongside of us. I gave a palms-up surrender gesture. He didn't react.

The truck rattled to a halt in the middle of a four-lane highway. I watched in the side mirror as black smoke spewed from the rear.

CHAPTER 3

Oblivious to the time, I flung the taxicab's door open, and collected my things. I dashed toward the throng of people waiting in the afternoon sun, by my family's crypt, in the Albany Rural Cemetery.

Since the Morgan family was part of Guilderland's original settlers, many were bewildered that our family's last resting place wasn't located in the Prospect Hill Cemetery on Western Avenue. I decided it was best not to tell anyone our crypt was won during the Civil War in an illegal card game.

When my great-grandfather, the family crypt's first occupant, had been laid to rest, a Union Flag had been draped over a hand-carved, oak casket. His grief-stricken bride sat next to the undertaker as their horse and buggy made the foreboding trek across gravel roads. Their arduous multi-hour-long ride would have been more relaxing than Franky's daredevil chauffeur attempt, which was followed by my brazen leap over the Northway's center divider to hail a cab.

My sneakers squished in thick damp grass as I circumvented a row of weather-worn stones.

"Hey lady!" The driver yelled. "My services ain't free!"

A man dressed in blue jeans and a black long-sleeved shirt slid out from the crush of people. He pulled a wad of cash out of his back pocket.

"Thanks," I yelled and hurried to the pillared stone structure where several people stood at the edge of an open metal gate.

Five years earlier, I had witnessed my father's casket being sealed into the wall. When I made the call to have my Mother's ashes locked inside I was informed, she'd be the last as the mausoleum was at capacity.

The elderly priest's frail voice was louder than the pounding in my head. "Did your cell battery die?" He extended liver-spotted hands that shook like they were possessed and accepted the box containing my Mom's ashes.

Lungs screaming for air, I cursed myself for being out of shape. I panted out the words: "Can you make this a quick service?"

The priest held up a tattered pocket Bible.

"Thank you for not making us wait any longer." Aunt Edna's distinctive one-cigarette-pack-a-day voice could be heard over whispered complaints from mourners. "Unlike Talia, my son had the good sense to call. He told me the muffler fell off his truck. A kindhearted state trooper stopped to help my poor Franky."

It wasn't my place to tell her the truth. No reason to worry a woman who had recently undergone extensive body transforming surgeries.

The fine hairs on the back of my neck stood up. A plump man in a tweed suit approached me. His bulbous nose, receding hairline, and posture reminded me of the character Gargamel.

"My condolences." He held out a meaty hand to shake mine.

I stared at the thick black hair on his knuckles as I shook his clammy hand.

"Unless you count massage parlors; there isn't much for me to do in this area." An elderly woman shouted.

She had the full attention of all two dozen mourners.

"Sure there's mall walking, dancing at the Senior Center, Tarot readings, and events held at the library. Heck, we can't do crimes like the surrounding areas. Sure we have misdemeanors, cheating spouses, break-ins, and a other infractions that happen anywhere people live. Except, those don't run the gossip mills like murder."

"Grandma Sanchez," a woman stage whispered. "Her daughter is behind us. And for the last time, Gladys died of a heart attack."

"That's what you say." The elderly woman raised her voice. "I was hoping to see Ezekiel here. Gladys bought that frilly shirt for their upcoming date."

The plump man in front of me scurried away. If it wasn't my Mom's funeral, I'd have bolted as well.

I adjusted my borrowed suit jacket. There hadn't been any reason for me to wear a suit in over a decade, and I swam in my aunt's clothes from her pre-liposuction days.

"Hands off!" The elderly woman yelled as she swatted at air and approached me. Her white hair was wrapped around tomato paste cans. Her wrinkled slacked skin was darker than mine, which isn't too difficult as the fur of a polar bear tans better than I do.

A woman I guessed to be in her twenties placed a slender hand on the other woman's slumped shoulder. Their outfits were a stark contrast. While the older woman wore a hot pink sweatsuit and lipstick two shades too bright for her complexion; the younger woman's floral dress was complemented by a pair of high heels, and a designer handbag.

"Please excuse my grandmother. She has dementia." The

young woman's voice was soft and gentle although her flawless face was haggard.

"Don't you man-handle me." The older woman wiggled out of her granddaughter's grasp.

I wanted to punch someone. Instead, I pulled hand sanitizer from my messenger bag. That slight movement caused a pain to run up my arm. The ER doctor told me I was lucky that the airbag hadn't broken any bones when I crashed my car into the telephone pole. Since I felt like a piece of discarded chewing gum, I figured the doctor was wrong on his assessment.

I used the hand sanitizer.

"We are sorry for your loss." The younger woman attempted to maintain her composure. My guess was that her grandmother was more active than she was. "I'm Cheryl Vaulkenberg, and this is my grandmother, Estella Sanchez."

"Yup, I'm Mrs. Sanchez and I got my teeth in for this." She gave a tooth-filled smile.

Their names were ones I recognized. The day of my crash, Mom informed me a woman named Estella had assisted in creating her dating profile. "My mother told me about both of you."

Mrs. Sanchez straightened up. "All good, I bet."

Whispers carried from behind them. A male voice said, "Easy bet for others to win."

"My granddaughter used to be a Wall Street broker." Mrs. Sanchez's doe-like brown eyes stared up at me. "I hear you used to be a waitress until a woman tossed a plate of mashed potatoes at you. Your swearing at her went viral."

The priest cleared his throat. I positioned myself next to Aunt Edna who was covered head-to-toe in traditional black mourning attire. She sniffed at me and scrunched up her face. "Is that the perfume I gave you for Christmas."

"No, it's the one Franky gave me." It wasn't a complete lie.

"Smells like burning rubber. Why in the name of all things green, did you get a priest in his nineties?"

"It was either him or an altar server."

The priest spoke in a frail voice, "Dearly beloved, we are gathered here today to join this man..."

CHAPTER 4

I dropped my messenger bag and ignored the skitter of contents against the wooden floor. One of Mom's lavender air sprays sat on the bay window. I moved it to the shelf under the microwave and drew the shades.

Nature's light muted by vertical blinds was a pleasant welcome for the migraine knocking at my skull. I slunk my way to the couch and its mismatched cushions. Years earlier, a novice hand had used dark thread to stitch a plaid patch across the back where my pet Schnauzer had chewed it down to the wood. Later that day, Bowser went to live with Franky. His plot of land near Thatcher Park was a perfect place for an energetic teething dog.

Whenever my cousin accidently left a door unlocked, Bowser would escape into the wilderness instead of a street. Fourteen-years-old and toothless, that Schnauzer still chased the hens.

I dropped onto the sagging couch and placed a pillow across my face; darkness followed. The front door opened and closed. One other person who had keys to my parents' house.

I slid the pillow down enough to see that Dozer was still in his all-black mourning suite. "Don't make me move!"

The soothing scent of his aftershave reached me first. That scent clung to him like the vines on the side of Mom's house.

"Migraine?"

"Uh huh," I muttered and slid the pillow back over my face.

"You dumped your messenger bag, again." The gentle quality of his voice was appreciated.

The entire day was a disaster. I knew my mother had been an active member of our community. That knowledge hadn't prepared me for the onslaught of mourners and their barrage of questions.

"Can you push this pillow down harder for me?"

"Euthanasia is illegal in the States," Dozer said as if that topic were part of an everyday dinner conversation. "Let's see, we have feminine products, a pocketknife, a bottle of migraine meds, and *A Guide to Old English* by Bruce Mitchell."

"One must be prepared for all emergencies."

The sound of the faucet running was a knife to my skull.

"What emergency calls for a dictionary?"

"Technically it's not a dictionary…" I stopped myself from

correcting him. It was as painful as the dim light I squinted into. "My minor was Medieval Literature."

"You didn't answer my question." Dozer 's knees cracked as he knelt next to me. A few grey hairs poked out of his buzz cut. In his mid-forties, his hair had for the most part kept its original black luster while my light-brown hair needed assistance from a bottle.

I gingerly accepted the glass of water as if it were a delicate decorated egg. Careful not to spill it, I downed the water and my migraine medication. "Have you any idea how often that has saved me? When I'm grocery shopping and a guy hits on me, I whip out that Old English hand-book and ask. 'Have you read *Beowulf?*'"

Having grown up the son of a socialite, Dozer was capable of facial expressions that leaned toward stoic. My comment received a laugh.

"That is the best rejection ever!"

His response was the emotional break I needed. "Glad you approve."

"I tried to hand you this at the VFW." He held up my flip phone. "Hector spotted it on the counter when we stopped to pick up the food."

Hector, Dozer's older son, was observant. Not much got past the two of these men. Maybe that's why Hector decided to work for a private investigator. The job offer was handed to him shortly after the world plunged into lockdown. With everyone stuck inside their houses, I didn't understand the need for a P.I. when spouses were separated by floors in their houses now miles of road.

"All that food should have fed an Army regiment." I grabbed my phone. "How does a reception go from two dozen people at the cemetery to over 100?"

"Your Uncle Sal live-streamed the burial."

"Ug."

"All of Franky's father's followers thought the funeral director's invitation to the VFW for food included them." Dozer slid onto the couch next to my legs. He placed a hand on my calf. "Imagine if his followers had been in the millions."

"Aren't you supposed to be comforting me?"

He squeezed. "Sometimes it's about distracting the mind."

My mind was already distracted. Mom had been emotionally distant my entire life. Dad believed it had been from childhood trauma. Despite her aloofness, Dad stood by her side until he passed away five years ago. Once he was gone, Mom all but vanished bouncing from one project to another.

A few months back I was thunderstruck when she contacted me. My Mom had been inspired her to have a fresh start in life when a woman named Estella Sanchez moved into the house next door. Details of the inspiration were hazy.

I choked back tears.

"Stop beating yourself up." Dozer pulled my hand to his mouth and brushed his lips against my fingers. "You know your mother's heart attack wasn't your fault."

I stared into Dozer's charcoal eyes and suppressed the thought of kissing my lips instead of my hand.

I told myself. *My hormones are confused.*

Dozer loosened his grip. I enjoyed his warmth a moment before threading my fingers on my lap.

"According to the Schenectady police," my voice pitched, betraying my emotions. I cleared my throat before continuing. "Mom's heart attack happened during our phone conversation. I found her doctor's number in the junk drawer and planned to call to see if she had had a heart condition that I didn't know about."

"Nice, you're proactive." Dozer flashed me the double dimple smile. In all the years we'd known one another, he saved that maneuver for high stress situations. He knew it was my kryptonite.

"How long do you think it'll take the doctor's office to return my call."

Dozer shuffled away. "Rome was built in less time."

"You're not funny." I tried to ignore the distinctive sounds of someone rummaging through items in the junk drawer. "Important documents are going to be in Mom's office."

"Paper and a pen. I need to write myself a note for later."

"Doesn't that phone of yours have an app for that?"

"There are things I prefer to have written the old-fashioned way." He returned to couch and held up a photo. "What's this?"

"Wow! That's old."

He tapped the image of three kids in 1980s mix-matched outfits standing in front of the Guilderland Library's brown checkout counter. "I get that. What was going on?"

"That's the summer I decided I wanted to be a writer." I pointed to the book I proudly held up. "*Hitchhiker's Guide to the Galaxy* wasn't age appropriate and I devoured every word."

Dozer winced. "You're what—seven in this photo?"

"There about."

He inched the photo toward me. "Who is everyone else?"

"The boy missing his two front teeth is Franky, the girl in the stripped shirt is me, and girl with the tilted cropped bangs is Stephanie Lauffenburger."

"What's this photo about?"

"Franky, Stephanie and I participated in the Guilderland library's 1987 summer reading program. Mom took that phone on the first day."

I didn't know if Dozer remembered Stephanie as they hadn't interacted that often. Most people describe her personality as "unique." Those are the ones who see her as an absent-minded individual who lacks focus. She's actually a complex individual whose invisible disabilities and high IQ created roadblocks for her to be successful. The lack of programs to help her during her formative years made things worse.

"The summer of 1987, we participated in a reading program. Stephanie made it a goal to read 54 books and I set mine at 52. We deduced that by reading more books than all the other kids and we'd receive awards for our efforts. Instead, we both received a badge stating we reached our goal. The librarian didn't believe that seven-year-olds read Edgar Allen Poe."

"The librarian didn't know you," Dozer said.

"Right. Stephanie and I were cheated out of awards while Franky was praised for going above and beyond his goal."

"Seriously?"

"Yeah. Franky signed up to read one book and read three."

Dozer shook his head. "They could've acknowledged you read more than the average child in your age group."

I didn't tell him that the unfairness still bothered me. "Franky says: The secret to earning awards is low standards."

"That's our Franky in a nutshell." Dozer pointed to a tow-haired boy who had tilted himself into the photo. "Who's this kid?"

"Photo bomber." I pushed my cell phone's power button. A glow flashed through the worn-down rubber keypad.

"Any idea who he is?"

"Why are you interested in the photo?"

Dozer used his smartphone to snap a photo. "It's a fascinating part of your past."

"Is that why you took a photo of a creased, dog-eared, picture?"

"Maybe."

My phone let me know the mailbox was full. "Seventeen text messages all from Aunt Edna." I flipped the phone shut. "The reading of Mom's will is Wednesday. I need to hire an attorney to be safe."

"Is that your way of asking me for help?"

"I don't want to impose." Even though I'm independent, I wasn't going to refuse help when it meant spending more time with my best friend.

"The private investigator Hector works for knows a guy who knows a guy..." Dozer smiled again.

"Stop smiling!" I nudged him. "It's weird when you do that." That lie received a raised eyebrow. It's fair to assume he saw the truth written on my face.

"Your mom wanted to make things right between you. That's why she gave you the house keys." Dozer's knees cracked as he stood up. He walked to the kitchen, opened the fridge, and struggled to hold up the door.

"Sorry." I rushed to his aide. "The door is kinda busted."

"Don't apologize. Got duct tape?"

"Doesn't everyone?" I retrieved a silver roll of duct tape from the junk drawer. "A little late in life to mend fences. Her work always came first."

I swapped out the duct tape for orange juice.

"It doesn't mean she didn't love you." Dozer used his knee to keep the door closed while he slapped the tape into place. "Easy fix." He set the roll on the spotless counter.

"You cleaned the counter."

"Stove, too."

The black glass reflected a shimmer. I twisted the top off the orange juice bottle. "What if I wanted more?"

"Hit the liquor cabinet. I don't judge."

"Dude." I was reduced to using a 1980s, cringeworthy word. "You know I rarely drink alcohol."

"And mixing booze with migraine meds is a bad idea."

"Oh my God." The jolt I felt was akin to shuffling my feet across a rug then touching an outlet. "Franky asked me to bartend for his new bar. He said you pulled a favor to get him that spot."

Dozer pulled his lips inward. He saved that maneuver for when he was avoiding unsettling news, like tornadoes.

I leaned closer. Since we stood nose-to-nose.

"The whites of your eyes have cleared up." Dozer batted a thick set of eyelashes.

"Don't you try to soften the blow, Mister!" I poked his solid broad chest. "I'm at wits end. Rip the tape off and let me have it."

Poor choice of words considering the fridge door was held closed by a single strip of duct tape.

"Franky pled a good case," Dozer said.

That was code for: bribery, whining, arguing, and reminding people of past digressions.

After two decades of friendship, you'd think we'd have no secrets. The problem was, Dozer grew up in the spotlight, and he learned to keep people at a distance to avoid creating a scandal. His secrets had a price attached, and Franky uses every advantage to get his way.

I wanted to know what dirt my cousin used to manipulate things to fall into his favor. For the sake of our relationship, I dropped the subject and stared at Dozer, hoping it was enough to make him cave.

He downed the orange juice without blinking.

"Franky told me he was going to a police auction." Horrifying images of fake dead bodies raced through my mind. "Is he really going to lacquer a chalk outline and pretend Raphael was murdered?"

"That's disturbing and not at all what your cousin pitched to our landlord."

My cell phone rang from the living room.

"Maybe it's good news," Dozer suggested.

I walked to the couch and picked up my phone. Franky's name flashed across the outer screen. I flipped it open and pressed speaker. "Good news?"

"Good news, nothing!" Franky's voice bordered on hysteria. "Bowser's missing. I tried to use the cat pheromone crap to attract our dog like the Internet told me too and… yeow!"

CHAPTER 5

The setting sun shone scarlet over the pumpkin-colored forest trees as Dozer pulled his black SUV onto a winding gravel driveway. A towering, red-leaved tree dripped water onto the high-pitched roof of Franky's 1908 single-story house. Its shutters, siding, and front porch were what set it apart from a modern-day trailer.

"What?" Dozer uttered. His vehicle came to an abrupt stop, feet from excavation equipment.

He was halfway to the mess when I exited the SUV and was struck by the scent of cat urine. I pulled my dress shirt over my face. It didn't help.

"Do you have a facemask in the glove compartment?"

Dozer ignored me. He looked like a crime boss in his mourning attire as he inched his way up to a towering mound of dirt that sat between a backhoe and the house. An opossum waddled past.

"Aren't those nocturnal?" Dozer asked.

"It might be the smell that brought it out."

Growls and hisses came from the backyard.

"I'm not investigating the noise." I had to draw the line somewhere.

A tubby tabby tranced by me. It stopped to give its back leg a few licks. I backed up figuring it was best to keep a safe distance from the hole and a possibly feral cat.

"I think he's going for an addition." Dozer stepped back from the hole. "Maybe a spare bedroom."

"No more taxidermy." I didn't want to go down this road again. Our grandfather had been a well-respected taxidermist who taught my father and my cousin the trade. Most girls in the 1980s received a doll for Christmas, I received a stuffed hamster dressed like Abraham Lincoln.

"If he opens up a shop, those posted signs are no longer valid and he'll need to fix that up to get a permit." Dozer pointed to a chicken coop that had been reduced to a barely viable grey structure where a one-legged rooster perched. The tabby backed up to a pristine shed, half the size of the house, and sprayed it.

"That's where he keeps his tools," I explained.

The front door of the house slammed open. The tabby climbed up a tree and hissed.

"Bowser's gone!" Franky shouted as he hurried down the

slanted steps. He was wearing a pair of palm tree-print, boxer shorts and nothing else.

"Dude!" I yelled. "It's fifty degrees. Put clothes on."

Franky carried the scent of a cherry blossoms as he padded to us. "I am wearing clothes."

I stifled a scream. "How about pants? A shirt? I'll settle for a bathrobe."

"My clothes are in the laundry. Are you going to continue to criticize me or are you going to help me find Bowser?"

"I'm sure he's chasing birds again."

"No." Franky scratched himself. "I fell asleep watching my soaps. When I woke up the back door was wide open."

"Did you call the police?" Dozer asked in an obvious moment of blank brain.

Franky's eyes darted to the excavator. "Are you crazy?"

Since my cousin enjoyed finding ways to skirt the law, he and the police had a twenty-six-year long love-hate relationship.

When we were in high school, Grandma Morgan started a betting pool as to how long Franky would avert incarceration. If he did more than a night in jail within the next year, I'd be ten grand richer.

That's when it clicked. "I need your attorney's contact information."

Franky waved his arms. "What does that have to do with our missing dog?"

I wasn't worried. This was routine. Bowser was a chicken chaser, and each time he vanished, I'd received a frantic call from my cousin insisting I assist in a search for the canine. Most of the time, he returned home tuckered out and hungry.

Not wanting to get into specifics, I said, "I have a legal matter."

"That's funny. You have a legal matter that your boyfriend can't bail you out of. This has got to be good."

A dog barked in the distance.

"Wait here." Dozer circumvented tree stumps and reached an overgrown path.

"What's really going on?" Franky scratched his thigh, leaving behind dark pink streaks from his fingernails.

"Could you not do that when you aren't dressed?"

Franky shoved his hands under his armpits. "It's a nervous habit."

"Wednesday is the reading of Mom's will. I want to make sure everything is fine."

His brown eyes went wide. "Did that guy she met on the dating app get everything."

"How did you know Mom was dating?"

"You know my sources are confidential. It'd be an injustice to betray them."

"Your mother told you."

A cat shrieked.

I pulled my suit jacket around me for comfort. "What did your mother tell you?"

"Okay. Look, your mom was lonely. So, my Mom and a neighbor—Sanchez, I think her name was—nudged your mom into trying a senior dating site."

An image of white hair strangling tomato paste cans came to my mind. "A woman at Mom's funeral commented about a blouse Mom had purchased for a special date."

"That's the rumor I heard." Franky rubbed his scrawny arms. "It's frigid out here."

Mind racing, I struggled to pluck out a single question. My cousin's constant movement threw me off. "You'd be warm if you put clothes on."

"Sue me for cleaning that cat stuff off of me. The internet site said this stuff attracts dogs. Instead, all I got was a gaggle of male cats."

The sounds of cats fighting grew louder. After a few unsettling moments all went quiet.

I pointed to his house. "That's what you get for taking the advice of an Internet site."

"Excuse me, Ms. Perfect. I am not hosing them down, again."

"Knowing Bowser, it'd have been a safer bet to leave out a bowl of pureed chicken."

"You monster." Franky gasped. "My chickens are for laying eggs."

There wasn't any reasoning with him. "Any gossip on my mom?"

"Yeah." That perked him back up. "Your ma met a guy named Ezekiel, a retired car insurance salesman from Arizona. They dated for a couple of weeks. That's why she wanted to talk to you and that's all I got. Sorry."

I pointed at the large yellow-orange object next to his house. "Another pool?"

"No. I found out you can have a cow in your basement if the head rests above the land."

I rubbed my forehead. The migraine fought to return. "I'm sure that law was revoked once PETA was founded."

"It's still on the books. And when I'm done, I'm getting a cow to have fresh milk every morning. You know how much I enj--.""

We were interrupted by the crunch of a vehicle's tires on the rock-covered driveway.

"Now what?" Franky groaned. "The last car to drive down here was driven by a teenage couple who claimed they thought this led to a hiking trail. At least when we were teenagers, we had the sense to drive out of the area. Man, last thing I needed was for a local to catch me out past curfew. Mom woulda roasted me."

My cousin deserves credit. He had been smart enough to drive out of town, but never remembered to add gas afterwards. Those occasions resulted in an early morning call from Aunt Edna for my dad to bring gas before he went to his taxidermy shop, until I bought my first car. That's when I became the predawn gas gopher.

"Yeah, and you still owe me gas money," I reminded him every chance I got about the fifty-dollar debt.

"Work at my bar and I'll make it up to you."

"Those are called 'wages' and you—" I stopped talking when a dented, gold-tone, four-door sedan swerved around Dozer's black SUV and stopped next to us.

"Bowser!" Franky tip-toed to the back window where our dog draped his out of the opened window. "You found him!"

Multiple green air fresheners hung on the rear-view mirror. The driver's door opened. A slender woman I estimated to be in her mid-thirties slid out. Her raven hair was pulled back in a tight black bun. Her crisp all-black outfit reminded me of military and her bronze complexion made me think she had Asian ancestry. While her perfume of choice was pine scented.

She spoke in a commanding voice, "Sir, I found your pooch running down the road."

Franky took in her attire and whistled. "Where are you running your undercover operation?"

She flashed a badge. "I'm mall security."

I chuckled.

"Ma'am, mall security is serious business."

That made me doubled over in laughter. It was a well-deserved emotional break.

Bowser rubbed a paw against my knee. "Good boy." I scratched behind his floppy ears. "Yes, you are."

"I haven't seen you here before." Franky leaned over the top of the car.

"You were smart to put your address on his collar."

The woman pushed her tinted sunglasses up her dainty nose.

I had that collar made special after the fourth time I retrieved Bowser from Animal Control.

"I'm Leah. That house under construction up the road is mine. I moved to Guilderland about six months ago. Once construction is completed, I'll be moving here to the Village of Altamont."

Franky leaned his head on a hand. "Are you named after the princess from that movie where a giant worm controlled the universe."

"Jabba the Hutt was inspired by a slug," Leah corrected him. "And he didn't control the entire universe."

I was impressed. This woman knows her movies.

Franky scrunched his face like he had caught wind of a foul smell.

Realizing his interest in her caused his brain to shut off, I chimed in, "Bowser misses you."

"Nintendo games?" the last word Leah spoke carried a tonal quality that was best described as a purr.

"Yup." I answered for the living statue. "He even played Pong."

"Atari. I'm impressed."

The mention of 1980s electronic games snapped him out of his stupor. "I'm opening up a bar in downtown Albany and have to pick up decor." Franky attempted to shove his hands in his non-existent pants pockets. His Adam's apple bobbed as he forced his hands onto his slender hips. "Need crime-affiliated stuff."

"Nice. A true crime-themed bar."

She had given my cousin her approval. This was only able to go two ways. Either one was going to drag me along. The woman tapped the roof of her car. "Schenectady has a police auction tomorrow."

Franky's face lit up like a child who had spotted wrapped gifts under a glittering Christmas tree. "I already have it on my calendar. We could go together. That is, if you're interested."

Leave it to my cousin to schedule a first date for an auction compiled of items confiscated in police raids.

While Leah and Franky hammered out details, I rubbed Bowser's belly. "Good boy."

"What'd I miss?" Dozer whisper in my ear.

His sudden appearance caused me to fall over.

"Where'd you come from?"

"I followed the chicken feathers. None were harmed." Dozer tugged his black suit pants as he squatted next to me and helped me up. "What's this about?"

He pointed to my cousin's goofy face.

I hummed the first few cords of the *The Twilight Zone* theme song before answering, "Meet the future Mrs. Franky Calderone."

"Number four?"

"He never legally married any of them."

"Smart women," Dozer mumbled.

My cousin had relationship difficulties. According to the Guilderland gossip mill: he needed a mother, not a girlfriend.

Franky's voice pitched. "You're studying to be a private investigator?" The woman hadn't answered before I was dragged in. "Talia! How great is this? I'll give you Pickle's number and on top of that this nice lady can help you research your ma's questionable death." He hooked a thumb at the woman. "What was your name again?"

"Leah."

Franky pointed at us. "That's my cousin Talia, and her friend Dozer."

We waved at the acknowledgement.

Leah gave Dozer a head-to-toe once-over and bit her lower lip as if she shifted to deep thought. "Lover?"

"Friend," I corrected.

"Too bad." She nodded towards the construction. "What's with the backhoe?"

"That?" Franky petted Bowser. Most likely buy a few seconds to formulate a lie. "The addition requires I expand the basement."

"There's limestone in this area," Leah commented. "The guys building my house had to pause construction to get a jackhammer."

"No kidding." Franky scratched his chin.

CHAPTER 6

The car rental place made me late for my meeting. Since my budget was pocket lint, I had the bottom end car for three days. That was enough for me to get my inheritance and buy a new vehicle.

I straightened my borrowed black suit jacket and stepped onto an ocean blue rug. Mr. Richardson's inner sanctum was an expansive room lit by a set of overhead fluorescent lights. An array of awards and photos were displayed on floor-to-ceiling bookcases, not a speck of dust visible. Behind a mahogany desk sat an imposing figure.

Vestiges of Mr. Richardson's rugged features hadn't faded from his weather-worn face. His thick, natural white hair matched his dress shirt. Deep-set diamond chips reflected rainbows from his gold cufflinks. His delicate, white gold wedding band was out of place in comparison to his fitted gray suit that must have cost more than my last car.

Leather crunched as I lowered myself into one of the chairs on the opposite side of the desk.

"Thank you for seeing me." Lacking confidence, I asked, "Would you answer a few questions about—"

An elongated frail finger shot up to silence me. It worked.

My right leg bounced in anticipation. Mr. Richardson remained focused on the door behind me. The minute hand of an old-fashioned desk clock clicked to the Roman numeral three; the door opened.

A balding man around five foot tall, wearing a sports jacket, polo shirt, and khaki pants limped into the room. He was pudgy in the middle, and when he sneered at me his gapped teeth showed stains from years' worth of smoking.

The creepy man who reeked of body odor sat in the vacant leather chair next to me. He was the guy from Mom's funeral who reminded me of Gargamel.

"Thank you, Ezekiel Knepp, for joining us." Mr. Richardson held up two sealed envelopes.

I reached for the one bearing my name. "That's it?"

"Yes." Mr. Richardson's professional demeanor didn't falter.

"What about Franky and Uncle Olaf?"

They were the two relatives I thought of who might inherit anything from Mom's estate.

Mr. Richardson shook his head. "Mrs. Morgan's estate has been handled in accordance with her wishes."

I accepted the nine-by-twelve yellow envelope. An object slid inside as I pulled it my lap. Ezekiel's pudgy face had a smugness I wanted to slap off. He leaned forward and farted.

The odor was worse than when Bowser ate beans.

Unfazed Mr. Richardson slid a document out of a third envelope. "Since you both have a copy, we will begin."

The reading didn't take as long as I had anticipated. Mom had bequeathed a box of toothpicks to everyone in the family.

She was a genius. Each relative had to sign a document that stated they accepted the sealed box as their inheritance and would not contest the will. One person was to receive a cash sum.

My mind had drifted on the thought of Franky opening the box to find tiny pieces of wood. Served him right for stealing my hair clips to hold the tight rope in place for his flea circus.

When Mr. Richardson arrived at Ezekiel, the smug expression vanished. I braced myself for more flatulence.

Mom's lawyer explained, "You, sir, are the recipient of Mrs. Morgan's life insurance police."

Crimson traveled from Ezekiel's collar up to his bald spot. "That's it?"

Expecting him to lunge at the elderly lawyer, I slid my hand to my messenger bag to grab my knife.

"Fifty thousand dollars." Mr. Richardson splayed his hands on the reflective wood. "That was more than generous."

I wanted to throat punch the ungrateful stranger Ezekiel. That policy was supposed to help me after my mom's death.

His hands slammed on the desk. I jumped. He was on his feet ready to lunge at the lawyer. Mr. Richardson reached for the phone. The two men stared at one another in a standoff.

An uneasiness gripped me. I needed to know who this man was and why my Mom had left him money.

"Sit back in your chair." Mr. Richardson remained calm. Ezekiel didn't move. The lawyer pressed a button on the desk phone.

His receptionist's chipper voice resonated, "How may I help you sir."

Ezekiel's eyes flicked to the source of the reply. He sat down.

"We'll be wrapping up soon." Mr. Richardson disconnected.

The man's light eyes narrowed. He steepled his hands as he spoke in an apathetic voice. "Mrs. Morgan acquired this insurance policy shortly before her death. She insisted that you be the beneficiary. Mr. Knepp, I'd like to know your connection to my client."

My pulse raced. My head pounded. More than anything, I needed to know if Mrs. Sanchez was correct in her assumption that my mother had been murdered.

The envelope in Ezekiel's hands crumbled. As fast as the anger had flared up, it appeared to vanish. He flattened his hands on the chair's curved wooden arms.

Mr. Richardson continued to read as if there hadn't been an interruption. "My only child, Talia Anne Morgan, receives my house, all of its contents, and my safe deposit box as well as all of its contents."

"Safe deposit box?" Ezekiel asked.

Mr. Richardson opened his mouth to continue.

"Which bank?" I asked.

Over the years, my mother had opened and closed multiple accounts. She was a bit of a free spirit who had many business endeavors and each one had a bank account. If her attorney didn't know, I was screwed.

Mr. Richardson stared at the document. His voice mournful when he spoke, "Sorry, Ms. Morgan. Your mother didn't give a location. I'm certain that was an oversight."

"That doesn't sound like my mom she is... I mean was..." Sadness, a vice on my heart, constricted my words into near sobs.

I grabbed a tissue from the box on the corner of the desk. Vision blurred by tears, I pressed the tissue to my eyes and forced myself back to the present.

"My mother taught me finances, banking, business management and--" My ramblings were cut off by Ezekiel.

"Are you sure that it?" He pulled a stained handkerchief out of his jeans' pocket to wipe his forehead.

"Mr. Knepp," The lawyer spoke before I regained my composure. "Is there something you'd like to share with us?"

Splotches of white shone through Ezekiel's maroon scalp. "Are we done?" His voice hit an operatic high note.

The elderly attorney leaned back. "As the Last Will and Testament is concerned, we are."

CHAPTER 7

A fine mist erupted from a plastic, egg-shaped scent dispenser, invoking visions of lavender fields. A mix of emotions grappled for my attention as my mind raced through the meeting I had with Mom's attorney.

"Ezekiel," I said in an exaggerated whisper. "What did my mom see in you, death farter?"

Minutes ticked by while I sat in the recliner staring at the blank TV surrounded by taxidermy animals and sundries.

Always an Immigrant a book written by Guilderland resident Mohammad Yadegari stared at me. I thought of Mom. She'd been born in Poland, landed in the U.S. as a child and insisted she was "out of place" here.

Ezekiel was the benefactor of my Mom's life insurance policy, the one she was healthy enough to qualify for weeks before her death. Yet, she died of a heart attack.

Instinct overrode my internal fight. Being a non-violent person, I called Dozer. He'd talk me off the ledge of violent desires.

He picked up on the first ring. "Chicken dinner?"

Leave it to this angel in human form to completely defuse me in two words. He knows I'm a frozen food package kind of chef. Who needs to cook when you can remove the premade meal from a cardboard package, pop it in the microwave, and tap a button?

"There's a new Mexican restaurant on Central." Dozer said in a sing-song voice. He knew he had me.

"There's always a new Mexican restaurant on Central Ave. I think the same family keeps reinventing the place to avoid negative feedback on social media."

"Is that a vote for a chicken quesadilla?"

I sighed.

"See you in twenty." He disconnected.

Yup, he knew me that well. I picked up the envelope from the floor and dumped the contents onto my lap.

A three-inch high, pale-pink envelope had been snapped shut by a metal closure. The date 09/12/68 had been written on it. I flipped it upside down. Two keys tumbled into my hand. I tossed aside the empty envelope, slid the keys onto one of my key rings, and set everything on the floor next to the recliner.

My cell phone dinged. My knee-jerk reaction was to let it go to voicemail. Since I had handed in multiple job applications, I answered in a forced pleasant tone.

"Thank you, I just won fifty dollars." A young female voice squealed. "There's a betting pool as to whether you'd answer the phone or not."

I held the phone at arm's length to protect my hearing and yelled my response. "Congratulations."

"I know. Right? I never win anything."

The woman didn't take a breath and missed my sarcasm. How anyone had the ability to spit all of that out that fast is beyond my comprehension.

"Why are you calling me?" I asked.

"Uh, yeah. I'm with a local news station and when we were filming the other day, your mom totally went down in the background. I didn't know the connection until your Uncle Sal posted the live footage at the funeral. He explained your family thinks she was murdered. That's why I had to call—"

"Wait? What?" I had to stop her. "He explained what?"

I was in stunned disbelief. My uncle thought my mother was murdered and posted it on the wild web of Internet mayhem without talking to me first. Franky was wearing off on him.

"Salvatore Calderone live-streamed your mother's service." Her voice was like a vocal roller coaster. "That old priest guy was absurd. His antics have racked up over a million views."

That footage she has might have something on it I could use. I forced myself to ask, "Is there any way you can send me a copy of the video?"

"Ew!" The woman's high-pitched shriek almost made me drop the phone. Before I was able to speak, the woman continued in a low voice as if she was trying to not be overheard. "You want a video of your own mother's death? Morbid."

I wondered if her end of this conversation was happening in the middle of a coffee shop. Social media trolls would be livestreaming my life into a full-on conspiracy theory viral spiral of hell.

That possibility kept me from telling the unidentified news woman the truth. I used a plausible lie. "I'd like to have a copy of the last moments of my mother's life."

A bell dinged on her end. A deep male voice yelled, "Number fifteen."

Forgetting the microphone was close to her mouth, the woman yelled, "Salami on rye? Yes. You can hold the pickle." After several moments of arguing the woman switched the conversation back to me. "I personally wouldn't want to see my mother die."

This woman's lack of emotional connection was appalling. I squelched a grimace.

"What will it take to get a copy?" I asked.

"Um... well... I can't do that."

"Why not?"

"Your Uncle Salvatore posted on all of his accounts—that your Mom might have been murdered and he pointed out her connection to the Raphael disappearance. Which makes this a major news story. I need an exclusive interview with you to impress my boss to go permanent. So, can I get a quote for my story?"

"Here's your quote." I hung up.

While my Uncle Sal's intentions were good, his actions weren't. Instead of letting me handle things the way I needed to, he enlisted the assistance of the Internet. Part of me wanted to know more and the other part wanted to strangle him.

One potential homicide in the family was more than enough. I opted for the old standby of counting to one hundred. When my rage had dulled to irritation, I listened to my voicemails. The first one was from the receptionist of Fabio's doppelganger. They wanted me for a second interview.

The job prospect jolted me upright. I jogged to the junk drawer to write down their information and glanced at the microwave. Its green numbers flashed 6:14. It was after hours. I played the rest of the messages.

After the fourth angry recording from an obscure relative, I suspected a toothpick had a cultural significance and I had learned several useful Yiddish insults.

Instead of researching "what does it mean in Poland to inherit toothpicks," I moved the folded step ladder to grab two sodas from the pantry, then I set them on the dining room table. Thoughts swirled like dancing leaves in the fall's wind as I folded the paper napkins into swans, and placed utensils next to them.

Heavy footfalls landed on the front porch. I tightened my ponytail and wished I had changed into my own clothes.

The door slowly opened, and Dozer strolled in. Sunlight silhouetted his muscular frame. I went breathless. In that moment,

I wanted more than friendship. I told myself it was the grief that caused my emotions to be out of whack.

Dozer kicked the door closed.

The clunk snapped me out of my fantasy. "Food?"

"Yup." Dozer set four bulging plastic bags of takeout cartons on the dining room table. His green T-shirt was neatly tucked into his blue jeans as he posed like a game show model presenting prizes. "Every chicken entree they had."

"Devine." I inhaled the savory scent of Mexican food. On top was a white paper bag of homemade nut-free marzipan. I set that on the counter for breakfast.

"Salsa." He snapped his fingers and walked to the fridge. "I'm not touching that duct tape."

"Check the pantry." I draped my suit jacket over the back of a wooden chair. "We're not going to be able to eat all of this!"

"The line cook from the restaurant that terminated you for the viral video works there."

Rule of thumb: When dating, make sure the guy isn't married and doesn't know where you work. That's why I avoid romantic relationships. I discovered a guy I had met through an Internet site was married when his wife showed up at my work. Nothing like a viral food fight and dropping the f-bomb to get you fired.

"Not Mark." I groaned.

"Yup. He heard about your mom." Dozer set an opened jar of salsa next to a container of fresh baked corn chips. "He got the owner to give you the employee discount to help you out. They send their condolences."

Not knowing what else to do, I sat down.

"Fancy." Dozer held up the paper napkin swan, sat across from me, and winked.

I didn't read into his actions. After the finalization of his divorce fifteen years earlier, Dozer hadn't really dated.

"Tomorrow, I'm going to contact a convent to donate stuff,"

"Items from your Mom's home?" he asked.

I opened a food container. Its contents sent me to my happy place. "If the head nun is interested in me, I'm joining."

"Mother Superior will love your outfit." Dozer poked his fork into his food.

I stared down at my blouse. A button had popped giving a full view of my green lacy bra and robust cleavage. It's not like Dozer hadn't seen that before—we had been to the beach plenty of times, but this felt different.

Embarrassed, I wanted to disappear. "I might have sat in the attorney's office like this."

Dozer's eyes remained on my face while I buttoned back up. The whirlwind of the past few weeks had caught up to me. All I wanted to do was take a breather to process it all.

The front door slammed open. Both Dozer and I jumped to our feet. Franky strolled in.

"What the heck?" I shouted.

Leah shut the door behind her. "I'm learning to pick locks for my P.I. training." She slid a metal object into what I assumed was a lock-pick set and tucked it into a side pocket of her cargo pants.

"Isn't she great?" Franky was wistful as he pulled out a chair for Leah and kissed her hand. "To think I wouldn't have met this fantastic woman if Bowser hadn't run away."

She sat in the offered seat.

I was dumbstruck. I had no idea he had the ability to be wistful and Franky was using manners.

I whispered across the table to Dozer, "We've slipped into an alternate dimension."

Dozer made a faint downward motion with his head. He was on my side.

"What's with the matching all-black outfits?" I asked.

"Is that dinner?" Franky rushed to the remaining chair, tossed aside the jacket, and flopped onto the seat.

"You're wearing a utility belt."

Again, I was ignored.

Dozer and I exchanged confused glances. Leah commandeered my chicken quesadilla and Franky stole Dozer's soda. My eyes involuntarily flicked to the marzipan bag that Dozer was already tossing into a cupboard. He had saved my breakfast.

"Why are you both here?" I leaned back in my chair.

Soda in one hand, Franky used his other to open a takeout container. "I was telling Honey Bear about your legal problem."

Since Franky didn't have any other romantic aspects, I assumed "Honey Bear" was Leah. I felt it was odd to dole out pet names after one date, meanwhile my cousin didn't. After all, he collects girlfriends like I collect dust bunnies. The difference was— my dust bunnies stayed longer.

Leah swallowed hard before speaking. "Sounds like Ezekiel is a professional con-artist, referred to in the trade as a 'vulture.' That's a person who preys on vulnerable people to take them for everything they can."

I was pretty sure "vulture" wasn't the technical term for Ezekiel. I wasn't going to correct a woman who carries a stun gun.

Franky reached over for my fork. "How did the reading of the will go? Did ya' get much?"

I was astonished. Franky hadn't been through the door for a full minute and already had me wanting to bang my head against the wall. Instead, I spit out the word, "What?"

"When Uncle Jonathan died, he willed his art collection to your ma and the tools of his trade to me. Plus, Uncle Levi's company fetched at least hundred grand when your ma sold it."

This prompted me to race through conversations Mom and I had after Dad's death. There hadn't been enough money to pay for his funeral services. That's when she opted to prepay for her own. The budget-friendly installment plan ensured I didn't have to bear that financial burden. I wished it had included a limo.

The memory of jumping over the center divider, to catch a taxi, while Franky's truck burned was fresh in my mind.

"The money from the sale of Uncle Levi's company was used up a few years ago. In addition, Mom had a fifty-thousand-dollar life insurance policy on herself. As for Dad's stuffed dead-animal artwork, that brought in a paltry amount."

"Wow." Franky spoke between bites. "That fifty grand will set you up for a while. Time to get a new couch."

I snagged a chip. "Ezekiel got that money."

"No way. Ma said they dated... what, two weeks tops?"

"Ha!" Leah slapped the table. "I knew it. That man is scum."

"What about this house?" Dozer set a glass of water in front of himself and one in front of me.

"House is mine." I glared at Leah.

She sipped my soda. "How about a savings account?"

"No savings account." I mulled that information over for a moment. When Dad died five years prior, Mom had several accounts. "She also left keys to a safety deposit box."

"Does Ezekiel have keys to this place?" Leah asked.

As far as I knew mom wouldn't give the house keys to a stranger. Then again, she left him her insurance policy.

"I don't know," I said.

Dozer pulled out his cell phone and sent a text message to someone. "We're changing the locks."

Franky reached for a crunchy chicken taco.

"Don't take anymore more." I swatted at his hand.

Franky motioned to the takeout containers. "If we don't help you eat all this, you won't have room in the fridge."

Dozer was a pillar of calm. This calamity was tame for him. In fact, I think he enjoys our banter. It brings back fond childhood memories of his five younger sister and holidays at the Wemple mansion.

"Ya know," Franky scootched his chair closer to the table. "It might be that the coroner is used to shootings, stabbings, and overdoses. That's why he missed a homicide disguised as a heart attack." He glanced at Leah whose facial expression was unreadable.

I let the comment slide. It was best not to point out Franky's shortcomings. Leah needed to figure things out for herself. After all, she was mall security.

"Murder isn't a joke." She held up a taco.

Franky appeared scared. Dozer inched his chair back. I followed suit. Best to keep oneself away from flying objects.

We all stared at Franky. He scratched his facial stubble. "Agreed. Murder is bad for your karma."

"Since when do you believe in karma?" I asked.

Franky mocked shock, and walked toward the kitchen. "I have always been a strong believer in that crap."

"His humor is refreshing." Leah stared at Franky like a competitive eater preparing to devour a plate of food.

Dozer held a chip covered in salsa. It appeared he wanted to respond. Instead, he popped the chip in his mouth.

Franky pointed to the fridge. "Did you know this is taped shut?" He pulled out his pocketknife.

"Don't!" I yelled, "The door is—"

Before I could finish that statement, Franky had cut the tape. The door crashed to the floor and slammed against the counter. "Oops." Franky sidestepped onto a pile of wilted kale.

My cell phone rang from the living room. I ignored Franky and followed the ringtone. I answered my phone, "Hello."

"Talia?" The deep, commanding tone gave me pause.

I forced out the words, "Depends. Who is this?"

The man identified himself as "Cory." There was a pregnant pause while he breathed into the phone. When he went into a car insurance speech. I hung up.

"Hold still!" Dozer's voice came from the kitchen.

"This door weighs a ton." Franky struggled to hold up the refrigerator door while Dozer picked up a roll of silver duct tape.

"Guys, set it aside and unplug the fridge," I suggested.

"We're good," Franky's strangled voice was a notch above a whisper.

I faced Leah to ask her for help. No such luck. The aspiring P.I. sat at the dining room table, recording the endeavor on her cell phone. "This is better than television."

A loud crash caused me to jump. Franky yelped. The fridge door banged against the bottom portion of the refrigerator taking Franky to the floor.

Leah was on the phone. Her voice cut into the whimpering. "Forty-one-year-old male, possible broken foot."

CHAPTER 8

"Unplugged," Dozer called from behind the darkened refrigerator; its ancient metal door lay flat under a bulging white drawstring garbage bag containing tofu, kale, and moldy food items.

I strode to the living room and flopped onto the couch. I chose to pretend the hard object pressing against my ass was a broken spring.

Garbage bag in hand, Dozer blazed out of the kitchen. "Whatever gelatinous mass was leaking splattered on my sneakers."

His green T-shirt and jeans were unscathed. I was grateful I had sat off to the side while he cleaned out the fridge. My borrowed suit was clean.

"Be back in a minute." Hinges groaned as he opened the cellar door. "Dumping this in the garbage can."

Overhead, several thumps seemed to respond to the door slamming shut. The to-do list was alreay backlogged.

I ignored the attic dwellers and stared at a blank television screen. Many hours had been spent in this spot watching the Cartoon Network while my parents remained asleep in bed.

I was singing the opening song of *Jabber Jaw* when Dozer sat down next to me. "You do know the television's off?"

"In my mind, it's on."

"Uh-huh." Dozer leaned away from me.

"Don't tell me you never watched the Saturday morning line-up on the Cartoon Network."

"You had me at talking praying mantis."

I snorted. "*Space Ghost.*" That was when I felt an internal weight grab hold and pull me down.

Dozer cuddled me into him his warm body. I barely registered his alluring scent when my eyes welled with tears. There were a few at first, and then I was overcome by a stream of uncontrollable sobs.

I cried into his chest until there was nothing left.

"I have no money. My live-in trailer needs to be cleaned out. My mom is dead. And to top it off, my cousin's foot might've been broken by a possessed refrigerator door."

"Franky's survived worse and Leah's by his side." Dozer rubbed my back. "Once you have your inheritance--."

I went rigid as the gravity of the situation hit.

Dozer removed his hand. "I forgot."

"It's an easy mistake to make. Ezekiel got Mom's life insurance money while I got this house and a set of safety deposit keys. I feel like I'm missing an important detail."

Dozer's laser-like focus bore into me. "Where are the papers?"

I shrank inside. It was like I was in front of my first-grade classroom being asked where I had hidden my unfinished homework, after I had claimed my dog ate it. To cover my nervousness, I pointed to the item in question. Instead of an oversized math book lying under a pile of discarded coats, it was a large envelope on the floor next to the recliner.

Several uncomfortable minutes ticked by while Dozer read over everything. I wrapped my arms around myself to make up for the lack of his warmth.

He struggled to tuck the documents back into the envelope. Dozer was unsettled too.

"When did your mom meet this guy?"

"According to Franky, they had been talking for a while online before they met up. Apparently, the relationship shifted to romantic a few weeks ago."

Dozer crossed back and knelt. He looked up at me and wrapped his smooth hands around my free hand. It was nice not to feel calluses. "The paperwork says her $50,000 life insurance policy was taken out two months ago. The beneficiary was changed afterward."

"What are you saying?"

His tone shifted to serious. "I think Franky's right. Your mom's death wasn't an accident."

My grieving bubble had been popped. A mixture of anger and a numbness I hadn't experienced before overpowered my senses. We lived in Guilderland, a growing town where homes sold quickly, and murder was limited to a rumored mob hit. We have a farm market in the library's parking lot, a National Park that overlooks the area, and a mall that accounts for most of the town's crime.

Dozer whispered, "There are people who have killed for less."

"It was a heart attack." I wasn't sure who those words were meant to comfort.

The nagging feeling chipped at my brain again. Did this guy

really murder my Mom in a way that her death appeared to be natural causes? If so, how was I going to find the truth? The most experience I had in taking on criminals was running out of the diner to catch a group of teenagers that had done a dine and ditch.

"The papers don't have heart issues listed. She was given a clean bill of health." He brushed a kissed across my forehead. "Unfortunately, it's going to take time. I'll make a few calls for you. In the meantime, we must be patient."

I didn't want to be patient. I wanted answers right then.

As I mulled over Dozer's words, I remembered the prescription pills. She was on medication for an invisible disability, and if you are on medication for something, you don't have a "clean bill of health."

Dozer's facial expression conveyed the question: "What aren't you telling me?"

I asked, "What about ADHD?"

Dozer smoothed out his shirt. "You never mentioned that before, and there's nothing in the papers about ADHD."

There was a major disconnect. My heart pounded. My hands trembled. "I found a bottle of ADHD medication…"

The rest of the sentence refused to be expelled.

"Okay." Dozer said. "We'll need to see when the medications were prescribed. She might've been diagnosed after the life insurance physical."

"I can do that."

Two of Dozer's sisters had been diagnosed as being on the ADHD spectrum, so he knew the ropes.

"This explains your mom's quirks. She was easily distracted, disorganized, was notoriously forgetful, and perpetually late. Those are major indicators of ADHD." He hesitated before asking, "Do heart issues run in your mother's family?"

I glared at him.

"Right. You mom was disowned. You can search old newspapers for their obituaries and--"

Dozer's cell phone gave a text alert. He paused to check the messages. When his head twitched, I knew something was wrong.

"What?" I asked thinking the worst. "Is someone hurt?"

"No one's hurt. It's Hector."

He tapped a response. Hector, Dozer's oldest son, was almost a carbon copy of Dozer. He was easy-going and strong-willed, and he packed a punch when necessary. While in high school, Hector had dreamt of going into law. He had met a girl he wanted to marry. Like most teenagers, he didn't take advice from any adults. He spent his trust fund on a European backpacking trip. Once his money was gone, so was the girl.

When he was finished typing a message Dozer said, "DNA."

Confused, I stared at him. He didn't respond.

"How is this an emergency?" I asked.

"When Hector was offered the job at the private investigator's office, he was asked about his ancestry."

A bit relieved, I commented, "That's intrusive."

"Agreed." His voice low, sadness flowed through his words. "If he can prove he's at least half-Mexican, Hector can take courses at no charge, through a certification program. Honestly, my thoughts went elsewhere when he brought up my birth family."

Hector had hit a hidden raw nerve.

"Since, my son is cut off from the rest of the family trust. He's gotta find a way on his own." Dozer held up the phone showing me an image of tracking history. "His spit is on its way for answers from one of those family search sites."

"How long will that take?"

"Up to six months." Dozer walked to the TV and pressed the power button. Nothing happened. "George took the test, too."

And there it was. The real reason behind his sudden mood shift.

"Plenty of time for you to tell them."

"No." Dozer spun around. "Sandy cheated on me with half of Albany County. That means she gets to tell them."

Dozer had caught his then wife kissing an attorney friend. Once it registered what he had witnessed, he walked out to clear his head and wandered into the bar where I worked. If she hadn't cheated, we might not have met.

"It's up to my ex to explain the discrepancies."

"I'm sure it wasn't that high a number." To change topics, I pointed to the wall. "TV won't work. The outlet's fried."

Dozer raised an eyebrow. I wish I had that talent. My forehead wrinkles every time I try to raise a single eyebrow.

I stood up to stretch. "We'll wait until your sons' results are back to tell them."

"We?" Dozer moved forward.

I remained still, a failed attempt to hide in plain sight. That "we" had been a slip, and he was all over it. His breath brushed against my face as he spoke.

"You said 'we.'"

"Slip of the tongue." I feigned innocence.

No such luck. I was being glared at. When the world shut down in 2020, Dozer switched to delivering his pastries, and I was roped in as a delivery person. It was during that time we spent together that I felt the chemistry between us.

Dozer's lips were dangerously close to mine. His breath brushed my face. A rush of desire swept over me.

My cell phone rang.

"Are you going to answer that?" he asked.

"After the day I had, no."

When my phone stopped ringing, Dozer's phone buzzed.

His facial expression shifted to annoyance as he swiped to answer his phone.

"Yo." He pressed speaker.

"Yo, yourself," Franky's voice boomed. "The doctor's signing my release papers. Leah will be taking me home soon. My home."

I cringed.

"Let me guess, you want me to let Bowser out for a tinkle?" It was best to use the dog as an excuse, instead of asking if he'd like me to return the borrowed excavating equipment to Leah's construction site.

"That'd be great." Franky hung up.

Dozer held up my purse. "He'd be lost without you."

Twenty-five minutes later, we pulled down the long driveway. Puffy, grey clouds inched over a waning sun, cloaking Franky's house in deep shadows.

"Whoa!" Dozer leaned over the steering wheel. "He's good."

The SUV's high beams reflected off a shovel propped against a pile of dirt. Next to that lay chunks of limestone. A chicken ran across the yard. Its brown wings flapped as it clear a mound of stone before it fell into the gaping hole. Two more chickens followed.

"They're more like lemmings," I mused.

"Is that another attempt at a swimming pool?"

"Actually…" It occurred to me that a fib might have been the way to go. Inevitably, I told the truth. "An enclosure for a cow."

The SUV bounced to a stop. We got out and approached the hole.

"Really? A cow enclosure?" Dozer asked.

"Yes. Franky found an obscure law that states that he can have a cow in the basement as long as its head is above ground."

"He needs to invest in a chicken coop first."

A chicken raced into the woods towards what I thought it was an injured coyote. The creature picked up speed. I contemplated jumping back into the vehicle. The animal barked.

Crunching sounds accompanied Bowser as he bounded down the leaf-covered hill. Chicken feathers stuck out of the dog's fur, giving him the appearance that he too was part bird.

"Again?" I chased after him. Chilled air lapped my face with a pre-storm heaviness that carried a fine mist. "Get back here," I shouted. The dog trotted up to me. "Your daddy needs a better lock." I gripped his collar.

"Is there a doggy door?" Dozer asked.

"No. I think he's figured out how to open the back door." I tightened my grip on the collar and guided the dog around the back of the house. We reached the steps and Bowser put on the brakes.

"Come on, boy."

He yelped. I picked him up. He wiggled in protest. I set him down and sat on the bottom step. "Everyone knows it's not the same as living with me." I scratched behind his ears.

Bowser rested his head on my knees. I plucked feathers out of his bushy eyebrows. "If you hadn't eaten Mom's couch, you'd have been able to stay."

A low whimper was his comment.

Franky had attached a chain to the side of the house for Bowser to run around the porch and side yard unattended. I hooked the chain to his collar and went to the back door. Years' worth of scratch marks marred the bottom half of the open door.

Bowser inched his way up the porch.

"Still an escape artist?" I scowled at him as if my angry face would have had any effect on him. Bowser licked my hand. It was difficult to stay angry at such an adorable creature.

"Ready?" Dozer strode up, giving the Schnauzer a quick pat.

"Bowser opened the door, again."

I made sure it was closed tight. Once I cleared the porch, I texted my cousin: "Get a deadbolt. Bowser's chained out back."

"Did you see this?" Dozer pointed to a chicken pecking at a strip of paint peeling off the shed's door.

I crept around to the wooden structure. "Rotting wood?"

"No." Dozer used the side of his foot to nudge the chicken out of the area and opened the shed's door.

Packed dirt muted my movement as I entered the darkened structure. The smell of mold clung to the air. Specks of light broke through pea-sized holes, giving the appearance of a star-lit, night sky.

Dozer hit the flashlight app on his smartphone. We stepped farther inside. It was large enough to hold a car.

Above a set of ropes dangled.

"Uncle Sal kayak is missing," I said.

"Probably at the lake." Dozer flashed the light over a corner where a heap of sawdust lay next to a dead mouse. The only other object in the shed was an abandoned volleyball-sized wasp nest.

"Disappointing." I closed the door as I exited. "I figured he'd have a Civil War cannon."

"Might be since he found Leah, he decided to give up his questionable ways." Dozer's suggestion was from a plot in a B-rated alien abduction movie.

Physically, Franky was taller, slender version of his Sicilian father while his personality was all his Mom's. In her sixties, my aunt still drank, swore, counted cards, and jay-walked. She believed that last offense wasn't a crime.

"He wants to make a nice impression," I agreed. "I'm concerned that once she dumps him, he'll return to his bad habits. I'm wondering where he hid the riding mover he borrowed from Mom. He's only had it for three years."

"I hope this woman stays. She seems to be a good fit for your cousin." Dozer closed the shed door.

CHAPTER 9

"Franky was right" is an admonishment you never say out loud. Fortunately for me, I had uttered those words while lemon-ginger body wash suds swirled down the shower drain.

The truth lay in front of me. My life was bat guano. I was a forty-one-year-old, unemployed woman who had inherited a safety deposit box and a borderline derelict house.

Water dripped off me as I stood on a bathmat starring at a foggy mirror questioning my sanity. My cell phone rang.

"Please be Dozer," I chanted as I padded into my bedroom and flipped my phone open. "Hello."

"Talia Morgan?" A woman with a thick, New Jersey accent yelled in my ear.

I fought to hide the disappointment in my voice. "Speaking."

I opened a dresser drawer and pulled out a pair of panties.

"This is Emily from Pickles Law Office. Franky Calderone explained everything to us earlier. My condolences."

"Thank you."

I pulled a pair of jeans out and tossed them on the bed.

"Mr. Pickles has a cancellation today and wanted me to check your availability. Since he and his partner Ms. Sar—" She cut herself off. "My apologies. Dust allergies. We're temporarily located on Congress Street in Schenectady."

It was as if the supreme deity had heard me. Franky's slimy attorney had an opening. Forget Dr. Watson, I had Pickles.

"Yes, I can make it." I reminded myself that I was one step closer to figuring out the truth. "When?"

"Now."

"Now!" My big toe caught on the crotch of my panties. Knocked me off-balance. I screamed as I fell onto the bed. The phone landed next to me. I spoke loud enough to be heard. "I can make it. What's the address?"

"I'll text it to you. And remember, you don't have to scream."

"Sorry. You startled me."

"Happens." She disconnected.

I dressed, grabbed my messenger bag, keys, and the envelope that contained Mom's will. I didn't have time to blow-dry my hair. Even though it was chilly out, I rolled the rental car's windows down and let the wind dry it as I drove.

Pickles Esquire's law firm was run out of the first floor of a 1930s two-family home. I climbed the peeling painted steps to the front entrance marked by a laminated, eight-by-ten computer printout that read: By Appointment Only. Thank you. Pickles.

Since I had an appointment, I pulled open the solid oak door and walked into the warmth. Unlike Mr. Richardson's spartan office, this one had a seedy, massage parlor vibe and reeked of musk.

I stepped onto a worn Persian rug, closed the door behind me, and followed the path to a metal desk behind which sat a woman in her fifties. Bright red lipstick smeared on her teeth as she chomped on a piece of gum. Her large fake boobs practically popped out of her blouse and her bottle-blonde hair had been teased beyond the Long Island psychic's voluminous updo.

"Emily?" I asked.

"We don't have any appointments with anyone by that name." The woman filed a hot pink, acrylic nail.

I tugged on my turtleneck, hiked up my southward roaming blue jeans, and introduced myself. "I'm Talia Morgan."

"Then why'd you say Emily? And what's with your hair? It's worse than what my mother had in the 1980s."

"Blow dryer broke." I finger combed my hair the best I could. "I was asking if you were Emily."

"No, I'm Lori. Emily is our file clerk who makes calls for me when I'm busy. As you can see, I'm busy."

"Okay…" I drew out the word like it was a question. "Emily called me to meet Pickles for this."

I held up the envelope that contained Mom's will.

"Ah, you're Franky's cousin. Such a shame that serial killer stole his identity."

Beyond the woman's hair was a quarter sized hole in the wall. I stumbled backward into a folding chair.

"Is that a bullet hole?"

"Disgruntled client." She shrugged.

"Talia." A soothing male voice called out. A slender silver haired suited man, about six feet in height strolled from the back of the house. A solid, black face mask covered a large portion of his face. "Any family of Franky's is family of mine." The crushing grip of the man's handshake sent a pain into my forearm. "I apologize for the delay. Franky has me busy these days."

I tried not to think about the New Jersey homicidal maniac who stole Franky's identity. All the women physically resembled me, and the killer was still at large.

"Thank you, Mr. Pickles." I flexed my fingers when he released my hand. I found myself wishing Dozer was there to ask questions. This was well out of my comfort zone. The only other time I needed an attorney was for my work lawsuit and that was an epic failure.

"Come into my office."

Mr. Pickles motioned for me to follow. We walked down a short hallway that smelled of cigarette smoke. I wondered who his slumlord was, and why hadn't the attorney painted over what appeared to be blood splatter on the ceiling.

I swallowed my fear.

Pickles motioned for me to enter a room to the right. "It's a temporary location inherited from a client in lieu of my fees."

I wondered if he'd accept payment in the form of pastries. Dozer made mouth-watering donuts. He'd hook this guy up with a dozen a week for life. I shoved down the thought of pimping my friend's food out for my impending debt.

Pickles unbuttoned his suit jacket as he positioned himself behind a dented, 1960s high-school teacher's desk while I sat across from him on a metal folding chair. An indentation on the rug next to me indicated this was where a bed once sat. It was safe to assume this had been the master bedroom.

"This is quaint," I said.

"It's temporary until my building is fixed up from the firebomb." Pickles held out a hand. "Do you have your mother's will."

"Firebomb? What firebomb?"

"It happens." He said it like we were discussing a snowstorm in December. "Now, about those papers."

Maybe a near-miss incineration was a minor inconvenience to this guy, but to me and the rest of the reasonable adult world, this was a big deal.

"Firebomb?" I repeated.

"Franky wasn't involved." He held up two fingers. "Scout's honor."

If Franky had been involved, I'd have known it was a prank gone wrong. This felt personal. Reluctance gnawed at me as I handed the papers over to the suited man. Maybe he'd find a loophole that allowed me to get the money and put the scam artist behind bars.

"Dated less than a month before your mother's death."

At least he was observant. That's when I noticed a red speck on his tan tie. I was optimistic that it was ketchup.

Pickles read over the documents, and I wrung the hem of my turtleneck as if it were a wet towel. If he didn't find a loophole and get me the insurance policy that day, I'd have to return the rental. Both of my legs bounced. I scanned the cluttered bedroom office for the musk air freshener.

The antique wall clock ticked the minutes away. Under it, a tilted shelving unit threatened to fall onto a pile of cardboard filing boxes marked "F.C." My cousin had eight boxes dedicated to him.

I tucked away that knowledge for a later date. On the long wall that faced the alleyway, a set of bullet-resistant windows had recently been installed. I tried not to think of Pickles' disgruntled former client and what his line of work might have been.

A long going rumor was that Jimmy Hoffa's remains were buried in the Schenectady area, I wondered if his skeleton was in the basement. My brain went to scenarios that involved Mafia snitches being tortured. The wall clock chimed. I stared at the shady man sitting before me.

"The timing of the re-write versus your mother's death, and this life insurance policy are suspicious."

"Re-write?" I leaned forward.

That was the first I had heard of a re-write. He pointed to a line at the edge of the document.

"See, your mother's attorney added this sentence."

I struggled to read the microscopic font. Sure enough, it had stated that Mom's will had been updated and referenced the original document.

"If you can find the original, we can negate this one." He flashed me a used car salesman worthy smile.

"Does that mean her attorney has the original?"

"Possibly." Pickles picked at a bandage on his left hand. "I'm sure he knows more than what he's told you. This clause indicates to me that your mother was experiencing a mental health crisis and/or was under duress. Mr. Richardson used a legal loophole to show he had your best interest in mind."

Pickles spent the next several minutes explaining what it meant for me. I pretended to understand the legal jargon and agreed my mom's lawyer was one of the best.

"What's my next move?" I asked.

"I want to represent you and my services won't be cheap."

And there it was. The thing I dreaded. He needed money I didn't have. Deflated, I slouched. The metal chair cracked as I leaned back. "Is there anything I can do?"

"Find the original." Pickles slipped his facemask back over his youthful face. "How did your mother afford Mr. Richarson?"

"I honestly don't know. He's been my Mom's attorney since before I was born. Why?"

Pickles eyed me with suspicion. "Fifty thousand was all your mother had for a policy?"

"Yeah." I had no clue where this was conversation was going. My family had always struggled for money. When I was a kid, Dad was a super couponer. Every trash day, he had me go through our neighbor's recycle bins for the Sunday's paper to get extra coupons.

"Why are you asking me these questions?"

Pickles jotted something down on a steno pad. "Franky told me your family wasn't wealthy. Yet, your mother had a high paid attorney on retainer. To me, that's motive for murder."

"What?" I jumped out of my chair. My hands on the edge of Pickles' desk, I leaned down. "Say that again."

A mischievous twinkle flashed in the lawyer's pale eyes. To him, this was a game. He stared at me for a few long moments before motioning for me to sit.

"Does your mother's family have a history of heart issues?"

I didn't budge. He thought my mother had been killed. His next words were spoken in a soothing tone, as if I were a rabid, emergency room patient about to have a limb amputated.

"This is important. Did your mother have heart issues?"

"We weren't close."

"Okay. If you can afford a private investigator, I'd recommend hiring one."

That was a loaded statement. After mentally going over a few numbers, I answered, "As soon as I move out of my trailer and shift money, I'll be able to swing $300 a month."

"We'll figure things out. Do you mind if I make copies of your mom's will and see what I can do?"

"How much is this going to cost?"

He leaned back in his chair. "Since your cousin is a preferred client of mine, consider this a favor."

"What do I need to do?"

He folded his fingers together. "Be thorough. Don't miss a single document when you go through your mother's personal belongings. Notify me of anything that stands out. Go to the library for old newspaper articles. Start with death notices of family members and once you have things set, I'll take a $300 retainer."

CHAPTER 10

When my Dad taught me to drive he drilled into me the importance of parking in a pull through spot. Even in my forties, I still coveted them as they make leaving easier and if a criminal lurked in the shadows this gave me a small advantage.

The library's overflow parking lot was larger than the library Franky and I frequented as children. It saddened me to think of how large our town had become and irritated me that there was no open pull through spaces. I loathed backing to spaces in while driving a rental car. I traversed through a sea of vehicles, winding my way around all three parking lots.

My anxiety level dropped a notch, on the third lap around, when I found a pull through spot. After the completion of the recent expansion of the Guilderland Library, I avoided visiting it. I blamed my absence on the presence of the Delta variant in our area. It was a safe way to avoid admitting that change makes me panic.

Moments later I was at the library's main entrance. A masked mother chased her wailing child out a set of sliding double doors and down the sidewalk. I ignored the indignant shouts, pulled an N95 face mask out of my messenger bag, and secured it in place.

I stopped at a set of red velvet ropes that guarded our once small town's biggest celebrity, Greulich's cow. For several decades the local icon had sparked many debates, as it had become a rite of passage for Guilderland High students to steal the cow from the roof of Greulich's Market as their senior prank. I checked its neck and found the groove where Franky had tried to cut off its head using a butter knife.

A muffled voice called out, "Potty around the corner."

I unzipped my jacket, stepped through the second set of sliding doors, and rounded the corner toward the conference rooms. The bright overhead fluorescent lights lit up the interior in a way that made me feel like I was outdoors. Adjacent to a café sign Stephanie Lauffenburger rocked back on her heels.

"Dude." She spoke through a royal blue and gold satin face mask. The movement made her 1960s, repurposed, winged glasses bounce. Her light-brown hair had been pulled into a waist long braid, it swayed to her movements. Knowing her unique fashion sense, I glanced down to her feet. A set of combat boots peeked from under a dress made of a lightweight purple, tie-dyed material.

"Dude?" I asked.

"Righteous." Stephanie's black leather jacket crackled as she tugged her hand-made, multi-colored quilted tote bag onto her shoulder.

Our paths crossed on a regular basis. It's bound to happen in this area, especially when you share interests and both of you are children of volunteer firefighters.

Unlike my complex family, hers was simple. Her father was an only child and her mother orphaned at a young age. They met while attending SUNY Albany. After graduating college, they bought a house in Guilderland, got married, and a few years later had one child.

"'Potty'?" Incredulity seeped into my words. It might have been lost behind the plain face mask.

"Old habit from Mom." Stephanie giggled. "This kid's mother was preoccupied and didn't notice her child bouncing as he pretended his toy dragon was pooping on the floor."

"Good call. So, what brings you out of hiding?"

Stephanie's autoimmune disorder and asthma meant she had been forced into seclusion at the start of the pandemic. We all handled the craziness of the lockdown in our own ways. She posted videos of bobbins spinning on social media feed with the tagline "As the bobbin spins".

"I sure didn't risk COVID to listen to a woman talk to her child's therapist. That was painful. Anyways, that woman claims her son is developmentally delayed because of an armored elf-like man and his farting pig."

That would make great fodder for a book I was thinking about writing. I pressed for details. "Was she on drugs when she saw these things?"

"She insists that drugs were not involved when both of them saw these things."

"Maybe paint fumes," I suggested.

"Maybe. You know, my publisher is on my case for another novel. So, I eavesdropped on the conversation for potential literary gold overload. I'll run this by my legal team first. Libel is a bitch."

Two attorneys in a week was more than enough for me, and I was pretty certain the way to make an attorney happy was to create more work in order to pay them more.

"No matter what you do as a writer, someone will always

attack your work." Stephanie tapped her temple. "People are convinced I'm crazy, so that story won't be too far of a stretch."

"True. Back to my question: What brings you out of hiding?"

Stephanie shot a thumb at the glass. "This town of Guilderland display. More than anything, I want to see how much information is incorrect."

"Acting like an Internet Troll?"

"Being a live action troll is a fantastic break from walking in circles around my neighborhood and writing. Also, they transposed two letters in your mom's maiden name."

"What?" I stepped forward to see for myself.

Deep-set lights illuminated the items that sat on glass shelves. A brief history of Guilderland was on display. While the Schoolcraft family and mine had a shelf each, Stephanie's had an entire shelving unit.

"That's not fair." I protested.

"To quote Monty Python: 'tis a fair cop.'"

"You do know that doesn't fit this situation?" I ignored Stephanie's bouncing foot and focused on the top shelf.

The first object was a book about Guilderland history by Alice Begley. Next was a black and white 1950s photo of Stephanie's paternal grandfather in front of the Western Avenue A&P. The towering fruit crates made it seem like he was closer to my five-foot-five frame instead of his six feet. I glanced over the other loose photos, faded scrapbook pages, and Stephanie's latest book.

I squatted to see the items on the bottom shelf. It was a grainy photo of the Guilderland Fire Department's grand re-opening in 1995. A tall man wearing thick rimmed glasses stood next to my father, it was Mr. Lauffenburger. Both clean-shaven men were in their ceremonial uniforms.

"Neat." I squinted at the fading images. "Dozer found a photo of us at the 1987 library reading event."

"Is that the picture where Cory Jr. photo bombed us?"

"How do you remember these things?" I asked.

"How did you forget the kid who wiped his snot on your shirt?"

"Some things are better off forgotten." I made a mental note to write his name down.

"I wish more people understood what goes into writing." She gave an overexaggerated eyeroll. "People think you write, publish, and poof you're rich. In two years, I've sold four copies at a royalty rate of one dollar and thirty-five cents each. Plus, over four dozen electronic versions have been downloaded during the free promotions." She sarcastically cheered, "I'm rich! Filthy rich!"

That's our Stephanie, making a joke to combat negative emotions. I knew well that many authors work a minimum-wage day job while their book collects dust on a library shelf.

"Oops," Stephanie jumped. "I forgot to tell you. There's a funding site collecting money to add a plaque to your telephone pole. It will commemorate the pole's 100th resurrection. That's ninety-nine more times than Jesus."

I changed the topic. "Is that a SPAMFAA photo?"

SPAMFAA was an antique fire truck appreciation group to which Mr. Lauffenburger belonged to as he had owned an antique fire truck. I pointed to a 1980s image of a man sitting behind the wooden wheel of a 1920s Fire Truck.

"Yeah, that's Dad in the driver's seat. The large, run-down hose cart behind the chemical truck was mine."

If she hadn't pointed out the fire apparatus, I wouldn't have noticed the plain-clothed Amish man standing next to the hose-cart. "Does that guy look like Gargamel to you?"

"Most people say my dad resembles a bespectacled Charlie Brown."

"I meant the guy in the background. The one whose dark hair is cut like his barber placed a bowl on his head for measurements."

Stephanie bent over and removed her fogged glasses to study the image. Keeping her glasses in hand, she stood. "He's the guy Dad was going to hire to restore my hose cart."

"I still can't believe you had a hose cart as a child."

"Why not? You had a taxidermy squirrel in lederhosen."

"Dad made that thing for Franky, not me." I narrowed my eyes.

"That's right, yours had a kilt and bagpipes."

I had to rein in the conversation. This picture was a potential lead and we had gone down the path of my father's roadside artwork collection.

"A few Amish communities still use hose carts."

That seemed obvious. Electricity wasn't involved and the concept was simple: you hitch a horse up to a cart, it pulls the cart that has a hose wrapped around the middle, and the horse pulls the cart to water, like a pond for example. The firefighters then place one end of the hose into the water and use a lever on top of the cart to pump the water out of the pond while another group of firefighters holds the nozzle end at the base of the fire. Less dangerous than a bucket brigade.

"I know and mine was from Pennsylvania." Stephanie's almond-shaped eyes became slits, hiding her blue irises.

"Neat. Do you know who the Amish guy is?"

"If my memory is correct, the cartoon character's doppelganger was a Mennonite out of Ohio. He specialized in the restoration of farm equipment pre-1900. He insisted my Dad restore my hose cart. The worn-out antique vibes added character and I refused to have it restored."

"Do you know his name?"

"A guy in Indiana was the go-between as that guy in the photo didn't own a telephone at the time. I think his name was Knepp."

A bell went off in my head. "Knepp?"

"Yes. That was it."

"Do you have a copy of the photo I can borrow?"

"I shave an electronic copy of it." Stephanie tapped her smartphone's screen. "Do you have air drop?"

I held up my flip phone.

Stephanie gave me a thumbs-up. "Emailing it now and this may be nothing..."

She put her glasses back on. "I'm working on a movie with the assistance of the Pine Bush preservation group your mom was involved in. If you haven't done so already, run your mom through a search engine. There's a fantastic black-and-white, 1970s protest picture of her chained to a tree to help save the Karner Blue butterfly."

"Is this going somewhere?"

"Yup." Stephanie was swaying. I was taken aback that she hadn't started before this. Her ADHD energy typically kept her moving. "I recommend you look closer at your mother's health. This doesn't feel right."

"Can you elaborate?"

"Sorry. I'm still thinking about that kid," Stephanie apologized. "Shortly before your Mom's death she asked me about ADHD medications. I explained to her that a little unknown potential risk is sudden death in people who have heart conditions. She didn't know if heart issues ran in her family and was going to schedule a cardiologist appointment. I don' know if she made the appointment but this sounds like medical negligence."

A child in a neon orange ballet outfit bounded by announcing, "I went poo-poo in the big boy's potty."

"Thank you for noticing my son's issue." The forty-something mother in a beige business suit nudged her child toward the exit.

The child held up an iridescent dragon. "Mommy, do you think the warrior elf will be outside?"

"No." The woman was shaking. She gave me an apathetic look. "My son's been convinced elves and dragons are real ever since he saw a man dressed like Peter Pan who borrowed a top from the Tin Man."

Wide-eyed, Stephanie cheered. "That's going into my book!"

CHAPTER 11

Lavender had been one of my favorite scents. Since my headache teetered on migraine, I edged toward despise. I yanked the batteries out of the air freshener as if I were tearing the stuffing out of a demonic doll from a disturbing movie, and slammed the machine into the kitchen garbage can alongside the other two.

Once Mom had discovered odor cover-up devices, she became obsessed. To her, it was easier to buy a case of air fresheners than to clean.

My stomach released a painful growl. I groaned. Food from my family for the bereavement period had trickled down to a carton of eggs from Franky's chickens. Those were yesterday's lunch and dinner. Today's breakfast had been the last nut-free marzipan cookie from Dozer.

I sat at the dining room table staring at a mound of historical newspaper printouts wishing I had read Nancy Drew books. That series might have prepared me for what I was up against.

Since the Morgan side of my family immigrated to the Albany area around 1700, I had fewer than two hours to weed through three centuries of information before the library closed for the night. Instead of skimming for pertinent information, I hit "print" on every item that mentioned either side of my family.

I was back to the black and white printout of Stephanie's Lauffenburger's e-mail. A younger version of Ezekiel stood between a giant metal wheel and an antique firetruck driven by a guy who resembled Charlie Brown.

"What is the connection?" I sipped black coffee from a cup decorated with an upturned arrow and the words, "I'm with stupid." My attention rolled to the ceiling. It was quiet.

The doorbell rang. I pulled my bathrobe tight before peering out the window and saw nothing. In case it was a neighborhood kid selling cookies, I cracked the door open.

A hunched figure sat on the top step. White, teased hair bobbed as the figure sang offkey in Spanish.

I knelt next to the older woman. "Mrs. Sanchez?"

Gaze fixed on the clapboard house across the way, she swayed to the song she was singing. When she finished her verse, Mrs. Sanchez's face lit up like she had run into a close friend she hadn't seen in decades. "Gladys."

I shook my head. "Does your granddaughter know you're out?"

"Oh dear, she's darning socks. Is that nice man you met on the Web treating you well? You deserve the best."

She placed a clammy hand against my cheek like a mother consoling her child. I reminded myself of her dementia. Instead of arguing, I pretended to be my mom and thanked her for helping me set up the account.

"Oh Gladys." She smiled. "I was worried. It's not like you to not answer my text messages. That's why I hopped over."

"Text messages?"

"Don't be ridiculous." She patted my hand. "You know I use Cheryl's cell phone to check on you. Speaking of which. I'd best get going before she worries." She brushed at her ankle-length floral print dress and made her way down the walkway. When she hit the empty driveway, Mrs. Sanchez pointed a sneaker-clad foot at a patch of lawn. "A gnome will spruce that right up."

"Yes."

I watched her navigate her way back to her home next door. "Mom's cell phone."

I rushed to the coat closet. When I identified Mom's remains the hospital had given me a transparent plastic bag full of her personal affects. I pulled out the hospital bag and dumped the contents out on the slate floor.

Her dress, shoes, pantyhose, makeup case, and inhaler were there. Her purse was zippered shut. I opened it and added its contents onto the pile. No cell phone.

I hurried to the dining room table where my cell phone sat. I flipped it open and dialed Mom. Her phone rang twice, then went to voicemail.

A generic message told me to leave a message. I ended the call.

"Two rings," I said to myself in disbelief. Someone had hit "decline." I dialed again.

This time, a man answered. "Hello."

My voice cracked as I spoke. "Who is this?"

"If you dialed me, then you know."

"I don't have time for your games. You have my mother's cell phone."

"Possession's nine-tenths of the law." He disconnected.

CHAPTER 12

Satisfied that I had gotten Mom's cell phone company to investigate her stolen phone, I went back to the table and began to read over articles. Birth notices, death notices, Franky's DWI infraction, the missing horse from our great-grandfather's farm, my parents' wedding announcement, and Uncle Olaf's arrest.

The man was worse than Franky. Uncle Olaf had stolen a goose from a local park for Thanksgiving dinner. The front-page article had a photo of the goose in a tuxedo.

The next printout was the article about Dozer's career-ending injury. I read through it:

> *A home invasion almost turned fatal when Stuart Wemple, a life-long resident in the town of Guilderland and owner of Wemple's Bakery, interrupted a burglary in progress. He had chased the intruder through four yards, when he hopped a wooden fence. There, Wemple was mauled by a vicious attack dog.*

My brain was stuck on the animal's description: "a vicious attack dog." That thing weighed at most three pounds. I continued to page C4 to finish the article:

> [...] *Wemple was transported to Albany Medical Center. Doctors are hopeful he will make a full recovery. The vicious animal was put down by animal control officers. Guilderland Police ask residents to lock their doors and to contact their hotline number below if they see this man.*

A full color photo showed a pale greasy-haired man. His sallow eyes were lost in high cheek bones. His thick lips were certainly purchased from a plastic surgeon.

The incident had hit Dozer hard. His home had been broken into and the intruder was at large. Then, there was the physical recovery that spanned several months.

In the middle of that fiasco, Dozer had taken too many pain killers and told me he wanted to whisk me away to places unknown. Since I'm terrified of commitment, I declined the offer. Soon after Dozer sold his property and moved from the Town of Guilderland to the City of Albany.

"Why must things be so complicated?" I shouted into the cluttered room.

It wasn't like the boxes of 1960s doll parts were able to answer me. On top of the shelf, above an out-of-date television set, sat the taxidermy armadillo who held an expression of judgment.

"I don't think so, Arny!"

The armadillo didn't answer. I pushed aside the thoughts of Dozer's perpetual tan body of perfection. There was no denying my desires to myself. No one needed to know the truth.

I popped a migraine pill, sipped my coffee, set the cup on the floor, and flopped onto the couch. "When my headache subsides, I'll read over the rest of the documents."

Shuffling noises carried from the entrance. I sat up. The door slammed against the wall. My head pounded.

I leaped to my feet, yanked the floor lamp with a force that pulled the cord from the wall, and positioned myself to fight. Not knowing what else to do, I did my best impression of a lion roar.

"Put that thing down before you hurt yourself." Franky hobbled on crutches.

Behind him, Leah clutched an object as she closed the door.

"Dude!" I slammed the lamp down. "Doorbell!"

"Who else outside of Dozer is going to come into to this rat trap?" Franky's left leg was wrapped in a surgical boot. He held it to the side as he lowered himself into the chair. "Besides, Leah needs to practice her lock-picking skills."

"She can practice at your place," I quipped.

"Are you crazy? I'm not chancing the dog running off."

"And why does mall security need lock-picking skills?"

"It's for one of my college courses." Leah set the package on the floor next to her.

This was news to me. As far as I knew, lock picking wasn't a legally required skill for private investigators. Curiosity got the better of me. "Where is the college located?"

"Virgin Islands."

Just when I thought things couldn't get weirder, my cousin brought us all to another sublevel.

"Why do I smell wildflowers?" I plugged the lamp back in.

"It's the new cologne Leah got me. She wants me to avoid the odor the orthopedic sandal causes, especially since I gotta wear it for six more weeks."

She exchanged a newspaper-covered package for Franky's crutches, set the crutches against the wall, and wiped her hands on her black shirt. I wondered if she owned clothing in another color, like taupe.

"Franky made this for you." She handed me a bagel wrapped in a paper napkin.

"Thanks." I bit into my gift. Melted cheddar cheese, crunchy bacon, and a scrambled egg made my taste buds dance. "From your chickens." I muttered through a mouthful.

"The eggs, yes. Everything else was store-bought." Franky pulled the lever that lifted the footrest and tugged his blue flannel plaid shirt out from behind him. "Doctor also said I need to use this thing when I'm not lying on my back." He undid the ties, set the sandal on the floor, pulled up the pant leg, and began scratching a leg that reminded me of Sasquatch.

"You're supposed to wear a sock with that thing."

"There's a foam cushion inside."

I wasn't going to say another word. This argument wasn't worth the energy.

"Nice new fridge." Leah called from the kitchen.

I hadn't noticed her move. "Dozer found it on sale. It even has a built-in ice crusher."

Leah returned to the living room and handed Franky one of my beers.

"Ain't she great?" Franky chugged his beer to the halfway point. "She even opened it for me."

Aghast, I stared at Leah. She stood next to the dining room table staring at the papers. This woman had the audacity to break into my home and steal beer from my fridge. She was perfect for my cousin.

"Why are you here?" I knew full well the food had a cost.

"Leah used vacation time to help me out and to do research for you." Franky withheld information. Since his new girlfriend present, I wasn't going to push.

"From the stacks of printouts on the table, I'd say you've been investigating, too." Leah picked up a document, then set it back down.

"After my meeting with Pickles yesterday, I went to the library and printed out everything connected to both sides of my family. That stack is all I have to go on, since I had to return my rental car this morning."

"That's a lot of papers," Leah said.

Franky tsked. "Our family was one of the first inhabitants of this town. We don't have articles, we have volumes."

He was confusing encyclopedias with newspapers, again. Not having the energy to correct him, I went along with his insanity.

"Yeah, there was more. The library gave the five-minute closing warning when I ran out of change to pay for copies."

As I said those words, I remembered the article of Franky's first DWI was on the table.

"Did my guy clear things up for you?" Franky paused. "You did say you met him yesterday? Or did my painkillers make me imagine that?"

"To answer the first part of that: Yes, he cleared up a few things and has worked out a viable payment plan." I shoved the rest of my breakfast in my mouth. "Need I remind you, mixing painkillers and alcohol is bad."

"Beer don't count."

Leah walked around the room scrutinizing every inch of my childhood home. She picked up knickknacks, a flea circus trapeze, and an empty tin can before she rounded back to the fireplace.

She flipped through the pages of *Always an Immigrant* and pulled out an envelope. "Interesting bookmark."

"Mom used everything from string to report cards to save her place."

Franky nodded at the envelope. "What's that?"

"A phone bill," Leah handed it to me. "Have you gone through her cell phone?"

The pages from June showed that her data and phone usage were both up and she was behind on payments.

"It wasn't in her belongings. When I called it, a man answered. Right after, I called Mom's cell phone company. They've opened a case." That reminded me that I had a voicemail. "Crap."

"What?" Franky and Leah asked in unison.

"I forgot about the second job interview."

I played the message again and burst into a fit of laughter.

"Are you going to share?" Franky's asked.

I put the phone on speaker and pressed play.

"Good morning, Tatyana Willies…"

There wasn't any need to play the rest of the message. A bit embarrassed that I had missed the greeting when I listened to it the other day. At least I wasn't alone in not getting that job.

Franky held up a newspaper-covered package.

"Leah and I went up to the Amish store by the cart company." Despite his shortcomings, my cousin knew how to cheer people up. "It's a queen-sized quilt made by one of our cousins."

He had that familiar mischievous glow. This gift wasn't an altruistic offer, it was bribery. I didn't care. I love handmade quilts. I got up, snagged the package from his hands, returned to the couch, and spoke to Leah who had a facial expression that indicated she was curious.

"Our grandmother, Sarah Hochstetler Morgan, left the community at eighteen to marry our Grandpa Morgan." Franky tapped his temple. "That's why I use newspaper as gift wrap."

"And churn butter." I tore off the newspaper and held up a folded quilt. The eight-point star pattern was made of blues, greens, cream, and white. "Seven stitches an inch." I rubbed the soft masterpiece against my cheek. It smelled of cinnamon.

"You both churn butter?" Leah asked.

"And hand-crank ice cream," Franky spoke to Leah. "Grandma Morgan kept some of the Amish traditions. Marrying our Grandfather was how she got out of the order she hated. You'd think having a kid out of wedlock at sixteen would've done it."

"What?" I nearly fell off the couch.

Franky whistled. "You missed out on all the best gossip!"

I wadded up a piece of the newspaper and tossed it at him. He hit it aside. "Don't throw objects at an injured person."

I tossed another wad of paper. It bounced off his big toe, skittered across the floor, and landed at Leah's combatboot.

"That's why you never made a sport team in college." Franky tossed a wad of newspaper back at me. It hit the top of my head. Satisfied he had won; Franky spoke to Leah. "My mother gets all the dirt. Don't know why people confide in her. She repeats it all."

Leah's lips twitched at the corner. I guessed we were on the same page for this one. My cousin hadn't fallen far from that tree. Franky continued talking. "Our Grandmother got sent to Ohio when her parents found out she was knocked up."

"She didn't go to Ohio to help a pregnant relative?" I asked.

"Grandma was that pregnant family member in need," Franky said. "Since she was the only child born to an Amish bishop, they had to shove this under a rug. So, she was sent out of the area where she gave birth to a daughter. Until a few months ago, no one knew."

"What caused the truth to surface?" Leah's expression was hard to read. If I had to guess, I'd say constipated.

"Dunno," Franky said over my response. He had the floor and was enjoying it. "The Amish are patriarchal. Since there were no sons, all of the bishop's belongings went to Grandma's Uncle Levi. Then when he died, Uncle Jonathan inherited everything which included the Amish buggy company. After Talia's father passed, that company should've been handed down to us." He pointed from himself then to me. "Instead, Talia's mother sold the company to a second cousin on the Amish side for pennies."

"That's the watered-down version," I folded a newspaper scrap into an origami crane. "Our grandmother was excommunicated when she married our grandfather. That meant we shouldn't have inherited anything. We figured she had juicy dirt on someone."

"I love our grandma." Franky wiped at his watering eyes. "A baby is one heck of an extortion item. When you meet her, ask her about the things she swiped as a teenager."

Being that Leah is a law-abiding citizen, it was my guess that our matriarch wasn't on her list of people to meet.

Franky must've had the same thought. He shrunk in his seat and glanced up at his girlfriend and struggled to backpedal.

As fun as it was watching him flounder, I knew this was the moment Leah chose to stick around or bolt. I did the one thing a loving caring relative would do, I helped dig the hole deeper.

"Yeah, our grandmother also stole from Englishers (that's non-Amish people) cigarettes, moonshine, and a llama."

"Llama?" Leah stifled laughter.

That was a good sign. Few found our family entertaining. In fact, most were disturbed by our shenanigans.

I explained, "When our Grandma Morgan was nine, she put on a stolen Englisher's bathing suit and snuck over to a neighbor's farm for a midnight swim in their pond. She lost track of time. To get home before anyone in the house woke up, she needed a ride. Since the horses were locked up, she borrowed the llama."

This was one of Franky's favorite stories. He pitched forward and used overexaggerated hand gestures as he spoke. "The next morning, her father asked why a llama was drinking at the pig's water trough. Our grandmother told him, 'It was God's will.'"

Leah was outright laughing.

Franky frowned. "This is the point when women leave me."

To my surprise, Leah stepped forward and kissed my cousin on the top of his greasy head. "Flaws and all."

This felt good. No one outside of our immediate family ever treated Franky like that. Maybe she'd stick around once she met our ninety-two-years-young grandmother.

"Speaking of family." Franky beamed. "I got my old man and a couple of his brothers to clean up The Bar for free. They felt bad about my foot. Plus, they set up all the stuff I won at that Schenectady police auction. We open tomorrow night and I still need a bartender."

"No way!" I protested.

"How are you going to pay for all of this?" He made a sweeping motion with his hands to the disastrous room. "You haven't had a job in over two years and that Ezekiel guy got all your mother's money. You start work tomorrow night."

"No. No. No." I protest. "The last time you volunteered me for work, a goat ate my car's floormats."

"Those bite marks were improvements." He scratched his chin in a way that doubled as a crude Italian gesture.

"Don't you use that language at me."

"What? I was scratching an itch. Besides, you love me."

"Like herpes."

"Ouch." He clutched his chest, mocking a heart attack. "Oh, and I gotcha a present at the auction." Franky jangled a set of car keys. "It's not as fancy as the one you totaled, but it's free."

Before I was able to respond, my cell phone rang. Pickles' name flashed on the Caller ID.

Attorneys never call on a weekend to give their client good news, unless the client was in jail. Since I was on the outside of metal bars, I pressed speaker. "Hello."

"Talia Morgan?" A man's voice spoke.

My cousin waved as if the man on the other line was able to see him. He whispered, "Turn it up so I can hear him better."

"Yes," I rolled my eyes. "Franky's here too."

"Franky! How's my favorite client?" That answer didn't settle my nerves at all.

"I'm doing great. Got you a possible lawsuit. The manufacturer of a refrigerator didn't use proper screws in the hinges, and I got a broken foot from their negligence." Franky held up his discolored foot.

"As much as I'd like to see the outcome of this," I interrupted the discussion. "It's the weekend and this is my dime."

"Yes, Ms. Morgan." Pickles gave a poignant cough. "I did some digging, free of charge of course, and discovered that your mother's original will includes Franky."

"No way." Franky stood up and fell into the recliner. His voice was strangled as he spoke, "I was written out of my Aunt Gladys' will? What jerk did that to me?"

I held up a hand. "That 'jerk' was my mother."

"Your mother loved me. Someone forced her to change that will." Franky stuck his tongue out at me.

"Real mature." I gave him the finger.

"Like that's any better." Franky held up both of his middle fingers.

"Mr. Calderone." Pickles' voice trailed off. For a few seconds, papers rustled on the other end of the phone. "I found a copy of the original signature page mixed in another client's papers file. Edna Calderone was a witness on the original."

"Ma is a force of nature who won't be happy about this." Franky stared at Leah who appeared to be in deep thought. She set her beer on the fireplace mantel and remained silent.

"What's all this mean?" I asked.

"Since your mother isn't available to answer any questions, I attempted to contact the witnesses," he paused. When the attorney spoke again, he lacked the confidence he typically exuded. "Raphael Guteriarz? I think Raphael's last name was misspelled."

"He's the guy I got the bar from!" Franky shouted louder than necessary. "What's he gotta do with this?"

"Here's the oddity," Pickles said. "The will had to be re-written because a couple letters were transposed in the last name of Olaf … yeah, I can't pronounce Polish last names."

I groaned. "He's Mom's uncle."

"That side of the family don't get squat." Franky blurted out. "They disowned Aunt Gladys when she married Uncle Jonathan."

"Exactly," Pickles said. "Mrs. Morgan added a failsafe into her will to prevent it from being contested. Her side gets nothing."

"Well, I'm not in there. I'll contest it." Franky slammed a fist into the soft arm of the chair.

Pickles stated in a matter-of-fact tone, "In the event we need to contest, I'm adding you to the list right after your mother."

"Aw crap," Franky whined. "You're risking Armageddon."

Pickles sounded cheerful as he said, "I'll draw up your will."

"Drink up, Franky," I joked. "This might be the end for you."

"Ha. Ha." Franky waved a hand. "Mom'll go after the co-signers first. Since one is dead and the other is in the wind, we have time to solve this mystery. Speaking of which, we gotta tell you what we found on this Ezekiel Knepp guy."

"I'm listening," Pickles said.

Franky's Sicilian heritage was showing as his hands talked faster than his spoken words. After several minutes of his tirade, he ended on, "Since this guy didn't exist until the late nineties, I'm thinking witness protection."

"More likely, he was born into an off-the-grid community." Pickles commented.

I began to say what I had learned from Stephanie when Leah interjected, "He dated other women who left him everything. They were all in perfect health and all died of heart issues. One in Springfield, Ohio, and the other in Charlottesville, South Carolina."

While I sat in stunned disbelief, Franky answered, "Wendy Walker, was a Mennonite who owned and lived on a horse ranch alone. She had limited interactions with anyone, and she didn't use the Internet. This Ezekiel guy also owned a winery and worked as a nurse in a psychiatric facility. When he received his inheritance from Camille Osburger, his profession was grave digger."

"I'm sorry," Leah said to me. "Sociopaths have been known to go to great lengths to alter themselves to hide in plain sight. Most people can't spot them."

"She's correct," Pickles confirmed.

This was a verbal game of Ping-Pong and I was a spectator suffering with whiplash. "You're all right, Mom was targeted. Unless, those are gold," I pointed to a box of plastic lids, "Mom was broke."

The click of computer keys carried through the phone. "I'm plugging this all into my computer," Pickles said as if he were reporting the weather. "I'll have to hire a P.I. to dig further."

"I'll do it," Leah said.

"No," I said. "While I appreciate your offer. This guy might me a serial killer and I put you at risk."

Pickles reminded me what his pay rate was and how much a licensed private investigator was going cost. Sticker shock hit.

I ended the call. "There's no way I can afford all of this."

Franky jangled the car keys, again. "Pay is minimum wage plus tips."

He knew he had me. I'd be broke in a few weeks, if I didn't take up the offer. This was it.

"Fine. I'm bartending. Not cleaning."

"Great!" He tossed the keys, and I caught them. "Be there tomorrow at 8 p.m. Doors open at 9. Close is 3 in the morning. You'll love the place."

CHAPTER 13

The word "Love" didn't do Franky's trendy, hot spot justice. Burgundy stained-glass light fixtures cast eerie shadows across a line of liquor bottles. In the center was a cash register that sat next to a decorative, horizontal, wooden crate.

I was almost certain that crate was from the chicken coop. Instead of holding eggs, it held bourbons from a local distillery. Behind the booze was a polished sheet of brass that ran the length of the bar. It reflected distorted images of us as if we were ghosts trapped inside a magic mirror. To top it off, the entire place smelled like a dumpster.

Dozer looked like he wanted to run out of the place screaming. If I didn't need the money, I'd have dashed out of the place too. I had anticipated a chalk outline, fake blood, and a coffin instead of a 1970s jukebox.

I spoke for the both of us when I said, "Franky's done a great job on creating a vampire dive bar."

Aunt Edna laughed. She thought I was joking. Her ankle length pink dress swayed as her stiletto heels clacked on the floor. "Always a kidder." She pointed silver acrylic nails at what I was certain were asbestos tiles. "These gems were hidden under that fake wood Raphael had installed."

Dozer flipped through the juke box's music selection. "Nice. This has a song titled 'Hole in the Wall.'"

"There's no way that's a real song." I sidled up next to him to see the options. Not finding what he referenced, I said, "You made that up to describe this place."

"It's a real song," Aunt Edna said. "Again, your humor. Oh, and don't worry about food."

"What does food have to do with music?" I whipped around to face her. "Franky didn't say anything about food."

Bait and switch was a typical move used by my cousin. He felt it was easier to apologize than to give too many details up front. I wasn't going to screw up food and beverage orders.

"Relax." My aunt waved a hand at me. "Since it's impossible to find help, the kitchen was converted to an office area. That way, Franky can do his work here in quiet."

At moments like this I wonder how Aunt Edna and my father had been raised in the same family and turned-out polar opposites.

I was more confused that relieved. "That makes no sense. Your son is a bachelor living alone in the woods with his senior dog."

Aunt Edna tapped a pack of cigarettes against the palm of her hand. "Don't forget the chickens. They make a ton of noise, and you know how sensitive my boy is."

Dozer shot me a facial expression that meant "Let it drop."

I shook my head. There was more. I wanted to find out what was really going on. "Aunt Edna—"

She cut me off. "My poor boy was behind schedule. Then, everything came together for his dream to become a reality."

I whispered to Dozer. "What was in that note Raphael left?"

His whisper was so low that I almost missed his words. "He said he was leaving and left the bar to Rick Olsen, our landlord. What I want to know is how did Franky pass inspection?"

"Who cares about the inspection?" I whispered back. "I'm more concerned about a woman in her sixties walking on heels made of sewing needles."

"Ahh, you two love birds remind me of my son and his girlfriend." Aunt Edna motioned for us to follow her to the back. "I can't tell you how happy I am he found Leah."

A cockroach ran over my sneaker. I elbowed Dozer. "Bribery. That's how he did it."

"Toilets are in here," Aunt Edna announced. "We have men's, women's, and a gender-neutral handicap room."

I thrust a finger at Dozer's face. "If there's a snake in one of those bathrooms, you're chucking it."

"Me?" He backed up. "Oh no. That's all you. I draw the line at reptiles."

"I'm not doing it."

"Hey." Dozer pointed. "What's with these toilet signs?"

"My boy is a visionary." Aunt Edna batted her thick fake eyelashes.

Each of the three restrooms had a different sign. The first two were the traditional 'Men' and 'Woman' stick figures on cheap plastic squares. The third door had the words "All Genders Welcome" scrawled across it in black spray paint.

Franky was more of a crayon vandal. I swiped at the sign. No paint rubbed off on my fingers. "Why didn't he use permanent marker?"

Aunt Edna lit a cigarette. "The street artist who was tagging the side of the building didn't have one."

Great. Instead of calling the authorities, my cousin had the vandal tagging private property paint a sign inside. This sinking ship had its mast above water. I squeaked as if I were a rat jumping off the tip into the Hudson River.

My aunt sucked on her menthol cigarette.

"Why are you smoking inside?" I tried to grab her cigarette.

She swatted my hand. "It's my only vice."

"Smoking isn't allowed inside. Franky can lose this place if you don't put that out."

I mentally kicked myself for speaking up.

"To get myself into a size eight, I had to give up bourbon." Aunt Edna released a smoke ring that floated to the overhead sprinklers. Nothing happened. That wasn't comforting, and neither was her passive comment about my weight gain.

"I'm a twelve." That was according to the pants printed on tag, although the frumpy sweater was at least a sixteen. Since the annoying tag had been removed, there wasn't any confirmation.

Aunt Edna gave me the once over. "Yeah." Her tone indicated disbelief. "If you're a twelve, then I'm a two."

"This is a 1970s mug shot of a Mafia crime boss." Dozer removed a picture from the wall.

Fixated on the rest of the establishment, I missed the wall decorations. Black-and-white mug shots had been cropped to eliminate the numbers at the bottom and framed to give the appearance of celebrities not of the twisted bank robbing and murder kind of fame.

"Where did he get these?" I asked.

"That Schenectady Police auction." The cigarette hung from Aunt Edna's lips. She tucked a piece of white hair under her brunette bouffant wig. "He figured he'd cash in on the local crime obsession. After all, it was rumored Raphael's disappearance was the result of a Mafia hit."

My stomach did a flip. "I'm not feeling well."

Aunt Edna scoffed. "If you get sick, go up to Dozer's apartment."

"Why don't you want me to use the bathrooms here? And what do you mean when you said Raphael might have been the result of a Mafia hit?"

"You have got to get caught up on the gossip. I heard from a reliable source that Raphael borrowed money from the mob to make this place happen."

"Is your reliable source the same woman who fit you for that wig?"

Aunt Edna flicked ash on the floor. "She's a pro."

"The pool table smells of urine." Dozer scrunched his nose.

"Once people are in, the smells won't matter." Aunt Edna quipped. "And they aren't rumors. My boy got confirmation from a pizza delivery friend."

"Wait Geoffery is back to delivering pizzas?" I asked.

Geoffery and my cousin Franky had been friends since the second grade. He was always tapped into the Guilderland gossip. Whenever Geoffery started a relationship, he went back to delivering pizzas. The tips were fantastic, especially the cash ones which he neglected to declare on his income tax.

"Until the pandemic hit, he dated this Russian woman who worked at a massage parlor. She's the one he got his information from. That proves it's true."

Just like Franky, my aunt latches onto an idea in her mind and refuses to budge no matter how insane it sounds.

Dozer busied himself by inspecting the painted wall.

I decided to check my work area. Clean beer taps hooked up correctly, I tested one. It spat at me.

"My genius son tipped the water ratio to earn more money on each mug." Aunt Edna's voice welled with pride. "That's a sound business investment."

I leaned my hands on the mahogany counter. A patron had carved, rude comments into the top. "Why didn't he have this sanded these down before refinishing it?"

"It adds character." Aunt Edna headed to the back door and opened it.

Dozer slid onto a barstool in front of me and read out loud. "Jerry wuvs beer."

I moved a stack of cardboard coasters over the words. "That's horrible spelling, not character."

Aunt Edna blew a kiss from the back door. "Hey, Dozer, we're counting on you to ensure all who enter are at least twenty-one."

The door slammed shut. The lock clicked into place. The stool Dozer had been using toppled to its side on the floor.

"I'm not a bouncer!" He ran to the back door and pushed on

the emergency bar. It didn't budge. "She jammed it." He ran out the front door. The large, storefront windows allowed me to watch him run towards the corner that connected to the side street, which led to the entrance to the back parking lot.

"That's my family." I reminded myself as I dashed into the men's room in search of graffiti.

Overhead fluorescent lights blinded me. Clean blue and white tiles lined the wall. Three sinks sat under clean mirrors. Two powder-blue cubicle stalls had easy-open doors. Next to them were three urinals. It was then I understood why men were faster in the bathroom: Most women's rooms had two stalls.

The door slammed open. "She's gone." Dozer leaned against the sink closest to the door. "She wedged a metal bar against the back door, and Franky's phone is off."

"This behavior surprises you?" I scoured the wall. "If my weasel cousin left a message..."

"Don't insult rodents." Dozer pointed to a handwritten message next to one of the mirrors. "For a good time, call Talia."

"I'm going to kill him!"

Dozer rubbed at the message. "Premeditated homicide has a longer sentence."

My cousin had used my vulnerability to talk me into bartending, a job I hadn't done since college and hated. Then, he dragged my best friend into the bedlam.

As I fumed over that last bit, Dozer's comment hit me. If was going to do anything, I needed clarification. "How does one get a sentence longer than a death penalty?"

"We don't have time. Familiarize yourself with the liquors. I'll take care of the smell and the graffiti."

By the time Dozer had cleaned my information off all the bathroom walls, I had the liquors and bar top organized. It wasn't like riding a bicycle. It was more like trying to cram your adult self into one of those metal desks in an elementary school.

Dozer set the stool back up and sat across from me. "Next week, Franky gets a new bouncer."

"No one will notice if we forget to open. This place has been boarded up for six months."

"Unfortunately, your cousin knows where we both live."

"And Leah's a lock pick." I leaned back to take in the set-up. Glasses, rags, jars of maraschino cherries, olives, and tumblers lined the area under a polished bar top.

Dozer went silent. His mind was elsewhere. His body relaxed. After a beat he spoke again, this time his voice carried a wistful quality. "We met in a bar not much better than this one."

"Yeah, and that creepy guy who touched me received a light sentence."

His back was rigid again. His jaw was clenched. The assault still bothered him just as much as it did me.

I picked up a prohibition era bottle of liquor and slid it onto an open shelf under the register.

"Franky said Olsen let him keep Raphael's stuff and this doesn't seem like anything he'd have on hand."

"No." Dozer checked his phone. "I have time to retrieve air freshers."

CHAPTER 14

If The Bar had been redesigned as a retro Disco Hall, I'd have been satiated. Instead, I was irritated over Franky's mafia motif. My touches were limited to placing coasters over crude words and lighting cookie-dough-scented candles in front of the elongated brass mirror.

"Everything in place is a nod to the Electric City, not the state Capital." I tossed the dish rag onto my shoulder.

Above thirty-watt light bulbs cast a dull hue onto the antiqued polished wood. The red glass lampshades had originally been the old Mongomery Wards diner in the long-gone Mohawk Mall. That must have been a Leah touch.

"Almost ready for the crush of people." Dozer sprayed the pool table with another hit from the air freshener. "We have offended the cockroaches."

"To Franky's Bar." I held up an unopened bottle of beer. "A place where New York's oldest residents visit."

"And that's how your cousin will spin it."

Dozer had walked the interior perimeter a dozen times by the time our first customer slithered in. He left a minute later when I told him we didn't serve chicken wings. Around eleven, Leah and several of her mall security friends arrived. She and the three guys were dressed in black. It's a slimming color. The side bulges on their cargo pants added padding in all the wrong places. I was comforted to know that Dozer had back-up in case things got worse.

Two of Leah's co-workers racked up the pool balls while a third tattooed muscular guy walked to the jukebox.

"Your boyfriend has quite the classic collection." The man pushed the buttons, plunked in a quarter, and 1970s disco poured out of ceiling speakers.

"I don't know how you're staying alive with that song," Leah shouted to the man and pulled up a barstool in front of me. "When Marvin's in the office, he plays that song on loop."

"How big is the office you all share?" I asked.

"Not large enough."

Marvin's head bobbed as he swayed in place. He shouted over the music, "I promoted the crap out of this place on social media."

Fists clenched Marvin began to hop. His movements were both disturbing and mesmerizing. He stopped all movement. A few beats passed before he thrust his hips in what might have been an Elvis Presley impersonation.

When he began gyrating, I asked Leah, "Is he having a medical emergency?"

"Dancing."

I set a beer in front of her. "That's not dancing."

She downed half the bottle before responding. "You don't want to be sober if he starts singing."

The woman sitting in front of me was a nice fit for Franky if he didn't ruin it. I pushed aside the thought of the guy who had stolen his identity and the local crime group that had tried to take down the culprit. All that group did was make things worse.

A man sat next to Leah and yelled for a shot of whiskey. I grabbed a bottle and a shot glass.

The man yelled, "Regular. Not flavored."

I set the bottle of honey whiskey back on the shelf, picked up the correct one, and poured a shot.

Leah leaned over the counter to talk to me. Her voice was difficult to hear over the music. "Franky forgot to tell you, that Bowser didn't escape that day you went to feed him."

"What do you mean?" I downed a shot of whiskey that burned my throat. The guy who had ordered it stared at me. I grabbed a clean shot glass and poured a drink for the guy. "On the house."

He downed his shot and left, brushing against a group of men in business suits. One of the men appeared to have had a bad experience with a traveling plastic surgeon. The three men surveyed the room and sat at the far end of the bar.

"Can I help you?" I yelled to them.

They didn't respond.

"Dozer's enjoying kicking underaged people out." Leah pointed to a crush of college-aged people as their hopeful beaming faces shriveled into juvenile pouts.

I agreed. He was enjoying this part of his job. A stream of middle-aged men poured in alongside a Cher impersonator.

Once I had served the easy-to-remember requested drinks, I set another beer in front of Leah. "What happened at Franky's?"

She motioned for me to lean closer. When I did, she whispered, "Your cousin's home was broken into."

"For what? He didn't have anything of value."

Then my brain went back to the missing excavation equipment. Since her property is where Franky borrowed those items from, I didn't mention them.

Leah pulled a napkin out of the holder. She set it under her glass bottle and gave me a look that said, "Do you think he'd have anything of value in that dump?"

A man next to her held up two fingers. "Beer."

At least his order was easy. I poured beer into two tall glasses, carried them to the end of the bar, and collected a ten-dollar bill.

"No tip?"

The man walked away. More interested in what Leah had to say, I pocketed the money and returned to her.

"There's more going on than we realized." She placed a hand on my forearm. "Also, be leery of the suited man, at the end of the bar. His name is Jackson. Surgeries aren't that slime ball's only obsession."

She glanced at my chest. When the heat kicked in, I had switched out my sweatshirt for a low-cut white T-shirt. Anyone who has tended bar knows the bigger the cleavage the bigger your tips. I gave my top a downward tug.

A robust African-American woman slid onto the stool next to Leah. Her braided hair was dyed magenta, and her makeup was simple. "I'm Henrietta." She waved. "Normally, I'd shake your hand. Since COVID, I avoid that pleasantry. Anyways, I live a couple floors up from here."

"That's a nice dress." Leah pointed to the white baby-doll dress that hugged the woman's beautiful curves.

"Thank you. Yes. This was supposed to be my laundry night. That's why I'm in this old thing." Henrietta batted full eyelashes. "I'm hoping people don't get the wrong impression about me, being that it's fall and all. I figured since Dozer is the bouncer, I'm in good hands. He's a perfect gentleman and we're the only women here, so there isn't any competition."

That hit a nerve. I force myself to nod in agreement. "Beer?"

"No. Thank you. I'm five years sober."

Henrietta leaned back and glanced at the closed front door where Dozer stood surveying the room like a sentinel. He was wearing a pair of faded blue jeans and the long-sleeve microfiber shirt that I bought him for his birthday.

The door opened. Another group of college students strolled in. Dozer checked their IDs and motioned for them to leave. Once the door shut behind them, my friend rubbed his hands together in an obvious attempt to keep warm. I wanted to run to his apartment and grab him a coat and gloves, if I had, the liquor might vanish.

"Dozer told me about the opening." Henrietta fanned herself. "It's been my experience that when a fine man invites you to a place, you don't disappoint him."

She adjusted her breasts back into the dress. I hadn't realized they had started to spill out and neither did any of the men.

I lifted my gaze to meet Henrietta's. "You're here for Dozer?"

"Yup. And I would've arrived sooner except my hairdresser ran late. I'm hoping I heard right, and our maintenance man is single."

Leah ran a finger over the carved graffiti that had emerged from under a cocktail napkin. The offensive phrase had been altered to read: "Book you."

"How'd you find a hairdresser on short notice?" Leah asked.

"She lives on the third floor." Henrietta pointed up. "I can get you a discount on lip enhancements if you're interested in plumping up those thin lips of yours."

Leah was about to speak when Henrietta cut her off.

"Okay, bartender, you gotta have information. Dish."

"A bit presumptuous." I grabbed a cocktail shaker.

Henrietta slid a compact mirror out of a powder-blue clutch purse. "When Dozer ran up the stairs to retrieve the box of candles, he called his son Hector to let him know he was roped into bouncer duty and wasn't going to able to talk to the woman he was planning on speaking to this evening." She added lip gloss. "The bartender is a close friend of his. That's all I got before a rude man pushed past me. I'm hoping that woman he wanted to talk to was me."

She was on the prowl. Anger bubbled to the surface. Even though I had rejected his advances, I didn't want Dozer to have a romantic relationship that did not involve me.

The words slipped out of my mouth, "He's gay."

A dozen heads pivoted in Dozer's direction as all the males in earshot scrutinized him. In unison, they nodded their approval.

Leah's lips curled at the corners. She was enjoying this.

"I'm not buying it." Henrietta leaned back and checked Dozer over like he was a prized steak. "I live one floor above him, and

I've heard him talking to both of his sons about this Talia woman. She clueless about his feelings for her. If a woman is that closed off to a man, he best move along and find himself an available woman of higher status."

All sound was gone. It was as if the cord to the speakers at a death metal concert had been yanked from the outlet. Dozer had talked to his sons about us.

Leah's lips moved. I stared at her. She snapped her fingers. At first, sound was muffled, and slowly ebbed into a mixture of a soft to loud incoherent mess. I tried to pop my ears until the sounds evened out. My IQ dropped to hover around that of a pecan.

I swallowed hard before responding to Henrietta. "What did he say to his sons?"

She shook her head. "I'm not one to gossip. However, I did hear him say he's loved this Talia woman for years, except she doesn't reciprocate his advances. One of his sons told him that she needed space since her mother died. Then the other son told him that this Talia person had commitment issues. Either way, they both told Dozer to wait for her. When she's ready, she'll let him know."

For a woman who doesn't gossip, she laid it on thick, and now everyone in earshot knew Dozer loved me and I was an idiot. Several dejected men left, and another group of men entered. Their attire was a mixture of 90s grunge and 50s beat poets. I allowed my gaze to sweep over the sagging pants of a Caucasian male whose T-shirt advertised the original Ninja Turtle movie. Holes lined the long-sleeved shirt that it covered, and his purple knit hat rested on top of a ball cap. *Why hadn't this fashion trend died?*

"Bartender." Leah snapped her fingers at me. "You might want to put that down."

My knuckles were white as I gripped the metal cocktail shaker. I eased it onto the counter.

Henrietta held up a twenty. "I'll have an orange juice. In one of them." She pointed to the hanging champagne glasses above my head.

I had been preoccupied by other details, such as the location of the fire extinguisher and adjusting graffiti that I missed a rack secured to the ceiling full of glasses.

I opened the fridge, pulled out the orange juice, opened and sniffed it. "Still good."

"Yo, barkeep!" Jackson shouted. "I was here first!"

"Excuse you!" Henrietta shouted down the bar. "Can't you see I'm having a private conversation here?"

Jackson ran a hand over his slicked-back brown hair. "Shouting to the bartender about your crush isn't private. It's rude."

Dozer stood behind him talking to a woman who appeared to be a teenager. The woman huffed out the door. Another underage person booted.

"Do you see this twenty?" Henrietta waved the bill. "I'm a paying customer."

Jackson leaned back.

As if on cue, Leah elbowed Henrietta. "That guy in the suit is divorced and doesn't drink alcohol."

"I don't usually go for guys who've had that much work done. Plastic surgery is a sign of vanity." Henrietta leaned over the counter to get a better look. "Oh, he's wearing a gold pinky ring, and that suit is expensive. Is he employed?"

"I thought you were interested in Dozer," the guy in the turtle movie shirt said as he slid onto a barstool.

Henrietta swiveled to face the man. "Our well-seasoned bouncer is occupied at the moment. That don't mean I can't seek out other opportunities."

"Whatever." The man pointed at the beer tap.

I grabbed a mug and poured him his drink. Foam spilled into the grate. I slid the wet glass to the man. "On the house."

"It's all foam."

"Its free!"

He complained about my incompetency as he walked away. That eradicated the guilt about his drink being nine-parts water. The music shifted from Disco to a Rock song.

I caught the words "Hole in the wall." Several patrons raised their glasses and cheered.

Leah reached over and plucked up a cherry by its stem. "Jackson works for a used car dealership and has no emotional involvement outside of his vehicles."

Champagne glass full of orange juice in hand, Henrietta slid off her perch. "Dozer has got to get over that Talia chick. If she ain't interested, he best move on."

I poured a beer for an impatient beat poet.

"Thanks." A full glass of actual liquid held tight to his chest, the beat poet vanished into the horde.

After I had given Jackson, and the husky guy next to him their non-alcoholic drinks, I sauntered back to Leah. "That guy is familiar. What else can you tell me about him?"

"A few years ago, he did a stint in a low-security prison. I caught him shoplifting last week and had to run a check."

I used a cotton rag to wipe up spilled beer. "What'd he lift?"

"Rogaine."

"A man who cares about his appearance." I tossed the dirty rag at the metal bin, missed, and it landed on a lit candle.

Flames shot up. I grabbed the fire extinguisher and hit the flames' base with foam before they got to the alcohol. Fire out, I snuffed out the rest of the candles.

Leah was next to me. She had shoved the mess into the metal bin. I glanced to the sprinkler system; it hadn't gone off. Another violation I needed to speak to Franky about.

"Hey, barkeep!" The free beer guy yelled as he approached me. He swayed. At first, I thought he was going to be sick. Instead, he tossed beer on me.

Part of the room was frozen in place while everything else moved fast-forward. Several males shouted. Pepper spray was deployed. A woman screamed. Then Dozer was carrying the jerk who tossed his beer on me to the exit.

I had never seen an adult carried by the back of a shirt and blue jeans. His arms and legs were stretched out, as he yelled, "I can fly! Woosh."

CHAPTER 15

I was exhausted, freezing, and reeked of beer. The overhead street lamp flickered on to off, plunging me into darkness.

"Albany budget cuts." I tightened my grip on my pepper spray. The streetlight flickered back on.

A towering graffiti-covered brick rowhouse loomed over me. I cut my eyes back to Franky's dream bar. The ambiance teetered on train wreck, and the jury was out on its clientele.

Raphael had created a serine place. My cousin had destroyed it by adding photos of former crime bosses and a pool table he found discarded on the side of the road.

I thought back to Dozer hauling a drunk out for tossing his drink on me. Leah and her crew went into mall security mode defusing the situation and helping us clean the aftermath of the fire I had caused. Thankfully, the overhead sprinklers malfunctioned. Leah said she'd have them fixed before the next weekend.

Water dripped from a planter secured in a fourth-floor wooden windowsill, mournful tears that carried a sharp pungent scent kissed a crumbling sidewalk. Discarded pieces of bubble gum morphed into a blackened polka-dotted pattern on the concrete.

"You're married!" a husky voice announced from above.

Morbid curiosity tugged my head back at whiplash speed. A light was on in a third-floor apartment.

"Do I want to know what Henrietta's up to now?" Dozer strode up next to me. The reflective pinstripe on his navy-blue windbreaker glowed under the streetlight.

The conversation we had flashed through my mind. I chewed the inside of my cheek as I debated repeating what was said.

Dozer elbowed me. "Five bucks on the used car salesman."

"Leah said he's divorced."

As if on cue Henrietta shouted, "You said you were divorced!" Articles of man's clothing rained down. "I don't tolerate lying or cheating."

A brown leather shoe bounced off of my car to the cracked curb. Dozer picked up a suit jacket.

"What are you doing?" I asked.

"Free clothes." Dozer slid into the jacket that hung on him as if he were a child playing dress up.

"That naked guy will march down here for his clothes."

"He'll go for a towel first." Dozer slipped out of the jacket, snapped a photo of the inside tag, then dropped the article on the sidewalk. "I want to know if this is a knockoff. The label isn't like the one Dad wears."

Thank God for pretentious parents. I've met Dozer's stepfather a handful of times and never once did he wear a tie that wasn't made from imported silk.

Incoherent shouts carried from above.

"Don't you gaslight me!" Henrietta's voice reminded me of an electric sander on metal. "Get out of my apartment, you cheater! And don't you dare take my towel!"

Dozer jabbed a thumb upward. "Fodder for your novel."

He was right. I was ready for more and my writing was a means to a new life. Vocalizing my agreement meant that once I figured out Mom's estate, he'd remind me every chance he had that I needed to focus on writing. I have plenty of drive, it's focus I lack.

"Use Frank as a character. No one will believe that he's a real person." Dozer gifted me his dimpled smile. "And we'll hire a literary attorney to protect you in case his mother sues you. Then, throw in your Amish grandmother, your Aunt Edna, this dump, and..." he paused. It was as if he contemplated each word. He shifted weight. "All you need is a love interest."

It felt like the acknowledgment of a love interest for a fictional character was the same as saying Dozer was my love interest, and I wasn't ready.

Light reflected off the few flecks of gray scattered in Dozer's hair. "It'd help you pay your bills."

I stepped off the curb, bumped into the dented rear of my car, and slapped the rusted trunk.

"Most expensive car I have ever owned."

Dozer crossed his arms. "The four different-colored doors give her character."

"Those increases the value of this gem as they make it less likely to be stolen." God, I sounded like Franky.

"Right." Dozer held that word out longer than necessary.

"You're enjoying this too much." I threw my messenger bag on the passenger seat and settled in behind the wheel.

A crazed naked man rounded the corner. Dozer motioned for me to leave. I drove off.

CHAPTER 16

In the pre-dawn hours, I lay awake, enjoying the warmth of my cinnamon-scented quilt and the darkness of my new bedroom. It was a pleasant change from the hard mattress, tattered comforter, and the streetlights pouring through the threadbare sheets I used as curtains in my musty trailer. Guilt gnawed at me as I thought about how easy it was to adjust to my current living arrangement. The only reason I had this luxury was because I had lost my mom.

I adjusted the down pillow against my aching neck. The nightmare of the opening of Franky's bar played on a loop in my mind, from the rude guy tossing his drink on me to the flames I extinguished. I pulled the covers to my chin as I attempted to relax. A loud thump came from the attic.

"Raccoons," I groaned and rolled out of bed.

My feet hit the floor mat and I recoiled at the unfamiliar texture. Every room of my trailer featured worn-out linoleum. This was going to be an adjustment. A thump sounded from the living room. I pulled my housecoat off mom's treadle sewing machine and padded my way toward the nightlight in the hall. To save money, my dad had installed nightlights throughout the house. That way, our home was never shrouded in darkness and every month we saved a minimum of five dollars.

I didn't care about the five dollars. I flicked on the overhead light in the hall and stood still until my eyes adjusted. Piles of boxes towered over my head. There was no way I'd be able to search through this hoarder's bounty for answers on my own.

A thump came from the kitchen area. I assumed this meant the attic creatures were attempting to escape. As long as they didn't visit me on the main floor, our co-habitation was fine by me.

I yelled up to the ceiling. "Enjoy the attic rude tenants."

The ungrateful animals gave no response.

I grunted at their insolence and shuffled into the kitchen where my black twelve-cup coffee maker sat next to a chrome barista-style, espresso machine. I figured if Dozer was able to toss a stoned antagonist out into the cold, I could face an intimidating garage sale find. Once I had everything set, I pushed a button. Frothy liquid spat out.

Hot liquid spewed at me. My housecoat intercepted the assault. In a frenzy, I slapped all the buttons. In the end, I pulled the cord, cleaned up the mess, and sloshed off to shower where I checked my thigh. All I had was a stinging, red mark.

Half an hour later, I was wrapped in my mom's tattered housecoat leaning against the clean counter, a cup of traditional coffee in hand. The doorbell rang.

"Please don't be a salesman," I muttered as I peeked through the cream-colored curtains.

The automatic, overhead porch light shone on a greasy, brown paper bag hovering in front of me. My mental state went from "I've been run over by a cart of cattle" to "I've won the lottery."

I swung open the door. A breeze carried the usual morning scents of fall and knee-weakening aftershave.

I shouted to a crouching figure, "Dozer!"

As he stood, his assessing eyes drank me in. "Did I catch you in the shower?"

I held up my coffee mug. "Missed that one by a few minutes."

"Dang."

I glowered. "Excuse you?"

Dozer's voice shifted to concern. "Are you okay?"

"I'm fine. My thigh hurts a little thanks to the espresso machine's murderous attempt."

"If it had wanted you dead, it'd have gone for your heart." Dozer handed me the bag and closed the door behind us. "When did you turn to fancy morning beverages?"

"Mom picked it up at a garage sale. I figured I'd give it a try."

Dozer removed his windbreaker and slung it over the back of a chair. He was wearing a long-sleeve, green plaid flannel shirt too big. While the shirt had me thinking "What the heck?" his tight blue jeans made me thing "He has a nice butt."

"Did you read the instructions?" Dozer removed the pot and stared at the inside.

"Garage sale items tend not to have instructions."

I placed one breakfast sandwich on an empty space on the table and began to eat the other one. Dozer ignored my near-orgasmic sounds while he worked on the machine. In a few moments, he had the thing whirring. "All set."

"Show off." In between bites, I asked, "Is this lumberjack outfit your Halloween costume?"

"After that guy left, Henrietta had me fix a leaking pipe in her bathroom."

My mind raced back to her admonishment at the bar. The thought of her hitting on Dozer upset me. Not wanting to make myself sick over all the what ifs, I asked, "Did she hit on you?"

"No." Dozer fumbled with the shirt's top button. "I can't stand buttoned shirts."

"Then, why wear it?"

"George gave it to me." He yawned. "The plumber wasn't available, so I duct-taped the pipes. I woke up to a flooded closet, and what I'm wearing was all I had available."

Dozer held up a perfect cup of espresso.

"How did you get that machine to work?"

He set his drink on the table. "I'll show you how to use it if you let me use your washing machine."

"Deal."

Concern plastered on his face, Dozer sat across from me and placed a hand on mine. "I'm sorry I wasn't able to be there for you when you lost your mom."

"I told you your sons were more important than me. We'll get through this."

Creases appeared at the corner of his eyes. "We will."

His actions, more than the words, comforted me. I knew he'd be there, no matter what—and that's what scared me. I involuntarily flinched. Dozer ran a smooth thumb over my knuckles. He knew me better than anyone.

We finished our meal in silence. Considering how I felt, it seemed fitting. The natural music of us eating and breathing had a calming effect on my tattered soul.

Dozer glanced at the stack of documents. "Research?"

"There's more I wasn't able to get." I tapped the obituaries stack. "Several of Mom's relatives died of heart attacks between the ages of fifty and seventy."

"What's this?" He held up a black-and-white printout.

"A printout of a picture from Stephanie Lauffenburger. Her dad almost hired that guy to do restore a hose cart."

"And you have this photo… because?"

I meant to tell Dozer about the photo instead I said, "Leah discovered that Ezekiel inherited businesses and insurance policies from other women. Plus, he didn't exist on paper until the 1990s. It turns out that Mom had another will. Pickles said that I need to find the original will to overturn this one so I can get that fifty grand."

"Impressive, and here I thought Pickles was only good for turning DWIs into parking infractions."

Normally, I'd argue. Instead, I changed the topic. "Mom's will was rewritten. Raphael was a witnesses. Plus, Stephanie's working on a movie."

"No more pixies." Dozer groaned. "One of her pieces is not worth killing over."

Stephanie's work was a unique blend of LSD-inspired images and flawed characters that virtually went nowhere. Yet, she never did drugs and had gained a large following of stoners.

Dozer held up the photo. "Back to this."

"Yes! That guy is a Mennonite from Ohio."

Dozer set the picture aside. "Didn't your grandmother visit Amish cousins in Ohio when she was a teenager?"

"Yes, and I found out that she had a baby and left it with her cousins in Ohio. They raised her as their own. Oh, and they owned a buggy production company that also restored antique fire apparatus."

Dozer raised his head. I had his full attention.

"Franky and Leah stopped over to give me an Amish quilt. That's when he dropped it on me that at age sixteen our Amish grandmother had a daughter out of wedlock. Plus, Pickles and Leah are both doing leg work on this Ezekiel guy. He's a serial dater who used various aliases and received money from those he dated after they died."

Dozer was on his feet. "Why don't you get dressed?"

I stared down at my bathrobe. There wasn't anything underneath it. I sighed.

CHAPTER 17

When Dozer had requested that I get dressed I contemplated shucking my bathrobe and staying that way. Those thoughts had gained in frequency. I needed them to remain thoughts. That's why when I wandered into the dining room, I had on a pair of mom's old bellbottom jeans, a sweatshirt, and a pair of beat-up sneakers.

Dozer stared at me. "Teal?"

"It accentuates my eyes." It also draped over my curves like a potato sack.

He set a metal travel mug in the center of the paper mess on the table. "I have to make a phone call. We leave in five." He vanished down the hall.

"Okay, lumberjack."

I stared down at an article from my teenage years.

The headline read: "Amish Bishop Hochstetler Death Ruled Homicide."

It was believed that my great-grandfather was securing a rogue horse into its stall when he fell and had hit his head on a wooden post. Grandma Morgan swore her ninety-five-year-old father had been murdered. Since Franky and I had been at her place when she had received the news, she brought us along to the desolate village's police station to contest their findings.

She had barged in speaking Pennsylvania Dutch like she was the mayor on a campaigning mission. She demanded to see the officer in charge. Confusion creased a middle-aged woman's face as she sat behind the reception desk observing us.

My irate white-haired grandmother was draped in an oversized Motley Crue T-shirt that hung over her spandex-clad, spindly legs. The odd scene was amplified by two terrified teenagers in matching Englisher pajamas acting as translators.

Since the Amish distrust outsiders, Great-Uncle Levi had secretly called Grandma from the Bishop's landline to let her know he had found her father dead. Until we started translating, all Franky and I knew was that our grandmother had dragged us out of bed to rush down to the county where her birth family lived. I pushed aside the article about my great-grandfather's murder and saw Levi's obituary underneath.

"Anything of interest?" Dozer asked.

"It's odd that they died so close to one another."

"Not may surviving relatives." Dozer picked up another printout. "This article says his sister-in-law returned to Ohio to be with her family. No maiden name given."

"From what I remember, she died a few years later in a buggy accident. Her family followed a stricter Ordnung. It was around dusk. The driver of the plow didn't see them. If they used a reflective triangle, they might not have been hit."

Dozer set down the paper. "Is 'Ore's dung' a painful disease?"

"It's pronounced 'ore-d-none-g' and it's the rules Amish are supposed to follow. The Hochstetlers were more liberal. They used reflective traffic triangles on the back of their buggies and the women are allowed to wear purple dresses."

Dozer slid his jacket on. "When this is over, I'll make you whatever meal you want."

"Mmmm … bacon marzipan."

"You couldn't resist."

"Your horrified expression was worth it."

He shook his head. "I'll toss my laundry into the dryer when we get back from the Yoder Manufacturing Company."

I glanced over a few more articles, including one attached to a 1980s, black and white photo of a younger and heavier version of my mom. She was chained to a tree in protest over the development of the Pine Bush Preserves. My mom, the endangered-species-loving activist, was wearing a tie-died tunic and bellbottoms.

Dozer grabbed the to-go container from the table. "Someone at the company might have information about your family that tie into this mess you're in."

"Need I remind you, we're both Englishers? We'll accomplish nothing."

Dozer held his phone between the two of us. "How about a compromise?"

"Depends on what you're proposing."

He grinned.

"Get your mind out of the gutter."

"You started it."

"Fine." I grunted. "Just tell me your compromise idea."

"We'll Facetiming your grandmother."

"That's a bad idea." I protested.

"Hello." My grandmother's voice came through the phone's speaker, while her nostrils filled the screen.

"Grandma, you're on Facetime, not speaker." I glared at Dozer.

"Sorry, Dear." The image moved until grandma's leathery, wrinkled, face stared back at us. "This phone Franky gave me isn't what I'm used to. Is that Dozer?"

"Hi, Grandma." Dozer waved back.

"Did you two elope?"

I was mortified. Dozer's on the other hand was wide-eyed. I pretended not to notice.

A male voice thick with a Polish accent yelled, "There will be no bagels for you in the afterlife."

"Shut up, Olaf." Grandma's image bounced.

Behind her a man swore in Polish. My grandmother set the phone down. A string of words were shouted in Pennsylvania Dutch.

"What did she say?" Dozer asked.

"May your cows produce sour milk."

"Nice." This comment came from the man who rarely swears.

The on-screen image bounced. Polish and Pennsylvania Dutch were thrown around like a verbal game of dodge ball until Olaf let out a shriek akin to a person with arachnophobia being confronted by a tarantula.

Grandma was on-screen again. She beamed like the Cheshire cat moments before Alice trotted off. "I tossed my hemorrhoid pillow at that buffoon."

Anyone else would've been horrified. As for me, I was trying to figure out how she had the strength to throw an object.

Grandma blew raspberries to someone off-camera. "May you trip on it and break a hip."

And with that comment, I spewed out the words, "He has questions for you."

I stepped aside.

"Hey!" Dozer shouldn't have been surprised. It's not a secret I'm coward.

I pointed to him. "Bouncer."

Then, I pointed to myself, "Chicken droppings."

"Yes." Grandma beamed. "Since both your parents are deceased, I give Dozer permission to marry you."

That wasn't what I had expected my grandmother to say. The last time I had spoken to her she asked about medical marijuana.

"We all know Franky isn't going to give me anything other than chickens." She gave a curt nod. "It's up to both of you to get cracking."

Dozer went rigid. I leaned over the phone.

"I need to ask you a few questions about your family's company. The one your Uncle Levi left to your son."

"You two better marry before I die."

"Grandma!" I shouted.

She gave an over-exaggerated eye roll. "The cart manufacturing and antique restoration business wasn't worth much. The land, however, was."

"Land?" Dozer and I asked in unison.

"Yes. That old place is owned by the Yoder family. Don't ask me which one. That surname is as common as Knepp."

Off camera, raised voices argued in in Polish. I recognized a few words. None of them were worth repeating.

Grandma shouted, "Shut up about your toothpicks!"

"Toothpicks?" I asked.

"Last week, he received a box of toothpicks from a deceased relative. He said it's a Polish insult. I told him that we're in America. This is an insult." She flipped the bird and hung up.

In stunned disbelief, I collapsed in to a chair. There was no denying it. The facts were in front of me.

"My Uncle Olaf is in the same retirement place as my grandmother. She'll murder him when she finds out he's the one who made the fake tombstone that was placed on my parents' front lawn when they moved in. He put Mom's death date as their wedding day."

"That's harsh." Dozer placed a hand over mine and squeezed. "If given the chance, your Grandma Morgan will slip a laxative into his food."

"I said 'murder him,' not give him diarrhea."

"It all depends on her mood. She might make him suffer for a few days before offing him."

Both were options I preferred not thinking about.

"The company probably has the answers to what Mom's will is protecting. You win. We're visiting the Amish."

CHAPTER 18

The SUV's illuminated clock turned to quarter after eight in the morning. During my two-year stint of unemployment, I'd grown accustomed to sleeping in past ten. I sipped espresso from an aluminum, to-go container.

If you drive like Dozer, the Amish side of my family lives about an hour away, while I've made the trip in forty minutes. Instead of demanding he pull over and let me drive, I downed the last drops of my drink, then set the empty receptacle on the excessive bellbottom material at my feet.

"You can use the cup holder." Dozer's jacket made a swishing sound when he pointed to the center console where his cobalt travel mug sat in the holder closest to him.

"Don't use logic on me before noon."

My words were a sharper than intended. Dozer tightened his grip on the steering wheel as he stared at the lengthy highway. Typically, he sloughed off my sleep-deprived snaps, but this one he internalized. His sons were both in need of his assistance, and I was eating up his time. I believed his mood shift was my fault.

Instead of reaching for his hand, like he'd do for me, I allowed a few moments of uneasy silence pass.

"I didn't mean to upset you."

There was a pregnant pause before Dozer answered in a distant voice. "If you're worried about my sons, don't be."

"Stop reading my mind."

"That isn't hard to do."

I tried to think of a pithy, noteworthy comeback, a statement to ward off evil in a room of demon-possessed teenagers. Instead, I closed my mouth and grunted.

"After this trip, we'll take a nap." Dozer hadn't meant to imply we'd nap together.

Betrayed by my mind I enjoyed images of his arms wrapped around me. I suppressed the thought as we passed a derelict barn. The moss-covered, concaved roof reminded me of a weighted tree canopy. Attached to the faded front door was a sign bearing the image of a white X inside a red square. Another farm building to be demolished.

"This town needs food—not more apartment complexes."

"Your distractibility is heightened today."

It was embarrassing to acknowledge that I felt like I was a cat chasing specks of dust in a room full of floating catnip bubbles.

"Your family has more secrets than you realize," Dozer said.

"Isn't that part of being a family?"

"Yes, but yours has more than a typical family." He faltered on the word 'typical' like he wanted to use another word. Since 'normal' didn't fit the Morgans, I accepted the substitution.

"Finally, something we excel at."

"A small cross to bear," Dozer said. "Talia, there are too many coincidences. Raphael, your mom, and now the Amish side of your family are connected by multiple strings. In addition, your Uncle Olaf is in the same facility as your grandmother. Why did he receive toothpicks, but your Grandma Morgan didn't?"

"All that's missing is a partridge in a pear tree."

That didn't even get a groan out of Dozer. He spoke matter-of-factly, "Someone on the Amish side of your family is bound to know something that'll explain what was worth killing the bishop and your mom over."

There was too much packed into that statement. We were both uneasy over my situation. I allowed my memories to shift to the child-sized carts Franky and I received as gifts when we were kids. They were miniature versions of what was used on the farm. One of those carts collected dust in my basement while my Aunt Edna used her son's for a medicinal herb garden. That's when it hit me.

Franky hadn't complained about toothpicks.

"I gotta send a couple of texts."

To limit the family drama, I sent a text to Franky and his parents. I returned my flip phone to my messenger bag.

"Do you have a plan on how to get the Amish side of my family to talk to us?"

"We walk in and ask questions about your great-grandfather's 1996 death and claim it's an unsolved murder." Dozer had a lot to learn.

"And what? Follow that with the announcement that my Englisher mother might have been murdered, then request to share information about the family business. That's a bad plan."

Dozer's nostrils flared, a sure sign he was agitated. I tried to change the uncomfortable conversation by pulling an envelope from the stack of papers at my feet.

"Leah found this old cell phone bill stuck in a book."

"Anything useful?"

I unfolded the document and scanned the phone numbers.

"Wow. There's one Mom contacted a lot."

I dialed the number, and hit speaker. After three rings, a woman's voice came on.

"If this is a telemarketer, we donate at church every Sunday."

"No. This is Talia Morgan and I—"

"Talia!" The woman yelled. "Oh! Thank heavens. I wanted to talk to you about—"

An older woman's voice cut her off. "If that's Gladys' daughter, tell her that Dozer's a hottie. I've got my binoculars out for their morning coffee and—"

"Grandma Sanchez!" The younger woman cut her off. "It's not appropriate to peek through our neighbor's window."

Mrs. Sanchez cackled like the Wicked Witch from *The Wizard of Oz*. "Who's peeking? I'm sitting in our living room for my own viewing pleasure." She shouted a few Spanish words, one of which referred to an oven.

Cheryl retorted in Spanish then switched back to English to address me. "Ignore her, Talia. Your mother's estate sent both of us a box of toothpicks. We had to sign a paper for it, stating that by accepting the contents of this box we will not contest the will. It also states that one person will receive a box containing a thousand-dollar cash prize." She shrieked. "No, Abula!" She hung up.

My mind whirled at the absurdity of that concept. A toothpick box wasn't large enough to hold one thousand dollars in cash and people willingly signed away any chance they had at a larger sum of money that didn't exist.

The corner of Dozer's lips were upturned.

I gave his biceps a playful poke. "Hey, hottie."

"Your mom was brilliant." He turned down the heat. "A thousand-dollar cash prize is a good incentive to sign away all rights to contesting a will."

I added the phone bill to the pile on the floor. "Let's pretend that Ezekiel's connected through my unknown aunt... Then why didn't he tell Mom who he was and ask for money?"

"Let's start by examining what we know. Your grandmother's pushing a hundred while this Ezekiel guy is around sixty. He's old enough to be her grandson. We know Ezekiel received other insurance policy pay outs. His motive to kill your mom is stronger if he knows the cart company was supposed to be his. He may think he can get monetary compensation by whacking everyone in your family for insurance money."

"Tact would've been nice."

The comment about 'whacking' everyone in my family had my nerves tingling, especially since it meant I was on the killer's list.

"It still doesn't make sense that my mom might have been murdered over a company she sold five years ago. And you missed a crucial detail. Franky."

"How? You sent him a text message."

That wasn't what I meant, and I had a feeling Dozer knew it; he was now in a playful mood. I refused to take the bait. "The cart business was supposed to pass to Franky and me. Since Dad didn't have a will, Mom got everything and Franky's place was recently broken into."

"I'm going to assume you missed telling me those details out of grief."

"No. I missed telling you about the break-in because Leah told me right before I almost torched the bar."

That removed his ammunition. Dozer tapped the steering wheel. "Valid point."

I opened the glove compartment in search of hidden candy.

Dozer shook his head. "Why are you rummaging through my glove compartment?"

I pushed aside papers, a factory sealed box of condoms, a miniature rubber chicken, and pulled out the remains of a package of butterscotch candies. "You always have candy for your sons."

The package had been rolled down to almost nothing as it had one candy left. I popped the sweet treat in my mouth, shoved the empty package back where I found it, and closed the compartment.

"I don't think there's enough to get Mom's case re-opened as a homicide."

"Try Pickles. He can order a copy of the autopsy report."

"Why did I follow Mom's prepaid funeral instructions and have her cremated?"

"Because you're a decent human being," Dozer said.

That's not how I felt. I felt like a chipmunk drunk on fermented berries trying to cross the highway in rush-hour traffic.

Instead of doing the sensible thing and calling Pickles, I sent him a long-winded series of text messages explaining everything I had learned. At the end of it, I added: "and that's why I think we need a copy of my mother's autopsy. Are you able to get a copy?"

A few moments later, I received a text message back letting me know he'd have the request drafted to be sent later today and to keep him posted on what else I found.

Since he was paid by the hour, I wrote back 'OK'.

"What are we missing?" I asked. "Ezekiel inherited a winery, a horse farm, and a place that dealt in afterlife accommodations. Sounds like an interesting party."

"It's not afterlife accommodations—it's a place that takes care of dead bodies."

"I prefer my interpretation"

The SUV slowed to a crawl behind a black covered Amish buggy. "Double solid yellow line." Dozer hit his four-way flashers. "We're in a fifty-five speed zone at eight miles an hour and twenty-two miles to our destination."

"It's us and an Amish family. You can pass."

Dozer scowled. "You know as well as I do, that many first responder horror stories involve vehicles illegally passing others. We are staying behind this family."

"My father and his fellow firefighters are the ones who told you those stories."

"Thank you for making my point."

"This is absurd. Over ninety percent of those accidents involved multiple vehicles and the only other vehicle, on the road right now, is a bunny rabbit."

"Double solid yellow line. I'm not breaking that law." Dozer's knuckles were white.

"No one will know." I waved in an attempt to use the Jedi mind trick.

"That doesn't work in real life. Half a tank of gas. I've got this."

CHAPTER 19

I tugged at my oversized turquoise sweater. The feel of it against my neck was aggravating me. "If I have to pee, you're pulling to the side of the road, Braveheart."

A yellow flash whizzed by the SUV's left side. I assumed it was a sports car. An object clunked against the driver's side. I gagged on the stench.

"Skunk!" I rapidly tapped the window button. "Why don't automatic windows have a speed differential like the old crank ones?"

"You can regulate the speed of your hand not the speed of the internal... oh this is bad." Dozer's window was half-way down. "It might be stuck on the side."

My head was out the opened passenger window. Fresh chilly air hit my face. Autumn trees lined a withering pasture. The rhythmic clomp of unshod hooves against asphalt soothed me.

"Wait... I can see in the side mirror a freshly washed black door. The skunk only bounced off." Dozer cheered.

"It's a sign." In-between gasps for air, I said, "Pull a U-turn. We'll go home."

"Nope. We're going to visit your father's former business."

I decided it was best not to argue. He was determined to meet the Amish side of my family and find answer.

"Oh yeah. They'll totally enjoy your green plaid flannel shirt, blue jeans, black jacket, and our new cologne."

"Fifteen miles to your family's cart company." His voice was hoarse. His cheeks glistened from his watering eyes. "We got this."

I leaned over the shift. "Speedometer says six miles per hour. The Amish driver is messing with you." That was the first time I had ever wanted Franky to be driving.

"Maybe their horse is tired."

"When you have your mind set, you can be an immovable object." I picked up the papers at my feet and flipped through them: Mom's will, newspaper articles, death notices, and a coupon for a free pizza at the joint on Western Avenue. I pocketed the coupon.

"Six miles an hour! Six!" Dozer's voice cracked. "These pacifists are as bad as your carny-dating, Amish grandma."

"There's a retired carny in the elderly care facility? Go Guilderland."

"No. Past tense. She dated a carny."

I was done. I demanded an answer. "What are you talking about?"

"The August before her sixteenth birthday, a carnival came out this way. She met this guy before her father shunted her off to Ohio. It's a gray area as to who was the bad influence."

It annoyed me that he knew this about my grandma, and I didn't. I tossed the papers on the floor. "When did you find this out and why didn't you tell me when we discussed her baby?"

"While you were changing, I called Franky. And before you get mad…"

He paused to give me a second to calm down. If we weren't stuck in a moving SUV, I'd have lost my temper. Chin up, I narrowed my eyes for emphasis.

"Already mad. Go on."

"I wanted to save time and see if he had useful information, on that side of your family to help us out today."

I rubbed at my right ear to massage away the pain. "You'd have better luck getting useful information out of a Magic 8 Ball."

"That Hasbro toy is why I called."

"What?"

"I pulled it off of a shelf and asked it questions. It kept telling me that the outlook was unclear." He grinned.

"That's wrong." My Aunt Edna's the one who collects fortune telling toys.

"Just you know, a carny did father your grandmother's child. That's useful information I obtained from Franky."

My anger drizzled down to annoyance. "You earned that point. Dozer fist pumped the air.

My cell phone chirped. I checked messages. "And Franky's pissed."

"Are cats still showing up at his house?"

"No. Leah discovered her rented jackhammer is missing."

"Where'd your cousin hide it?"

"He didn't." I let that statement sit for a minute before my brain switched tracks. "It amazes me that you got custody of both your sons, but your ex was able to take your trust fund."

Their divorce had been finalized well over a decade before I had this revelation. If this was any indication of how my mom's mystery was going, I needed to pack up and leave it to the professionals, who were not in my budget. Oh, how far I had fallen. I was considering hiring Leah to help.

"Trust fund money?" Dozer slowed to a near standstill, distancing us from the black Amish buggy. I hadn't realized he had inched up on the slow-moving vehicle.

"Your ex-wife bragged about getting your trust fund money."

"That trust fund." Dozer shook his head. "If I had that money, I'd hire a good attorney to help you out. Pickels doesn't appear to be that useful. As far as what happened to the family trust, my Mom didn't want Sandy to get a penny of her money so I never received any of it."

Talk family secrets. Dozer dropped an unexpected landmine into my lap.

"What?" I asked.

"Everything I've ever had I earned through my hard work. My ex got the money I had saved for a second pastry shop. My Mom held onto what supposed to be my money and divided it between my sons for eighteenth birthdays."

Just when you thought you knew someone as well as yourself, that person tosses you a curve ball that makes you feel like a pile of steaming elephant dung.

My phone dinged. I had forgotten I was holding it. The shock of Dozer's words kept me from checking who was texting me.

"You're as poor as I am?"

"That's a matter of perspective." He danced around the answer. "I keep a fire-proof box hidden under my bed. Once a week, I add money to it for emergencies."

"Isn't that where you hide your pistol?"

Most people find it odd that he has a pistol permit. They think the deep-seated terror from the paparazzi he encountered as a child is erasable. Those nay-sayers hadn't seen Dozer's therapy bills.

"Are you going to check your messages?" he asked.

"Digesting the fact that your sons have blown through two dollars was more important."

"It was one million and that might be Pickles."

The only million I had ever seen was sand granules.

"More likely it's a pissed-off relative upset about toothpicks." I checked my phone. "Oh, just as bad. They're Messages from Franky and his parents."

"What's the news?"

He ignored me.

"Leah talked to Grandma Morgan. Her baby was named Rebekka Yoder."

That name mocked me. It was one I should've known. I went over that part of the text again before reading the rest. "The baby was given to an Amish cousin whose family specialized in making Amish buggies."

"More buggies." Dozer pointed to the one we followed. "They aren't that sturdy."

"Anyways. Aunt Edna and Uncle Sal refuse to open their box until Franky checks it for explosives. Meanwhile, Franky says his had a note in it that read "box number fifteen.""

Dozer released a hysterical laugh. At first, I thought he was reacting to the vehicle in front of us.

"Holy crap!" I shouted as the scheme hit me. "Mom told him the safety deposit box number."

"He's the 'lucky' winner."

"That hurt." Too many load questions bogged down my ability to speak any of them."

"I'm guessing you have the bank's name." Dozer and I did a fist bump. "Your mom was awesome!"

"A bit paranoid too. I mean, my mom created a postmortem scavenger hunt. All I need to collect do is collect clues, and piece them together, to find the buried treasure."

I stared at the scenery as we inched along. Overgrown fields gave way to shutterless farmhouses. The plainness of the buildings made me think Amish.

Paint peeled off the side of a house obscured by a crumbling structure. Between them, a juvenile tree poked out of an antique manure spreader. Several feet away, a flock of sheep stood next to tilted grain silo. The nearby faded red barn reminded me of a movie involving an axe murderer.

The chill was getting to me. Since I didn't want to marinade in eau de skunk, I rolled my window up to an inch from the top.

"Dozer, there's an abandoned home and its driveway isn't weed infested."

"A safe pull-off point." He skidded alongside the buggy and pulled down the gravel driveway. "Let me see those papers again."

I handed him what I had. His brow furrowed while he remained in deep concentration. He flipped through several pages.

"Your lips move when you read."

He ignored me. Since there wasn't anything else to do, I pushed aside my bellbottoms to retrieve the book I use to fend off creeps. I ran a finger over the silver tape.

"Why is there duct tape along the length of the spine?"

I ignored him and reminded myself the original pronunciation of house had an oo sound.

"Hoose and moose—not house and mouse."

"I'd rather chase a seasoned cannibal down a dark alley than listen to Old English translations."

"That was Chaucerian English." I corrected.

Dozer knocked his head against the steering wheel. I stashed my book into my messenger bag. When I picked my head up, I saw movement from the side of the leaning silo of New York.

A man wearing overalls, a wide-brimmed straw hat, and work boots emerged. Determination plastered his face as he approached the front of the SUV. A lit cigar hung from the corner of his mouth. The muzzle of a shotgun was aimed at us.

My attempt at ducking under the dashboard failed when the seatbelt tightened its grip.

I yelled, "It's the seasoned human-eating, axe murderer."

The man cocked the gun. "I'm giving you skunk-scented trespassers to the count of three to get off my property."

Hands raised, I shouted, "I'm too fat for a stew."

Dozer set the papers on the dashboard. "Ted?"

The man lowered his weapon. "Wemple?"

My voice cracked as I yelled, "You guys know each other?"

The next thing I knew Dozer was standing in front of his vehicle giving the man an elaborate handshake.

"Hold up!" I fought to unbuckle myself. Once free, I climbed out of the SUV, tripped on the bellbottoms, regained my composure, and marched to the men. "What is going on?"

"This is the culinary genius who got me interested in the field." Dozer nudged the older man, who dropped his cigar on the ground.

When Dozer had regaled me with his culinary school exploits, he had described his mentor as a man who loved cigars. When Wemple's Nut Free Bakery opened, he introduced me to several of his old classmates who had joined him in that celebration.

"After my quadruple bypass, I retired." The man used his beat-up, steel-toed boot to grind the cigar into the ground. "Since Stuart was my best student, I sent him a three-pound bag of candy when he had his event."

They both chuckled.

My eyes flicked between the two of them. They were laughing. When neither let me in on the joke, I said, "I'm lost."

Dozer explained, "They're sugar-free."

That meant nothing to me. "I'm even more lost."

"Sweets." Dozer tugged at the hem of his jacket. "There's a brand of sugar-free gummy candy that works like a laxative. Since I was bit on my backside..."

He stopped there. My guess is he saw my appalled facial expression. He didn't finish his explanation. Instead, he rushed out the words. "They're in a safe place."

Ted ran a hand over his unshaven face. "How long you two been dating?"

"We're not dating," I corrected him.

"Right. If this isn't a romantic rendezvous, what brought you two out to my slice of heaven?"

Dozer quipped. "If this is Heaven what do you call Hell?"

Ted pointed his gun at the barn. "In a few years, I'll have this place set to farm corn. Now, tell me what brings you out this way."

Dozer gave him a quick overview of the past few weeks.

"My condolences." Ted rested his shotgun over his left shoulder. "For what it's worth, I'm not liking this duck you've got quacking here."

"It's more of a mystery than what happened to Raphael," I said.

"A man who left behind a note stating: 'I'm done with this festering pile of excrements. Off to Aruba' Isn't a mystery. It's a man who's pissed off and wants a life."

"Is that what the note said?" I asked Dozer.

"There was more to it than that."

Of course, the news media had announced it was a murder, it made for better ratings in an area where everyone is oddly connected. I didn't want to think about the number of times stories were embellished for the sake of ratings.

"There was a case, in the mid-nineties, the news media messed up that still bothers me." Ted shook his head. "An Amish bishop was murdered. The day it happened the news channels said he was killed by his own horse. At the time, I owned the only non-Amish bakery near where the incident occurred and a few weeks later his grandson stopped in to pick up donuts for his family. It turned out the Amish Bishop was struck multiple times by a hammer."

This was my family he was discussing. I leaned against the SUV's warm front as I processed this new information.

"You knew the grandson?" Dozer asked.

"Jonathan Morgan was a good seed, a bit of an odd duck though. His taxidermy art obsession was the tip of that iceberg. He was a wreck after several of his family members died under questionable circumstances."

If felt good to have a tangible morsel from outside the Morgan gossip mill. "Do you know what happened?" I blurted out with a bit more zeal than intended.

"Don't get out much? Do you?" Ted asked.

Not wanting a stranger to know the truth, I went with the most plausible lie. "Research for a book I'm working on." I gave my best charming grin and hoped I didn't come across as a patient fresh out of electroshock therapy.

"We all gotta start our trades somewhere." Ted shrugged. "About five years back, the Morgan guy died of cancer. Dang fool didn't go to the doctor, and it caught up to him. I ran into him at the supermarket a few months before. He was a walking skeleton. Told me he thought someone was after his family. Talk about paranoia."

My dad believed we were being targeted and never told me. I was stunned. "Did he say why?"

"Said the buggy company was on a two-hundred-acre family farm. Back in 1995, some guy tried buy the company and the bishop refused the low-ball offer. Turns out Jonathan was the bishop's grandson and he got everything when he died. The Amish relative was smart and made a will. Why a man who was dying of cancer didn't is beyond me."

I was going to speak up when something crawled up my pant leg. I released a high-pitched squeal and danced around. "Get it off! Get it off!"

Unfazed, Ted used the gun's stock to knock the creature off me. "That chipmunk likes you."

"Easy for you to say."

I kicked at the retreating rodent.

"Good seeing you again." Dozer and Ted did that elaborate handshake, fist-bump good-bye thing.

Ted slapped Dozer on his back. "When's your wedding?"

CHAPTER 20

Overhead, the garage floodlight lit my immediate area. Crisp air carried the faint scent of burning wood. Tiny windows peered from the top of white garage doors as if they laughed at my fatigue.

I slid the final box out of my garbage-find-of-a-car and slammed the trunk shut. It bounced back up. Three tries later, I felt a twinge of satisfaction when the trunk stayed shut.

Things would've gone faster if Dozer assisted me in moving my stuff from my trailer to my childhood home. After I met Ted, the guy Dozer had received his pastry training from, I realized how dependent I was on others, and I needed to be able to hold my own.

A couple of days had passed, and I alone had moved all I was keeping from one place to the other. Items left behind were part of the package deal to the next owners of my trailer. As I slogged to the walkway, a sleek black cat rubbed against my leg. I attempted to shoo it away.

Instead, the defiant creature waltzed up to my car and jumped onto the hood. A teal, bedazzled collar flickered in the sunlight as if it were made of precious gemstones. In general, having an outdoor cat was a bad idea. Living near acres of uncultivated woods was even worse. Foxes, fisher cats, coydogs and woodchucks had been known to roam the neighborhood. A pissed-off woodchuck is as dangerous as the carnivorous fox.

The cat gave her leg a few licks before trotting to an evergreen barricade. There she snaked her way between the divide and vanished into darkness. On the other side lay the lawn dotted with deteriorative gnomes. The side motion light flicked on. I was certain the cat thought those painted plaster creatures were lunch.

"Enjoy!" I tightened my grip on the box of dishes and stared at my house.

Above the front door, a bare bulb served as a porch light. The architect my parents hired to design the raised ranch created a 1970s masterpiece to withstand extreme New York winters. His creation included an alcove instead of a traditional porch to protect the inhabitants from the elements. A rusted milk jug occupied a corner spot perfect for a reading chair. I had begun to make necessary adjustments to embrace this place as my own.

A familiar shaky voice cut the thick night air. "Darn gnomes!"

I adjusted my position to watch Mrs. Sanchez approach. She wore a knee-length, mauve nightgown, and a floral shower cap.

"A housewarming gift." She held up a hunched lawn gnome.

"Is it mooning me?"

Mrs. Sanchez stepped back a few feet after she set the two feet high grotesque creature on the ground.

I stared down at the painted plaster piece. The mooning gnome was wearing a blue robe and a matching pointed hat.

"I painted him myself," Mrs. Sanchez smiled.

"Why are there dark streaks in his white beard?"

"He's a zombie."

The pride in her voice reminded me of a child who had created their first volcanic eruption of baking soda and vinegar.

"When I was fourteen, I relocated to this area from Puerto Rico by accident." Mrs. Sanchez kicked a sandaled foot at the asphalt. "When I arrived in New York City I told the guy at the bus station I wanted 'Amsterdam' instead of 'Amsterdam Avenue' where several of my cousins lived. The guy didn't ask for clarification. And that's how I wound up in the City of Amsterdam."

I set the heavy box down. "What does this have to do with a painted plaster statue?"

"Lots of people took cash under the table jobs to survive. I mostly did house cleaning and farm work. It was my ticket to a new life." Mrs. Sanchez pointed to the box in front of me. "If you're cleaning out, you're going to want a dumpster."

I chose to pretend that conversation hadn't just happen and slipped my hands into my sweatpants' pocket for warmth. "When you were at my mom's wake, you mentioned murder. Were you referring to my mother?"

"Oh no. I was talking about the guy in Albany. Word is he got killed over shady business dealings involving counterfeit items."

Raphael didn't seem to be the type to get into anything illegal. I wasn't going to let that slide.

"That doesn't sound like the guy Dozer knew."

A set of brown saucers peered up at me. The prospect of gaining juicy gossip perked her up. "He knew the guy?"

I didn't want to destroy what little entertainment this woman had by retracting my statement. "Yes, he did."

"Then he knows that a downstate guy acquired a few items from a shipwreck and duplicated them. I know that because I overheard Ezekiel talking on his cell phone one night. He even mentioned the house they hold the stuff in." She leaned forward and attempted a whisper. "Folks in this area don't know how clearly their voices carry. You'd be amazed at the things people talk about."

A door at the Sanchez house slammed shut.

"Grandma!" Cheryl yelled.

"My granddaughter is divorced," Mrs. Sanchez said. "I'm trying to fix her up with Anotelli. He's got a good complexion, a steady job, and his uniform compliments his physical assets."

I was embarrassed for Cheryl.

"Um—"

Mrs. Sanchez put a hand up. "Before you judge me, my granddaughter needs a good distraction. She's been trying to find her birth father and I don't have the heart to tell her the truth. That's he's a deadbeat. I hope that DNA test doesn't have any matches."

Cheryl huffed as she approached. Her aqua-colored pajamas depicted a pattern of leaping orcas.

"I'm sorry, Talia," she said in-between breaths. "My grandmother loves to sneak out at night, and I'm afraid the coydogs will nab her."

"Those puppies ain't got nothing I can't handle." Mrs. Sanchez shook a gnarled fist.

I didn't think her fists were a viable means to fend off a wild animal. However, they did give me better insight to the sheer frustration her granddaughter felt.

"In case of an emergency, I carry a knife."

"My late husband carried one of those too." A glint flashed across Mrs. Sanchez's eyes. "It belonged to his sister. She bought it as a means for protection when she crossed the border. When my husband inherited it, he used the knife to scrape the calluses off his feet and—"

"Grandma!" Cheryl yelled, cutting her off. "We don't talk ill of the dead."

"It ain't talking ill of the dead if it's the truth," Mrs. Sanchez stood, hands on her hips. "Your grandfather, Carlos Sanchez, drank a bottle of Scotch every time he gambled. Then, one night he lost everything in a poker game. A few days later, he departed this world."

"Cancer?" I asked.

Mrs. Sanchez shook her head. "Hit by a bus."

There was no safe response to that statement. If I had heard this nonchalant death admonishment when Mom was still alive, I'd have thought it was a joke and produced a sarcastic remark. Now that I knew the pain of losing a close family member in an instant, I felt an emotional tug for the frail woman standing before me.

Mrs. Sanchez clarified. "I didn't push him."

"Please tell me I heard you wrong."

"He had a few too many and chased after our neighbor's pig." Mrs. Sanchez was on the move. "Come on, Cheryl, let's find the telescope. Maybe that man of hers has a brother you can date."

I watched the women enter the house.

"At least my new neighbors are friendly." I told the zombie lawn gnome.

Dozer's black SUV rolled to a stop not far from me. He emerged and sauntered to the front walkway, a six pack of beer in hand.

I put the lawn gnome on the retaining wall near the Rose of Sharon, picked up my box, and walked up to the house where my angel in blue jeans and a black windbreaker stood.

"Did Levi spill any family secrets?" Despite how futile our trip had been, Dozer insisted on playing detective while I moved in.

Dozer pushed the door open. "Three coats of polyurethane."

"You're as bad as Mrs. Sanchez." I entered the house and set the box down next to the coat closet to mark the labyrinth's entrance.

Boxes of my stuff stood five-feet high. A pathway between the stacks led and racks of items let to a floor lamp, a 32-inch DVD-TV combo, and taxidermy artwork. My father had squirrels dressed in eighteenth-century clothes to recreate the signing of the Constitution of the United States, a cockroach from a trip to Manhattan, and an armadillo Christmas stocking holder.

"Mrs. Sanchez is in another zip code." Dozer locked the door behind us. "The secret to a high-quality cart is three coats of polyurethane."

"I told you the trip was a waste of time."

"No entirely." He set the six pack of beer on the kitchen counter. "Your mom didn't sell the company."

"What?"

"Your Great-Uncle Levin's will stated his belongings were to be divided among all surviving descendants of the bishop, including the granddaughter in Ohio."

Confused, I grabbed a beer.

"He knew about the baby?"

"Yes, and you as well as Franky. All we have to do is locate the correct Yoder family and we're golden."

"That's like trying to find a needle in a box of needles."

"We'll have better luck if we can get your grandmother to talk."

I knew that wasn't going to happen any time soon. I waved at piles of boxes. "Wanna help me search for the missing safety deposit keys?"

If you don't mind, I'd like to stay the night in case any issues arise."

"As much as I want to say 'yes', I'm going to have to decline." It felt wrong to refuse his offer, but I was on my way to being an independent adult and I didn't want a setback on day three days of my transformation.

"Let me know if you change your mind." Dozer sat on the couch, propped his feet on a box, and reached between the cushions." He held up a screwdriver. "Do I want to know?"

"A hidden weapon." I suggested.

"Right."

CHAPTER 21

A scratching sound broke into my sleep fog. My first thought was *Dozer's searching for the keys.*

I remembered that I had politely refused his offer to stay the night. My next thought was of the attic animals. Content, I wrapped the quilt tighter around me and inhaled the faint scent of cinnamon.

Sharp successive taps came from the front of the house. I blinked. Creeping fingers of moonlight reached through the blinds and touched trinkets on top of the 1980s oak dresser. While my insides raced, I reached for my cell phone. It wasn't there.

Confusion hit. A trace of moonlight hit the nightstand allowing me to see the hands on the analog clock sat at one thirty.

The shuffles grew louder. Metal clanked.

"They have to be here," a gruff male voice complained.

A loud crash came from the living room. I slid onto the floor. Frantic, I patted the area for my phone.

An indistinguishable voice cut through the echoes of my heartbeat. "On the TV."

I reached for the jeans I had worn the night before. Light flashed on inside my room. I eased my way under the queen-sized bed's underbelly.

Faint vibrations rumbled against my stomach as two individuals stomped into my bedroom. Inches from my face a knockoff brand's logo blazoned a set of pacing high-top sneakers.

A male voice swore in Spanish.

"What?" A baritone voice asked.

"House is empty. She must be at Wemple's place."

I had a brief glimpse of relief. Neither heard my movement.

The baritone voice increased his volume. "We'll have to finish her off later."

"I'm not deaf." The other man shouted back. "English is my third language."

The high-top sneakers closed in on my nightstand. The owner of them grumbled incoherently.

I clamped a hand over my mouth to keep from screaming. The nightstand's drawer slid open. Its contents clattered onto my bed. A tube of lipstick hit the floor and rolled next to my cell phone a foot out of reach.

"We don't get paid enough for this mess."

"Agreed. This hoarder's home is more like a house of horrors." The high-top man knelt.

Side pressed against a center set of metal legs, I clenched my hands into tight fists. I was prepared for a fight.

A large hand pressed against the floor mat. This was it. The moment he dropped to eye level he'd kill me. I choked down a whimper.

"Bad to the Bone" started to play.

The hand vanished. The baritone voice said, "Hello." He stood. "Yeah, that chick isn't here. We got one item on your list. Do you want us to torch the place?"

Tendrils of terror crawled through me while I listened.

"Cops are on their way." The baritone voice spoke. "We'll try again later. Then kill her."

I focused on my breathing until I saw the cuffs of black pants over matching polished black boots. My first thought was that this was a different group to kill me. I whimpered.

The individual knelt next to the bed. Fingers curled around the dangling blanket. I stifled a scream. The blanket vanished. That's when hope became the angular, Mediterranean face of Officer Anotelli.

His voice was full of concern as he asked, "Are you okay?"

"Yes."

I forced myself to slide out from under the bed. My legs were like wet pool noodles. I sat on the floor to gather my composure.

Next thing I remember, I was wrapped in one of my blanks sitting on the back of an ambulance, blinking into the lamppost light. A police officer handed me a warm heavy paper cup.

"It'll help calm your nerves."

I gave a shaky nod.

Antonelli asked. "Do you have any enemies who'd like to harm you?"

"No."

"Did either of them say anything to you?"

"Not to me." I paused. "One mentioned they had an item on the list. They weren't able to find the others."

"Do you know what he meant?"

"My mom died last month." I sipped the blackened unsweetened coffee. "She left me everything except her life insurance money."

Anotelli wrote on his notepad. "Who inherited that?"

"Ezekiel. I think his last name is Johnsonville. No, that's a hot dog." I pressed a thumb into my forehead in an attempt to force the name out. "All I can think of is sausages."

Anotelli's expression exuded compassion as he spoke in a soothing voice, "This has been a traumatic experience. Take a few deep breaths and steady yourself before you tell me what you remember."

I wanted to tell him everything that had happened. Instead, I set the coffee next to me. "That's revolting."

"That's candy compared to the coffee in our break room."

Anotelli's humor was a welcome comfort. He handed the cup off to someone else.

"In order to help you, I need to know more details. You said the men wanted to kill you. Can you elaborate on anything that might help us?"

That was the straw that burst the dam. I blurted out everything that came to my mind: Mom's death, the ADHD meds, the last minute change in her will, my new job as Franky's bartender, having to move, the guy Mom dated who got her life insurance policy, having to clean out old stuff to make room for mine, and even Dozer's gummies.

Anotelli soaked in every word. Once I was quiet, he asked, "What was Ezekiel's relationship to your mother?"

A barely audible click and a low buzz reminded me that his body camera was recording. Vanity kicked in. I wiped the crust from the corners of my eyes and pulled the blanket tighter to cover up my pajamas.

"They were dating."

I berated myself for leaving that part out. Again, I went on a tirade dumping everything I knew about this guy to all who were in ear shot. It felt good to get it all out, even down to the news intern who contacted me for an exclusive quote.

"I'll need the name of the news station and the woman who contacted you." Anotelli's tone was firm yet gentle.

Embarrassed that I hadn't thought to ask her those questions, I stammered, "She didn't give me either."

"Do you have a copy of the will?" he asked.

I noticed his eyes were a darker shade of brown than Franky's. "I left them in Dozer's vehicle."

"Dozer?" The shift in Anotelli's vocal tone was unmistakable. "Do you mean Stuart Wemple?"

"Yes."

"Yarwood," Anotelli hooked a thumb at me. "She's dating the pastry chef who got bit by the rat sized dog."

"No way." The blond buzz-cut cop stepped closer to us. "Wemple makes the best nut-free Marzipan. My kid keeps begging for it. Is he opening his bakery back up?"

That's the Smallbany spiderweb for you. No matter where you go in this area, you will always run into a close connection.

I gave the answer Dozer had many times before. "Not sure. There are staffing issues."

"Staffing issues are everywhere." Yarwood shook his head. "Let him know, we're rooting for him."

"I will."

Once those words slid out of my mouth, a horrifying thought crossed my mind... What if Dozer and Franky went into business together?

"Wemple's a great guy." Anotelli shifted his stance to that of Alpha male. "Has this Ezekiel guy made recent contact? Has anything unusual happened?"

"Define unusual." I pointed at the mooning lawn gnome.

Yarwood crouched in front of the decoration. "Is this blood?"

I explained, "He's a zombie."

Anotelli's hand rested on his side weapon as he stepped back and sized me up he probably figured I had escaped from an asylum.

"The gnome was a gift from Mrs. Sanchez," I explained.

Yarwood lifted the decoration by the pointed hat. "It has a hidden camera."

He passed the now upside-down decoration to Anotelli. He opened a compartment on the bottom. A memory card slid out.

"Mrs. Sanchez is brilliant."

"He thinks I'm brilliant?" Mrs. Sanchez's hunched form approached from the hedges. She was wearing a black leather outfit. Her white hair slicked back giving her the appearance of an elderly version of Trinity from *The Matrix*.

"Gram!" Cheryl circumvented lawn ornaments. "Get back inside!"

"It's Anotelli!" Mrs. Sanchez shouted.

"I don't care if it's Santa Claus. You get back here this instant."

Cheryl hiked up her ankle-length chartreuse dress and lifted a foot over a cluster of religious statues. "Why is Mary wearing a facemask?"

Mrs. Sanchez shook her head. "It's getting to be winter and I didn't want the Blessed Mother to catch influenza or worse COVID."

Cheryl demeanor exuded a need for a decades-long Barbados vacation.

Anotelli chimed in. "How kind of you. Have you thought about wool blankets to keep them warm?"

Mrs. Sanchez's eyes lit up. "I hadn't thought of that."

"Don't encourage her!" Cheryl shook a homemade statue-sized facemask at Anotelli.

"He's got a valid point." Mrs. Sanchez tied on a black Zorro type mask. "We can't have Baby Jesus get sick if he's going to save the world."

She shuffled toward to her house. Neon chip-bag clips kept the leather outfit in place. Once the women were back in their house, I smiled at the nice police officers standing at military rest.

I tried to sound casual when I spoke. "She has dementia."

CHAPTER 22

Caffeine-infused comfort gurgled from the coffeemaker. I was moments away from my first real cup of the day. A faint pop and a shift in a white glow let me know that a bulb in the overhead fixture had died, as had my feelings of safety.

My home resembled a California supermarket after an earthquake. Sliced empty carboard boxes lay on top of broken dishes, dolls, wooden pieces of a Backgammon game, playing cards for poker night, and a pile of pillow stuffing. I moved back to the safety of the kitchen holding the torn dustcover of Immanuel Kant's *The Metaphysics of Morals*.

I tossed part of Kant's legacy into the kitchen's garbage. This hoarders' heaven made it impossible for me to identify all the missing objects. I berated myself for not changing the locks sooner and leaned against the counter next to my charging flip phone.

The doorbell rang. I snatched up the nearest thing that might serve as a weapon and darted for the door. I was going to fight.

"Returned to finish the job, you Nimrod!"

I tightened my grip on the raised spatula. A familiar male voice called out from the other side of the door.

"It's me!"

The kitchen utensil clattered onto the slate floor. I opened the door and flung myself into the man's arms. Being brave was on hold. I had Dozer. He kept a grip on me as he walked me backward into the house.

"Leah heard about the break in from one of her coworkers and called me."

That's all he needed to say to turn me into a pile of mush. I began to sob. Dozer ran a hand over the back of my head. His gentle kiss landed on the side of my neck. A rush of desire ran through me. I told myself it was the adrenaline.

"Two men broke into my home, ransacked the place, and stole Arny." I released Dozer and wiped my snot off his dark jacket. "Sorry. I got your nice, black shirt wet."

"Water dries. The main thing is that you're okay."

We were in the living room when I heard a male voice behind us, "Who's Arny?"

In the entranceway stood a man in his forties wearing faded jeans and a blue-paint-stained sweatshirt.

Unsure of what just happened, I stared at the man, He set a black case on the slate floor.

"Put the control panel there." Dozer pointed to the wall. "Arny is the taxidermy armadillo, Christmas stocking holder, that her father made for her when she was a child."

"Right." The man kept a hand on the doorknob. "Right," he repeated.

Few people grow up in a family as eclectic as mine. If it weren't for my dad's family members, I'd be a full-fledged hermit not by choice.

"You're safe." Dozer mistook my reaction and rubbed my arms. "While Earl installs the alarm, I'll help you clean things up."

"Okay." I stammered and walked around the corner to get my coffee mug. A thought crossed my mind. I faced Dozer. "Since when do alarm systems people do installations at seven in the morning?"

"They do when it's an old friend paying you an extra grand," Earl yelled from the entrance. "And two dozen Boston cream donuts. My wife will have my hide if I don't get those."

"Hey," Dozer shouted. "It was half a dozen."

"Better make it three," Earl corrected. "My son's visiting from college."

"Ugh," Dozer grunted. "I'll make it an even six and Talia's helping me."

If I helped in the kitchen, it'd be a disaster of epic proportions. My culinary skills consisted of removing an item from the freezer and popping it into the microwave.

"I'd poison the guy."

"Nah," Earl responded. "If you tried my wife's cooking, you'd know I've got a stomach made of steel."

Dozer reached for the coffee mug.

I swatted his hand. "Mr. Wemple! You know I don't have the money to pay you back."

"Consider it a gift. Want espresso?"

"Are you making it on Satan's prized machine?"

"I'll take an espresso." Earl peeked around the corner. "Nice, you have a fancy barista machine like the one my wife bought a few years back. When she couldn't get the thing to work, she sold it in our garage sale to a lady for five bucks. Man, people buy the strangest things."

Dozer and I stared at one another for a moment. I waited for the machine to finish brewing Earl's drink.

"Can you describe the woman?" I handed him the cup.

"Thanks." He walked back to the entranceway, and I followed. "Not well. I was switching out the Christmas lights for Easter decorations when we had our sale. I want to say the woman was in her early seventies. I do remember she was arguing on her phone in Polish. Then, she spoke fluent English to my wife."

"Are you positive it was Polish and not Ukranian?" I asked.

"Yes, ma'am." Earl set his espresso on the floor next to his paint-stained plastic stool. "My wife had four years of Polish as a foreign language in high school. She shocked the woman when she answered her. A guy named Olaf was harassing this poor woman over some inheritance she'd gotten. That's when I left the conversation. Whatever was going on was her business, not mine."

There had been contact between my mom and her Uncle Olaf a few months before her death. "Do you know what inheritance?"

"Again, that was none of my business."

I wanted to get more information out of this guy without tipping him off that this woman was my mom. "Anything else noteworthy about this woman?"

"The woman thought the machine would make a cute gift for her daughter. Said they had been distant. She wanted to make up for lost time. Then she dragged me in by asking about antique fire apparatus."

That was an unexpected statement. As far as I knew, we didn't have any antique fire items in the garage.

"How did the conversation turn to that topic?" Dozer asked.

"A buddy of mine is storing his 1890s hose cart in my garage." Earl reached for a pencil. "That's why we had the sale. Needed to make room for the eyesore. The Polish-speaking woman asked me about the restoration company we used. I figured there'd be no harm in it, considering the woman had a friend who owns a 1905 cart. I gave her the contact information for Ezekiel Knepp. He's this Mennonite a couple of the guys have used for restoration work. He's a bit creepy, but good."

"Creepy how?" I asked. "And did she say who had the 1905 cart?"

"You ask a lot of questions." Earl erased a mark from the cream-colored wall.

To hide my true intentions, I repeated the lie Dozer had told Ted. "I'm a writer working on a mystery novel about the area. This story is unique."

"Good deal. That Stephanie Loufer … um … yeah, that local writer who does science-fiction, has her heart in the right place, but honestly, we don't need pixies in this area. Let's get a good wholesome mystery."

I gave him the thumbs up.

"Make sure to put me in. I want to be ten years younger and have a thick mane of hair." Earl tilted his head, light reflected off the scalp visible through the thinned area. I didn't respond. He continued talking. "Just so you know, Ezekiel resembles the bad guy from *The Smurfs*. If that ain't enough, when he gets nervous, he farts."

A mixture of anger, excitement, and despair washed over me. I clutched Dozer's arm. I didn't want to tip Earl off that there was more to my questions and kept my mouth shut. All this time we thought Mom had met this guy on an Internet dating site. Instead, they met by chance from information given to her at a garage sale.

Dozer gave me the "I know" death stare.

I blurted out, "Do you have his contact information?" I stepped back to gain composure. "It'd be research for my novel. My dad was a volunteer firefighter, and my experience is with modern fire trucks."

"A buddy of mine tried contacting him last week for a job. Got the phone out of service message." Earl faced us. "If you don't mind, I'd like to get back to work. Unless you're good for time-and-a-half, then I'll stay all day chatting."

CHAPTER 23

Around noon, I was still in my flannel pajamas when Earl announced, "Alarm is set."

The idea of having a security system and a new door lock was comforting as well as unnerving. The feeling of safety was gone, and I didn't know if I'd ever recover it.

Earl handed me a notepad and a booklet. He stared at one of the headlines and read out loud: "'Cow Gone Missing In High School Prank.'" He shook his head. "I still can't believe some teenaged bonehead tried to butcher the fiberglass cow to make burgers."

I placed the instruction manual on top of the article. "We all did silly things as teenagers."

"Not that silly." He called back as he exited the house, "Any questions you have, ask Dozer."

The front door clicked closed behind him.

The toilet flushed. The bathroom door opened, and I yelled down the hall, "You missed saying goodbye to your friend."

I used a napkin to wipe at a grey smudge off the table. I was annoyed at the hundreds of gradient gray ovals dotting the interior of my home. The police had hit every surface like the house had been a murder scene. Talk about overkill.

"What are you doing?" Dozer leaned against the fridge.

I instantly thought of how sexy he was in his sneakers, tight blue jeans, and a black long sleeve shirt that hugged his body.

"Removing finger-print dust." I tossed the napkin aside. "That's it. I give up."

Dozer's cell phone buzzed. "Yo." There was a pause while someone spoke. "Yeah. Grab food on your way." Another pause. "If you want. We have espresso." He ended the call.

To keep myself from staring at Dozer I surveyed the mess. For decades the house had been a disaster, so it was difficult to see the carnage left by the intruders.

"Why does the couch have a gash on the side? They even cut a cushion. These guys need a therapist."

"They probably thought you hid an item inside."

That made no sense to me. "They stole a stuffed armadillo!"

"I didn't say they were intelligent."

"Did you insult my father's artwork?"

"There's no peaceful way out of this argument for me." Dozer adjusted the surviving cushion into place.

"We're not arguing."

"This feels like an argument to me." He set the floor lamp up. It fell behind the couch. "Duct tape won't fix that."

"It's not an argument. I'm a bit emotional. It's not every day you figure out your mother was targeted by a deranged serial dater or killer or whatever he is, and your house gets ransacked by two guys. FYI: One of those intruders answered his phone while inside my home."

"There's a third person is involved and--"

I didn't let him finish his statement. "Oh, let's not forget that trip to Amish country. We were passed by a snail."

"Are you done?" Dozer asked.

"Your driver's license needs to be revoked." I tossed the notepad and instructions into the junk drawer. "A snail!"

"Talia," he picked up a wad of pillow stuffing. "There was no snail. And what do you mean: 'He answered his phone'?"

Dozer sat on the good side of the couch in deep contemplation as I told him everything and he bombarded me with questions.

I broke. "The more you ask, the more this conversation feels like a police interrogation instead of a friend helping me out."

He flashed me his dimples.

"You fight dirty."

"Use what you got." He was at the table across from me. "Someone saw the lights and called 911. Which is how this third person knew. He had a police scanner and called the intruders to get them out. They found one of the items on top of the television. Which we know was the aardvark."

"Armadillo. The aardvark was… forget the aardvark." I didn't want to explain Arny's distant cousin.

"We know Mrs. Sanchez has binoculars. She probably used them to do a good deed." Dozer stood up. "Nothing makes sense. Unless they thought you hid valuables inside the stuffed animal."

"Mom only kept that thing because I liked it."

Dozer leaned against the kitchen counter and crossed his legs at the ankles. "Why?"

"Instead of Elf on a Shelf, we had Arny on a shelf."

"You're joking?"

"Nope." I leaned back. There was no way to maintain a serious conversation. I decided to go into as much detail as possible. "Mom sewed seasonal outfits for Arny. The day after Thanksgiving, he was in full elf attire. That included a hat and a matching skirt, both adorned in copper bells."

Dozer attempted to remain stern-faced. But I saw the thin line of crow's feet twitch. He was on the verge of losing his composure. I went for a quick jab to finish the job.

"At the end of every Thanksgiving dinner, the armadillo was recruited to by Santa to be an elf for the season. Many mornings Arny sat on the bathroom sink holding a letter, just for me, from the big man himself. Nothing screams Christmas better than that."

"You never cease to amaze me," Dozer said. "Did your cousin have a matching elf?"

"Franky!" I raced to dial his cell. I pressed speaker when he picked up. His voice indicated I had woken him.

"This better be good."

"Arny's been stolen!"

"No way!" That woke Franky up. "What happened?"

I explained the break-in in detail. "Now I have a new alarm system."

"That code better be easy for us to remember." Franky yawned. "When my place was broken into, they cleaned out all your dad's taxidermy equipment I kept in my shed. To make things weirder, they stole that German squirrel art your dad made me when I had my appendix out."

That image is what sent Dozer over the edge. He laughed for a good five minutes before he composed himself. "Your dad taxidermied a squirrel and put it in lederhosen?"

How this was a surprise, at this point, was beyond me.

"Yeah," Franky answered. "It even held up a miniature plastic knackwurst."

Dozer laced his fingers behind his head. "Is that an Amish thing?"

"No." I set the phone on the table. "Grandpa Morgan learned the trade from trial and error before he taught my dad. When we were kids, Dad and a friend had an animal artwork sidebusiness."

"The guy was a nut." Franky interjected. "He insisted the family carriage business was half his because he worked with Uncle Jonathan on the taxidermy art. Can you believe it? That carriage business existed for a hundred years before they ever met. Then, one day he dropped dead of a heart attack. Good riddance."

Dozer grabbed the pad of paper and a pen. "What was his name?"

"Hold on," Franky yelled. Rustling paper sounds came through the phone. "Ah ha!" My cousin was on the line again. "His business card was in the Rolodex your old man gave me. It was under 'T' for taxidermy. Man's name was Cory Jackson Sr."

Both Dozer and I leaned in.

"Jackson?" We asked simultaneously.

"Yeah. His son, Cory Jr., was that kid who made fun of my reading material, then killed my fleas."

Dozer rubbed his temples. "There are so many things I never knew about your family until now."

"Hey." Franky snapped. "I spent an entire summer rolling around in poison ivy in order to have enough fleas for that project. Then this numbskull killed them all. Charloette was about to lay eggs, too."

Only my cousin would have that concern.

"The summer you were supposed to be reading books," I reminded him.

"Are you still mad you didn't get an award for reading over fifty when I read three?"

I didn't answer.

Franky tsked. "See, that's what I'm talking about. Set your standards low, and you'll never be disappointed."

I ended the call.

"We're in over our heads." Dozer tugged his shirt over his blue jeans. "Do you have a card for the officer who handled the break-in?"

I pointed to the fridge where I had used a magnet to hold Anotelli's business card.

Dozer spent several minutes on the phone, recapping what we had learned. While he was on the phone the doorbell rang.

I waltzed over, and pulled back the curtain to see Hector's stern face on the other side of the glass. He was a younger, more slender version of Dozer clad in black leather. I glanced behind him and saw his motorcycle. I opened the door. He strode by me, carrying a brown paper bag and carrier that held chocolate shakes.

"Anything useful?" Dozer asked.

"Yes." Hector walked to the evil machine and had a perfect shot of espresso in seconds.

"How did you do that?" I was jealous.

"I pushed the start button." Hector pointed at the machine.

"No." I leaned in to see what he was pointing at. "I've pushed that button. Okay, this confirms it. That machine hates me."

Dozer handed me a sandwich. "What have you got for us, Hector?"

"Prior to 1996, there's no records of this Ezekiel guy. Not even a birth announcement. Either he was from an off-the-grid group or he's in witness protection."

He poured the shot into his shake.

"Leah already found out he's from an off-the-grid group." I nibbled on a piece of bacon. Hector's expression told me he had missed the memo. I waved the bacon. "Franky's girlfriend, Leah, is studying to be a P.I. Plus I have Pickles."

"Did you say you have Pickles on retainer?" Hector asked.

"We're off-topic." Dozer retrieved a glass from the kitchen cupboard. "We need to find out who this Ezekiel guy is, what he's after, and how the taxidermist Jackson ties in."

"I have notes on my phone." Hector pulled out his smartphone and read: "Ezekiel Knepp. No priors. No convictions. Fingerprints not on file. Inherited two estates from unmarried women. According this his driver's license, he was born September 15, 1958. Current bank account has a holding of $500. Drives a purple mini-van. Has connections to Ohio and Indiana."

Hector set aside his phone. "We know that part because he sent a money order to an unknown individual in both of those states a couple days ago. I have the women's information if you want it."

"Yes, please." I snagged a hash brown. "Anything else?"

"This guy knows how to cover his tracks. It's going to take a miracle to open your mother's death as anything other than natural causes."

"We'll have to prove everything ourselves," Dozer said.

"Have you talked to any of your mom's friends? Gone through her papers? Contacted relatives?" Hector had learned the art of asking questions in rapid succession.

I had learned the art of overexplaining everything. "Stephanie Lauffenburger said she'd been working on a movie that ties into the preservation work mom was involved in. Mrs. Sanchez is certain

Mom had been dating Ezekiel. As far as papers go, I have her cell phone bill. No keys to her filing cabinets."

"Yeah, I heard about the movie," Hector groaned. "Another big corporation wants to develop part of Pine Bush. Stephanie decided to create a fake documentary that involves a bridge troll."

Dozer nearly spit out his shake.

"That obsession is my father's fault." I used a paper napkin from under the microwave to wipe his face. "When we were kids, he made Stephanie a taxidermy squirrel pixie dressed in a medieval Bulgarian barmaid outfit."

Hector shook his head. "I'll chalk that up to information I never needed to know."

I went slitty eyed. "You're as bad as your father."

That made both of them smile. If I didn't know better, I'd swear they were brothers.

"Anything else?" Hector asked.

"We have a phone bill from June." I handed Hector the phone bill. "Mrs. Sanchez was the person Mom contacted the most."

"Estella Sanchez? The woman who wears tomato paste cans in her hair?"

"How'd you know?" I asked.

"A few years back, she dated my boss."

Hector scribbled a note on the phone bill.

Dozer choked. "Olsen?"

"Yeah, and I'll return this when I'm done." Hector held up the document. "You've gotta be careful who you date in this area or you might wind up dating an uncle."

"Or cousin," Dozer added.

My jaw dropped. He wasn't going to let me live that one down. "We were fifteen and there was no way to know that we were related."

Dozer gave me a playful nudge. "He was cute though."

Hector tapped on his cell phone. "Whatever I missed, I am fine not knowing."

CHAPTER 24

I ignored the banter between Dozer and his son. They had opted to clean up the worst of the mess left behind by the intruders. In all fairness, I had started to assist in cleaning up shattered porcelain, boardgame pieces, and other sundries until Hector accidently dropped a container of ultrafine glitter onto Dozer's head.

That was my cue to leave. I chose a more soothing atmosphere and ventured into Mom's untouched home office in search answers.

Rows of shelving units and cabinets lined the walls. In front of them, was more stuff. I shuffled sideways between stacks of labeled boxes that stood a head higher than me. My hope was that the musty cardboard boxes didn't fall on me leaving behind a blood-stained pair of blue jeans and a *Ghost Buster's* T-shirt.

The first box I opened was marked "1972 Cart Inventory." I assumed that meant it was connected to Dad's company. Inside I found receipts from haircuts, gas stations, fast food places, and even a groomer's bill for shampooing a cat named Jellyfish.

To me, this was news. "My parents owned a cat?"

Dozer's voice carried from the living room. "Was it made of gold?"

"According to the bill, she was a domestic long-haired mix."

"Keep digging," Dozer and Hector said in unison.

I set the box on the floor. After two more boxes, I realized they all had been mismarked. I pulled one down that was labeled "Crap to sort through 1986."

Inside was my father's satin-lined, albino skunk-skinned hat. I tried it on. The all-white tail trailed to the back of my neck. It made it feel like my father was there.

I held up a one-eyed doll head. "Miss Suzy."

Yeah, I was reliving my childhood.

"We need you to stay focused?" Dozer tugged at a single strawberry blonde tuft that stood out from Suzy's otherwise bald head. "What happened to her hair?"

"Franky reenacted a French Revolution execution." I pointed to the red marks on her neck. "She was Marie Antoinette."

Dozer placed the head on the closed laptop sitting on the computer table. I caught myself yearning to run my hands down his dark shirt and along his tight blue jeans. I forced the intrusive thought from my mind.

"That explains the decapitation. What about the tattoos and haircut?" Dozer's words snapped me back to the moment.

"Duh. She shaved her head to avoid catching lice and the ink is a cluster of prison tattoos."

There were parts of my life I hadn't disclosed to Dozer. It wasn't fear that kept me from discussing those things it was how insane they sounded. Unless you were there to experience these anomalies, you'd probably label our entire family as crazy. These were the untold truths I kept from my best friend out of self-preservation.

"Right." Dozer set the rest of Suzy's tattoo covered remains next to the head. "Was this before or after the flea circus?"

"After. Since Franky had created a stadium for our stuffed animals to watch a show and he no longer had fleas, he built a guillotine."

I held up the wooden metal object in question.

"Why is there electrical tape over the blade area?" Dozer asked. "And how did he acquire the necessary items to build this? Never mind. I don't want to know."

I set the killing instrument aside. "Stephanie's father was a carpenter. She was the one who helped build that monstrosity. Even helped test it on carrots."

Dozer adjusted his position. Ultra fine sparkles landed in the box. He wiped at them. More fell.

He shouted to Hector, "I hope you understand why I didn't allow glitter in the house when you and brother were kids."

"Who puts an open tube of glitter in a box labeled: Sales Receipts?" Hector was learning Mom's filing system.

Dozer muttered something about a bonfire.

I caressed his ashen cheek. "We'll get through this."

He kissed my fingers. I recoiled.

Dozer blew out an exasperated breath before speaking. "You, Franky, and Stephanie were close?"

"Depends on your definition of close. Our dads joined the Guilderland Fire Department at the same time and since the three of us were months apart, we gravitated to one another."

I pulled out another stack of papers. One fell to the worn wood-patterned linoleum.

"Once you're emotionally in a better place, we'll get a dumpster to tidy things up."

Dozer held up a large gray faded envelope. The thickness was consistent with a novella manuscript and the tape holding the flap down had lost its adhesive. He flipped it to face me. An undiscernible message had been scrawled across the front.

I suggested, "Blackmail photos?"

"Have you ever heard of a blackmailer using a peach crayon?"

"If it was Grandma Morgan, sure."

Dozer ignored me as he slid the document out and read over the first page. His worried face shifted to delight. "We got it!"

He kissed my cheek. "Hector," he shouted and hurried to the living room. "We have the original will!"

My cell phone rang. It was Franky. I didn't bother with pleasantries when I hit the talk button. "I found the original will."

"That's awesome! What were we supposed to get?" Franky paused. "Wait. You need someone. Leah and I can come over to give you emotional support."

Shocked by his sudden ability to be an observant empathetic human, I let myself digest that revelation for a beat.

"Dozer and Hector are doing what they need to do while I sit on the floor in Mom's office--"

"Never sit on the floor in that room!" Franky interjected. "A stack of boxes might fall and smash you. That'd be worse than that guy who died trying to climb a mountain while he was wearing summer clothes in December."

He got me to laugh.

"Now that you're laughing again, send me a copy when you can. I gotta tell ya, Leah hit pay dirt! I'm in love, Talia. When we get married, I want you as my best-man. Well, best-woman, on account well you ain't a guy and—"

"Franky!" If I didn't shut him down, the rambling would last into the night.

"No need to get angry." He tsked at me. "The nefarious taxidermy guy was the father of Cory Jackson, Jr., the kid who wiped his snot on you at the Guilderland Library reading group in second grade. Anyway, his dad had a vendetta against your dad on account he thought your dad stole the business from him. Plus, this Cory Jr. guy is none other than the guy Henrietta kicked outta her place for being married and he's single."

"No way!" I pulled the skunk hat off and set it on the desk. "I gotta call my attorney."

"I already put a call into Pickles to let him know all the developments. He thinks this is all connected to this Knepp guy. It's a matter of how. Now that you have the will, I'm guessing we'll figure this out soon."

Dozer rounded the corner. "Is that Franky?"

I hit speaker. "Dozer's holding the will."

"Lay it on me!" Franky's voice came through flip phone.

Dozer held up a handwritten note. "If you had a smartphone, I'd be able to hold this up for..." He stopped. "Talia, that glare reminds me of my mom when she's angry."

"Uh-hu."

Hector poked his head in. "Your mother left a note explaining that she hid the original will because she suspected her life was in danger."

"Why?" Franky asked. "She wasn't wealthy."

"You're getting glitter on everything." Dozer shook the paper off sending the sparkle dust onto me.

I brushed it off. "Right now, you two are worse than Franky!"

Hector shrunk away. Dozer explained, "When your mom's Uncle Olaf reappeared in her life. He accused her of stealing family jewelry. She re-wrote the will to have everyone sign off on contesting it. She wanted to make sure you and Franky were covered."

Franky shouted. "All I got was a number written on a strip of paper. Remember?"

Dozer knelt to the phone. "That's the number to the safety deposit box that contains the inheritance left to you and Talia. Gladys' protection of the both of you was ironclad. All we have to do is figure out which of the local banks has the deposit box and find the keys."

"Talia, you're as bad as Grandma Morgan." Franky chortled. "She loses her hemorrhoid pillow once a week and she sits on it."

CHAPTER 25

Hands red from the biting edge of the seasons' shift, I stood on the front walkway, breaking up pizza crust for the squirrels. When I was done, I wiped my hands on my pajamas to clean off the crumbs. A creeping figure round the hedges. Instead of running inside the house and cowering, I waited until the person set off the garage's motion sensor light.

It was, Thursday my last day of rest before I had to work at Franky's bar, and I wasn't in the mood for visitors.

I shouted, "Mrs. Sanchez, what are you doing here?"

She made the quiet motion and tip-toed to the bottom of the stairs. Yellow and red tomato paste cans were visible through the white bunches of hair. Ripley's had nothing on her.

Mrs. Sanchez motioned for me to get back in the house. "Quick, before Cheryl knows I'm gone."

I had already learned this woman made Tropical Storm Irene an inviting adventure.

Once inside, I kicked my house slippers off and Mrs. Sanchez flopped on the couch. Her sneaker clad feet dangled over the edge.

"Got any plans for this evening?" she asked.

"I'm working. Make this quick."

"Nonsense. You work at The Bar tomorrow." She had to correct me.

"Why are you here?"

"To tell you that Cheryl and I got our hair done today and your break-in was all the talk." She giggled. "Good thing that mooning gnome trail cam caught images of the bad guys. They were driving a monster of a truck. One of the girls carried on about how the Guilderland police found that vehicle, this morning, in the trailer park on Carman Road. She knew this because her brother was at the liquor store, buying whiskey when a couple was discussing what happened. Can you believe it?"

"Did they say where in the trailer park?" I braced myself for the news I didn't want to hear. They were in my old neighborhood, the place I had lived for the better part of five years and had moved out of the day before the break-in.

"In front of a baby-blue trailer that had been cleaned out. The ladies said the owner got herself a ranch house."

Whatever these guys were after, they tried both my mom's home and my trailer. Until they were caught, I wasn't safe.

"How's the structure?"

"Glitter?" Mrs. Sanchez hit the couch cushion. "I wish I wasn't wearing a dress. This stuff will wind up in my underwear."

I didn't want to think of her undergarments. "The trailer?"

"Let's just say whoever owns it better have it insured."

If it was a bad as my car, I was selling it for scrap. A question boiled up inside. "Did they contact the owner?"

"The owner of the park is on vacation. I guess the owner of that trailer will be getting a call soon if they haven't already."

I thought back to the ignored messages waiting for me on my phone. I agreed. She didn't need to know it was me.

Mrs. Sanchez leaned in and whispered, "I hear we are in the center of the Smallbany Triangle, where major crimes almost vanish like the ships in the Bermuda Triangle. Except in the mall. I think that's because it's on the edge."

Most of Guilderland's crime was connected to the mall. In recent years, our town's population had exploded. It grew too fast and the crime rate had gone up. Apartment complexes were now the rage. Our town had grown into a place I didn't recognize and had earned the unfortunate nickname of 'Builder Land."

Mrs. Sanchez puffed out her cheeks. "Toward the end, your mother and I grew close. You need to remember both of your parents loved you. For that, I ask you to keep digging. You'll see I'm right. Ezekiel's a bit odd but nice."

"Is that why he stole my mother's cell phone or why he got upset over the safety deposit keys?"

"Those don't add up. I think we're missing a clue."

"Or you haven't got one," I muttered.

"What?"

"Nothing."

"As I was saying," she continued. "Your mom insisted she had to go to this store in Schenectady. It had a couple of your father's taxidermy pieces for sale. She said his art is unique enough to spot anywhere and that you enjoy those creepy creations. Collecting your father's artwork for you was her way of trying to make up for lost time. Speaking of lost time, I gotta go."

Mrs. Sanchez got up to leave. I rushed to the front entrance and blocked her exit. "You're withholding information."

"Duh. If the aliens are listening in, I don't want them to gain access to my thoughts."

"Aliens aren't real."

"Says you. Now, move before Cheryl notices I'm missing and calls the police again. Too many calls to them and I'm in a nursing home." Mrs. Sanchez tugged the edge of her pink dress.

I fought back to scream out of frustration.

"If I go to a nursing home, Cheryl loses my income and she'll have to move."

Reluctant to move, I stepped aside. "We'll talk later."

"When I can sneak away, sure."

After Mrs. Sanchez left, I slipped the deadbolt and thought about contacting Dozer, the proud owner of a pistol. He'd camp out at my place for security purposes. I flopped on the couch. A scent akin to rotting roadkill wafted up. I stood and pulled up an orange cushion. Wedged against the back was a moldy burrito. The last time I had a burrito was when Franky and Leah had visited. This was a back burner project. Exhaustion tugged at me.

The ringing of my cell phone jolted me awake.

I flipped the phone open and answered, "What?"

"That's how you greet me," a familiar male voice retorted.

"Sorry, Dozer. It's been a day."

"It's about to get worse."

There was no possible way this day could get worse. "How?"

"Cory Jackson was the guy you brought charges against when we first met."

"This doesn't sound like a coincidence."

"Nope." Dozer metered his voice. "What's even more interesting is how Henrietta got hold of your mother's phone."

"How is that possible?"

"I ran into Henrietta in the hallway. She had a box of electronics to be recycled. On top was a red phonecase. I remembered your mom had one like that, so I offered to bring the to the box recycle center for her. When I flipped over the phone, I saw your mom's contact information on the back. That's why Henrietta thought Jackson was married. Oh, and she told me she talked to the bartender..."

There was no need for him to finish that statement. I cut him off. "I'll be over soon." I disconnected.

CHAPTER 26

I was one clean pair of panties away from having to do laundry. A bra, a pair of blue jeans, and a long-sleeve green shirt all passed the sniff test.

The Wisconsin bobblehead cheese dog nodded from the top of my dresser.

"Don't judge me," I told him.

If he had answered me, I'd have lost the remnants of my mind. After a long conversation with Antonelli, about my trailer having been broken into, my head felt like it had been shaken not stirred. I did the quick, college hair-care regimen of brush and pull back into a ponytail. From on top of the nightstand, my cell phone made a strange noise, an indication its end grew near.

I reminded myself to check the messages later and grabbed the possessed electronic device. I slung my messenger bag over my shoulder and set the house alarm.

A black cat bounded by on its way to Mrs. Sanchez's yard, knocking over a St. Olga statue in the process.

"Patron Saint of vengeance, please be kind to me." My Catholic upbringing forced me to say a quick prayer. I hoped that short request was enough to avoid the wrath of the former Ukrainian Queen.

Since my car lacked a Bluetooth connection, Leah had given me an earbud she picked up at the mall. She was the first of Franky's girlfriends to buy me a gift. This woman had earned major points even more when my cell phone automatically connected.

I called Dozer as I pulled onto Western Avenue.

He answered with a question. "Pizza again?"

"You paying?" I don't know anyone who refuses the food of the ancient Roman gods.

"A pepperoni is already on its way."

His knowledge of me created a rush of desire that curled my insides. I reminded myself that we were just friends.

"Pepperoni. I'll be there in twenty."

"Make it thirty. You're already knee-deep in debt to Pickles."

"Why must you make sense?" My speedometer hit fifty-two. This rebel wasn't chancing a ticket. I tapped the brakes.

Dozer cleared his throat. "That strip is forty, not fifty."

This was beyond strange. There was no way he could know

my speed. I confronted him with the most logical explanation. "You put a tracking device on my car!"

"No. You sucked in air."

The light at the corner of two gas stations went from green to red. I hit the brakes. A silver SUV with a giant hot dog on top plowed through the light. I heard the sirens of several police cars in pursuit. A metallic clank came through the earbud. Dozer grunted.

"I've ridden shotgun while you drive. When you realize you're speeding you suck in air."

Flashing lights appeared in my rear-view mirror. A siren blared as a paramedic sped by in the direction of the wiener vehicle.

"I think those amateur crime fighters are up to something. Gerald's vehicle is headed toward the mall and the hot dog is still attached. What was the clanking sound?"

Dozer mimicked a night-time radio announcer. "Donut mixing bowls and spoons have entered the drying-rack phase."

The light turned green.

"Any for me?"

My car lurched forward. His answer was cut off by the distinctive sound of a fire alarm.

The phone was silent. A car in front of me was doing thirty. I switched to the left lane to pass. A horn blared behind me. The Guilderland Fire Station on my left was a blur as I sped up.

"Dozer!" I called out.

There was no response.

My mind went to the burglars—they were after my Dozer. The rattling sound my car made reminded me that it wasn't made for speed. I tapped the break to bring the speedometer down from ninety.

"Henrietta's apartment is on fire!" Dozer disconnected.

I made it to Albany in record time. Several blocks away, I smelled the smoke. I jumped a curb and parked my car. Flames and smoke towered the Victorian rowhouses. The mingling sounds of shouts and rescue vehicle sirens blocked out my thoughts as I snatched my messenger bag from the back seat and ran.

My heart pounded hard enough that it felt like my breasts were going to burst out of my bra. I ignored the pain and darted to a barricade that had been propped up on one end of the street. It closed rescue workers in and was supposed to keep everyone else out.

I ducked down an alley and snuck in through the open back door of a restaurant. Cooks yelled at me in Korean. Diners swore at me in English. Confused, I apologized in Yiddish.

I darted past a wooden podium where the head waitress held tight to a stack of menus. The woman's reaction didn't matter to me as Dozer was in danger. I darted out the front door.

Focused on the billowing smoke, I pushed through a crush of people gathered on the sidewalk. Several bloggers snapped photos of the scene. Others recorded their verbal assaults at the first responders, while the first responders instructed people to move out of dangers' way.

A woman yelled, "I have rights!"

A first responder remained calm as he said, "This is for everyone's safety."

The bloggers ignored the precautions and kept recording as a cluster of bricks crashed down on Dozer's SUV. The windshield shattered. Another group of red bricks crumpled the hood. The SUVs alarm joined into the chorus of sounds.

I needed a better view. Hundreds of people had gathered against the barricades and down the street. I was shoved. An elbow jabbed my ribs. A woman shrieked. There still was no sign of Dozer.

A blur of red Albany fire trucks emerged from the haze. Reflective tape lit the movement of firepersons laying down hoses. A firewoman climbed an extended truck ladder. A mist of water and ash poured down.

I called Dozer's cell phone. It went to voicemail. Deafening noises surrounded me. Heart racing, I scanned the pandemonium.

"Dozer!" I screamed.

Standing next to a fireman in his reflective gear, Henrietta's white knee-length baby-doll dress and blue jeans were out of place. Light reflected off the silver flicks in her hot pink hair as a camera crew closed in on her. A uniformed police officer motioned for them to move back. I weaved through the chaos toward set of concrete steps a dazed Dozer stood.

All my thoughts flew the coop. I pushed through a gaggle of teens and shoved aside a traffic cone. I wrapped my arms around Dozer's neck and kissed him.

Sweat, smoke and the small of his knee-weakening aftershave clung to his moistened skin. He kissed me back. The lips I had longed to touch were soft and gentle. Dozer pulled me tight against him. That's when my senses kicked in. I released the kiss and pushed back.

"Hey!" he shouted. "You started it."

Sirens screamed in the distance.

"Get back!" a fireman barked.

Dozer and I stepped onto the curb. He held objects in his hands. My mind wasn't processing what he held.

"Get back!" the fireman repeated.

Dozer asked him, "Got marshmallows?"

CHAPTER 27

"The windows stay open so that doesn't marinate." I pointed to my graveyard-reject car.

You'd think that diving thirty minutes with the windows down home would've eliminated the odor. No. The mingling scents of smoke and the unpleasant gift left by a homeless person clung to the inside like a spiderweb to a tree.

Dozer gave a noncommittal shrug. The entire ride had been in silence. Neither one of us wanted to discuss the fire, the toe-curling kiss, or the homeless man Dozer had ejected from my vehicle. (Pro tip: Don't leave your vehicle unlocked in downtown Albany.)

House keys in hand, Dozer opened the front door to the fully lit paradise that smelled of pizza. I inhaled the sweet, comforting aromas of my own home. It had taken me a several weeks to accept that reality. This was my home. I pressed the four numbers to turn off the alarm. Nothing happened.

"Isn't that beep supposed to turn off?" I pressed the numbers again. The beep continued. "The universe despises me!"

The ever-calm Dozer nudged me out of the way, pressed the disarm button, then the numbers. A rapid succession of beeps followed. The alarm light flashed green.

"What the hell?" I asked.

"Did you read the instructions?"

"No. I read the sticky note that had the four-digit code."

Dozer set his things on the couch. "That's why you read the instructions. Even Franky went over the instructions when I gave him a copy of your house key."

I tossed my things next to Dozer's fire-resistant box and prepared to argue. One look at his and I knew it was pointless. He was a mess. Blackened handprints covered his dingy white shirt that hung over the top of his paint streaked sweat pants. He waved his teddy bear, and I melted.

"Mr. Binky." I reached for the stuffed toy.

"You remembered," Dozer said in a low voice. He leaned closer. His warm breath grazed my lips. I moved closer. His hand trailed up my side and around the small of my back. I leaned in.

"Yes." My voice trembled. I licked my thumb. "Hold still." I attempted to rub a single glittery piece off Dozer's soot covered cheek.

"How do you still have glitter on you?"

Dozer grunted and wiggled from my grip.

There was some good old-fashioned guilt for what I had done. That was replaced by relief and another emotion I was unable to peg. In that moment, I admitted to myself that I wanted more, and I was terrified. Dozer set the one-eyed teddy bear on the couch next to his baby blanket.

"I'm astonished you remember." The tone of Dozer's voice betrayed him. He was hurt. This was more than losing his home. I was going to wait to tell him about his vehicle.

I picked up his most prized possession as if I was picking up a cracked tea cup. An arm had been sewn back on by black thread. "I prefer to think your birth mother panicked."

Dozer's moved to the kitchen.

I needed to be there for my friend. I set Mr. Binky on top of the couch. "Whatever you need, I'm here for you."

A cupboard thumped open. I followed the sound. On the kitchen counter sat a drying rack, a blender, a coffee machine, a few other items, and a landline phone answering machine combo. My mother had shared the same distain for electronics as I did, yet she owned a smartphone. I froze.

Before the fire started, Dozer told me he had my mom's cell phone. For a split second, I contemplated asking him if he had it in the fireproof box.

He pulled two glasses out of the drying rack and set them next to the barista machine of doom. "I told you that ten years ago."

An internal battle waged over when it was appropriate to ask about Mom's cell phone. I leaned against the counter to hold myself up. All her photos and contacts were potentially gone, which paled in comparison to the loss of all Dozer's possessions.

My hands were splayed on the counter. My fingers lost their color as I pressed down to hide my heartbreak. We had too many setbacks, and the holidays were around the corner. Our first Thanksgiving without my Mom, and Dozer's was homeless.

"How could I forget?" I did my best to tamp down my sadness. This conversation wasn't about me. I needed to focus.

Dozer's adopted mother was somehow related to Abraham Wemple, an American Revolutionary War colonel. All my knowledge, about this guy, was limited to the inscription on the Western Avenue historical marker.

A member of the Wemple family belonged to The Little Sisters of the Poor, a Roman Catholic woman's religious group dedicated to assisting the elderly and poor. At the time of Dozer's birth, the organization had a place in Latham that doubled as a senior living facility.

One day, a novice nun found a carboard box containing a teddy bear and a newborn baby boy swaddled in a blanket. A single word was written on a corner of the faded blue cloth, "Niño."

Through skillful marketing ploys, the news media remained oblivious to Ms. Wemple's involvement in the infant's care. The barely twenty B-list actress hired people to locate the birth family. When that search proved unsuccessful, she legally adopted the baby and named him Stuart after a children's book character. It's understandable that he prefers his nickname.

I mentally recapped those highlights while Dozer rummaged in the liquor cabinet.

"Any word from Pickles?" he asked.

"Nothing."

He released a high-pitched whistle and held up two bottles. "Tequila or rum?"

I pointed to the rum. He put that bottle away and opened the tequila. Oh, yeah, he was mad at me. Instead of yelling, he went with the drink I had no interest in drinking.

"Any hits on the DNA tests?" I was a donkey's backside for bringing up that low-blow question. There wasn't any topic change to save that conversation.

"Wish they had spoken to me first." Dozer's voice was controlled as he answered. "Six months later and they've—"

"Wait a minute." I did my best traffic cop stop-gesture impression. The severity of the evening's events required humor to ease the tension. "They just told you this about a month ago."

"Yeah. They didn't want me to stop them. If I had paid attention when I read the text message, I'd have seen the tracking information showed it was sent when that Guilderland crime app scandal hit." Dozer examined the clear liquid. "Gold label? Who's the sugar daddy?"

Now he was the one changing the topic.

"It was a gift." I figured two could play at this game. "Have you prepared your sons for the revelation they aren't full brothers?"

At that moment, I went down a deep dark rabbit hole I might

not recover from. Where was Franky when you needed a real distraction?

"High school biology class prepared them for that." He drank tequila straight from the bottle. Several swigs later, he set it on the counter.

"What aren't you telling me?"

He poured me tequila into a glass. "Recessive genes. George has red hair, freckles, a cleft chin, and pale skin, all compliments of Sandy's second husband. The man who she allegedly met a month after I caught them in bed together."

There I went, making an ass out of myself, again. Sandy's second husband had been arrested while entertaining himself in a house of illrepute. That multi-jurisdictional police raid had made national news. Dozer still hadn't answered my question.

"You said you wished they had talked to you first. What is there to know?"

Dozer held up the bottle back. "Tastes like blackmail." The corner of his lips hinted that they were about to move. Now, he was being playful. "Who'd you get dirt on?"

"You're avoiding the topic."

"Remember when I told you my adopted mother hired a P.I. to find my birth family?"

"Yeah," I sipped my shot, and coughed.

It had been seventeen years since I had touched hard liquor and that was at a party. Hangover headaches never impressed me, they are why I stick to soda and an occasional beer.

Dozer patted my back. When I had caught my breathe, he spoke with a sadness I'd never heard from him before.

"My birth mother was a Jane Doe."

His gaze was back on the tequila bottle. That was my cue to come clean.

I tapped the label. "This was my prize for winning the infamous Franky-Talia college bet."

Dozer's jaw open and close several times before he said, "How does this make sense? You tended bar and he worked at a sewage processing plant!"

CHAPTER 28

Dust motes moved in a sliver of light, breaking through a crack in the closed blinds. My hair gave off a lingering scent of smoke. Even though I didn't hear a sound, I knew Dozer was asleep on couch. I hugged the down pillow that had belonged to my mother. The hangover headache crept in and dulled my desire to move from under the Amish quilt into the disaster waiting for me.

Internal fireworks blasted my emotions into a dizzying mess. I knew our relationship was right. I also knew I was going to Hell for kissing Dozer as his apartment building burned.

As I lay in bed, I recited several Catholic prayers. To cover as many bases as possible, I threw in a couple of repentant Hebrew prayers as well.

The basement door slammed shut. I jumped up and slipped into my housecoat. On my way to the living room, I brushed against stacked boxes. Opened shades gave my place a warm glow.

"Clean." Dozer dropped a basket of laundry on top of a rumpled sheet that barely covered the couch. "I need to pick up a few things at the mall. Wanna join me?"

"How are you this awake?"

It was a fair question. The man, standing in front of me, had drained a quarter of the tequila bottle before I went to bed. The two shots I had made me topple-tipsy, and I felt the aching aftermath to my core. Yet, my friend had the centrally heated house smelling of baked goods, had done laundry, and wanted to go shopping.

"How are you standing?" I grabbed one of my thongs from the laundry basket and thrust it into my fleece housecoat's pocket.

He crossed his arms over the fine hairs of his muscular chest. Not wanting to get caught leering, I moved my gaze to other parts of his body and wound-up staring at the lion tattoo peeking from the side of his boxershorts. All these years, I thought he went commando. I was disappointed.

Dozer pretended not to notice me staring.

"Want my hangover cure?"

"Yes!" I said a bit more forcefully than was necessary. "First, would you mind putting my laundry on my bed. I'd like to …"

I paused. My lacy black bra was draped over the edge of the basket. As far as women's undergarment care is concerned, this man scores high on the clueless meter. After a second, I regained my composure. "… fold them."

"Once you're dressed, we're going to the mall." Dozer pulled his clothes out of the pile.

"How about the Salvation Army?"

The last thing I wanted to do was to go to the mall. It was a luxurious, multi-level shopping center that has its own branch of the Guilderland police force. Most of the calls that come from there are for shoplifting, gang-related activities, as well as fights over the last free samples at the Chinese fast-food stand.

"Ahem," Dozer's soft voice gently brought me back to the moment. "You're leering?"

He caught my fixed gaze lingering on his buttoned fly. Who wears boxer shorts that have an obstruction? My mind was in all the wrong places.

"Hangover." I grabbed the basket, started out of the room, and bumped into the recliner. "Any word on The Bar?"

In my mind, Franky had called me a chicken for not making a move on Dozer. I agreed.

"Leah did get the sprinkler system fixed; so The Bar is water logged. Whatever that means. Albany's Fire Department stopped the fire from spreading to the connected building, too. From what I understand the cause of fire involved a curling iron."

Dozer closed the gap between us. I wanted to say not now. Instead, I groaned. He brushed my hair out of the way. His soft lips trailed down my neck. Morals be damned. The laundry basket slipped from my grip.

"Ignore it." Dozer pulled me close. Our lips met and I forgot all about saying those Hail Mary's.

My arms were wrapped around him as we navigated our way through the pile of clothes. I kicked aside the empty basket. We were at the bedroom door when a loud thump emanated from the living room area.

"Ignore the raccoons." I brushed my lips against his neck.

A loud crash made us pause. Through a haze of construction material, I saw my grandmother's Amish-made nightstand resting on the recliner closest to us. On top, sat a dazed raccoon.

Above, two smaller raccoons teetered on the hole's edge. In a blink, that section of the ceiling gave out. The two animals fell onto the pile of clothes.

Dozer and I stood stunned spectators of squealing fur mayhem. My senses kicked in. I grabbed the empty laundry basket and tried to flop the thing over a baby raccoon. I missed. The second baby charged at me. I backed out of the way.

The coffee machine gurgled as I zoomed through the kitchen, and into the pantry. Brandishing a broom, I darted back into the living room where Dozer stood on the couch holding the only intact cushion as if it were a gossamer medieval shield.

Mamma raccoon slashed at it. Stuffing fell out. Dozer swung the deflated cushion.

"Careful!" I yelled. "They might have rabies!"

Dozer leapt to the slate floor in front of the fireplace and snatched up the poker from the hearth. The baby raccoons climbed on top of the recliner. I swatted at them. The one on the back of the recliner had a strong grip on the broom's bristles.

"Hey!" I shouted.

The raccoon yanked back. I held tight.

"Not today!"

"Over here." Dozer opened the sliding glass door and stepped onto the frost-covered, wooden back porch.

The racoon let go. I stumbled several feet through the open office door and stopped short of a shelving unit.

Dozer stepped farther onto the back porch. "Here, kitties."

His breath a fine mist in the November air trailed upwards.

I waved the broom. "They aren't cats!"

The raccoons advanced into the morning light.

"That's it, follow my voice." Dozer's soothing tone reminded me of a father coaxing a child away from danger.

When the raccoons were on the back porch, Dozer darted down the steps. I closed the sliding glass door. No time to lose, I rushed to the front and opened the door as Dozer rounded the garage.

The raccoons closed in.

I left the door opened and cussed as my bare feet hit the icy walkway. I sidestepped to the frosty, brown grass and met Dozer part way.

He doubled over panting. "No."

I followed his wide-eyed stare. The answering machine kicked in. I hadn't even heard it ring.

My Aunt Edna's voice came in loud. "Talia, your cell phone keeps going to voicemail."

Dozer shook his head. "She has the worst timing."

"No, those raccoons do."

A car horn blared. Windows wide open, I had a clear view of the mother raccoon gnawing on the steering wheel.

"No!" I screamed.

Stuffing flew out a back window. The baby raccoons were shredding the seats. My aunt's voice droned on about a liquor delivery at Franky's place. The car horn honked again.

Dozer asked, "Did a raccoon just poop on the dashboard?"

"Yup."

Aghast, we stood, transfixed, watching my car's demise.

CHAPTER 29

Artic attic air nipped at my face as I stood under the gaping hole. I tightened the belt on my housecoat. A clump of pink insulation landed at me feet. I was grateful that only a nightstand and three raccoons had fallen through.

"Duct tape will fix that." Dozer stood in his boxershorts sipping coffee.

Those are words no homeowner ever wants to hear unless it actually pertains to the heating system. "Mr. Maintenance guy, you know better."

"I used it on the pipes in Henrietta's apartment."

"And that's why your apartment flooded."

"It was a temporary fix." Dozer handed me his coffee mug, disappeared into the pantry, and returned with the step ladder. "As long as there are no more animals in your attic, the tape will hold."

"It'd be easier if you place plywood over the hole. You can use the access ladder. The pull-down cord is in the entrance of my old bedroom."

I shuffled to the kitchen, set the ceramic mug on the counter, and opened the freezer door. A package of frozen waffles was on top. I tossed four into the microwave and pressed the popcorn button. Granted, four minutes is excessive. Pressing two buttons was easier than three.

"Animal control might take the call."

Dozer was on the top of the ladder, standing on his tiptoes. His fingertips grazed the ceiling. He shone a flashlight into the attic. "No glowing eyeballs."

"Using a flashlight like a beacon will only help you see hanging bats."

"You have bats?" He struggled to maintain his balance.

I groaned, hit the stop button on the microwave, and pulled out the hot waffles. "Hot!" I dropped them on the counter and blew on my fingers to cool them off.

"That's not cooking," Dozer said.

"Toaster's broken and my professional chef is on strike."

"I'm not on strike." He held out a hand. "Pass me the duct tape so I can fix the ceiling."

Instead, I handed him a waffle. "Dad kept plywood in the

basement. Slap one of those over the hole from the attic side until I can get a professional to fix it."

"I am a professional." Dozer pulled a roll of duct tape out of the junk drawer.

"No.!" I reached for the roll. "Don't you dare."

He whispered, "Fresh, baked muffins on the stove."

"You don't play fair."

He kissed my nose.

"Fine."

Driven by hunger, I made my way to the stove. On top sat a decorative holiday tin carrier. I slid the top off. Six blueberry muffins were nestled inside.

My cell phone rang. I unplugged it from the wall, flipped it open and hit speaker. Franky's disembodied voice was near hysterical.

"What is going on over there? You missed my delivery!"

Hangovers when you're in your forties make a fair competition for migraines. Having your car destroyed by a raccoon family is horrifying. Getting berated by my weasel cousin on top of the other things is akin to being attacked by wolverines.

I gave him the cliff notes version of my morning. The recap zapped the energy from the actual events, especially since I left out the kiss. That part felt wrong to discuss.

"And that's why I didn't get your mother's message."

"Racoons destroying my car is an excuse I'd have made up in high school."

I admit it, the scenario did sound like a Franky tall-tale.

"Look." He was on the verge of a tirade. Instead, he paused and used a calming technique. After a few moments, he spoke in a more palatable tone. "The delivery guys saw the wreckage and left. Now, I won't be able to open tonight."

"If you are tripping on acid, I will call a rideshare and beat you to death with the tattered couch cushion."

Dozer knew I'd never kill anyone. He also knew it was time to set the couch on the curb.

"There's plenty of time to throw a post-fire party before the demolition and think of the free publicity that a break-in rave party will bring."

There was no getting through to him. I yelled, "Talk to your honey about this plan!"

I flipped the phone shut and set it on the table. It felt good to be able to pass his insane idea off on to another woman.

Dozer called to me, "What's the weasel up to now?"

"Illegal drug party."

"Again?"

"Always a profit angle." I made my way to my bedroom leaving a trail of white powder in my wake. Since we were going to the mall I needed to scavenge through Mom's old clothes.

Dozer leaned against the wall. "We could finish what we started, or I can call a rideshare to go shopping. It's your call."

Thirty-five minutes later, I regrated my decision as we strolled down the center beige-tiled walkway lit by cloudless daylight coming through skylights. My romantic relationship apprehension that had once been an invisible boulder of dread had faded to a faint flutter, and I was still reluctant to take that final step.

I berated myself for being a failure at romance and wondered what this amazing man saw in me.

There were scores of women available and yet he chose me. At that moment, both of us were dressed in sweatshirts and jeans. His was an emerald green. Mine was grey had a cartoon image of a rainbow unicorn on the front.

"You had to wear that sweatshirt."

I batted my eyelashes. "It was either this or a light up, singing, Christmas tree."

He squeezed my hand. "Good choice."

Hordes of people converged on the food court where mingling odors hit my nose. Pizza was the first one I identified. Next was cinnamon rolls.

"Pretzels." I pointed to a young child carrying one larger than his head. "I haven't had one in a while. Do you think they give out mustard dipping cups?'

Dozer released my hand to tap out a response on his cell phone.

"It's not the Altamont Fair." He had to remind me.

Attending the Altamont Fair is a family tradition. The five day long annual fair has been one of our area's main attractions in the month of August since 1893. It has a small carnival, rides, food, games, and farming expos, to name a few of the exciting things to experience. Every year since I was old enough to eat solid foods, I enjoyed the warm, salt-covered pretzels dipped in mustard. That fair is one of my favorite places to go, and Dozer knew it.

Beyond the sea of cluttered tables and lines of impatient hungry people was a group of loitering senior citizens. They had converged on a woman standing next to the Asian food stand. She was wearing a pair of khakis, a royal blue shirt, and an N95 mask. She balanced a tray of free samples on one hand and used her other hand to hold up a piece of meat on a toothpick.

Each elderly person snatched up a free sample off the tray. They then shouted commentaries. This was the seniors' version of a wine tasting.

A woman's voice cut through a heated debate on saltiness. "We can't go until I get my sample."

"Who puts that much spice on chicken?" another complained.

Dozer stared at his phone. "Olsen has left the building,"

"Your landlord?" I asked.

"Yeah. I had him to check for your mom's cell," Dozer showed me a picture of a smartphone's shattered screen. "It got stepped on by one of the firefighters." He pocketed his phone. "In my haste to evacuate, I forgot to turn off the home frier and caused a secondary fire."

"One of the first things fire departments do is turn off the electricity to a building. How did this happen?"

"By the time the power was shut off, there was already a fire in my kitchen. Also, an accelerant was used."

I was confused. "How did someone break your apartment and dose your place in gasoline?"

"No. Where the fire started."

The strange odor came to mind. "The flower bed dripped liquid onto the walkway. I hadn't thought anything of it at the time."

Dozer was back to tapping out messages on his phone. "I'll be a moment."

A teenager in sagging blue jeans waded through the gaggle of seniors and snatch a sample off the tray. He sauntered to the end of a winding line that led to tacos. It was nice to see normal life was returning to our area even if it involved rude behavior and a public display of stained underwear.

A hunched-over, elderly man wheeled his oxygen tank to the pleasant samples woman. His loud words indicated that he needed hearing aids. "Got ketchup? The hot dog guy ran out."

Above the clamor, I heard Mrs. Sanchez's voice, "What do you mean one free sample per customer? I got rights."

"I don't make the rules." A tired voice replied. "You can take it up with my manager."

Mrs. Sanchez shook her fist at the cinnamon bun guy and shouted something in Spanish.

The elderly man tapped his oxygen tank. "They don't even have ketchup."

Mrs. Sanchez shouted, "Communists!"

A stocky man in a New York Yankees baseball cap rushed by me. His posture indicated military. Dozer was at his heels. They circumvented the crush of people around the corner toward the escalator. A group of congregating teenagers converged on a nearby seasonal kiosk, blocking my view of Dozer.

"Crap."

I jogged to keep up. Dozer was at a full run. I rushed past a calendar kiosk before I stopped. There wasn't any way I'd be able to close the gap.

I stared at a shop window display of a mannequin in a slinky, electric-blue bandage dress. Although the knee-length skirt was a classy mermaid-cut, the rest of the skin-tight garment hugged the mannequin's unrealistic curves in a way that left nothing to the imagination. The spaghetti straps of the high-end dress seemed out of place as the accessories were a faux-fox-fur purse and a metal-studded, leather dog collar.

"Where's the coat?" I vocalized my distaste for the out-of-season eyesore.

I craned my neck to see over the crowd. Dozer stood across the way at the lingerie store.

"Men," I groaned.

"Tell me about it." A silver-haired woman dressed in a floor-length jeans skirt and a long-sleeved turtleneck held up a brown paper bag. "Last week, I asked my husband to pick up a face mask. Instead, he bought me a G-string from that store. I put the lingerie on my face to prove a point. He thought it was sexy."

That was too much information for me. Before another word was uttered, I hurried away.

When I caught up to Dozer he was transfixed on the ball-cap man fondling bras.

I approached. "Dozer, If this is your idea of a good date--"

"Not now," he pointed.

I looked in the direction he had pointed. A man in jeans and an emerald-green windbreaker held up a bottle of perfume to a woman wearing my mother's one-of-a-kind engagement ring.

"Ezekiel." His name a guttural sound from the depths of my existence rumbled into a low growl. I was ready for a confrontation.

"No." Dozer had a firm grip around my waist.

"He killed mom!"

Dozer tightened his grip. "Until we have more evidence, the Schenectady Police Department's ruling of national causes stands."

His lips brushed against my ear, sending a prickling sensation went south of my belt.

"Stop confusing my body."

I pulled at his fingers. He kissed my neck, causing a rush of desire to overshadow my anger.

"Calm yet?"

"No." I protested.

Another gentle kiss landed on my earlobe, another on my neck. We edged into the gray area of lewd.

Ezekiel hurried to another store. Dozer released me. I side-stepped to follow. I wasn't going to let Ezekiel get away with murdering my mother. Dozer pulled back on my jeans.

"Let go of my belt loop."

"Easy." Dozer pulled me against him.

"Doze." I was pissed off to the point that I didn't even use his full nickname. I fought against a tightness around my waist. For a pastry chef, he had serious strength. It had to be from all those flour containers he lifted.

"Nope," he said.

"Let me go."

"I did that once. Now, we're back here."

Dozer's strong grip tamped my impulse to kill. My body began to shake.

My chocked words were lost. I tried to say, "We need to make pay for what he's done." But it came out as, "Ug."

Once my convulsions had subsided, Dozer moved his hands to rest on my hips. I felt like I was on a drifting boat unable to find my sea legs, and he was keeping me steady.

Mrs. Sanchez broke through a group of people. Her outfit of choice was a neon orange sweatshirt, a pair of grey sweatpants, and pastel pink, rabbit house slippers.

Her voice hit a shrill note, "Yoo-hoo. Mr. Hotty Pants."

Not far behind her, Cheryl raced to catch up. She was dressed like she had been trading on Wall Street in a classy A-line burgundy dress, casual shoes, and a black coat. Her dark hair was pulled back at the nape of her neck and her makeup was flawless.

"Grandma's been itching to get out and I figured the mall was the best place for us to go."

"A nice man bought this for me." Mrs. Sanchez plunged a fork into a plastic to-go container of General Tso's chicken. "He made me promise not to use colorful Spanish around children."

Cheryl held up a cinnamon roll. "This as a condolence prize."

"My deal is much better." Mrs. Sanchez peered into the shop window and beamed. Of all the places for her to catch us at. My face heated up. She waved a piece of broccoli. "Did you two finally hook up? And what's with the glittery unicorn?"

"No more glitter," Cheryl's voice was stern. "The other day, my grandmother wound up with glitter all over the back of her dress and now all our clothes have sparkles. She refuses to tell me how this happened."

I did a once over. Sure enough, both of their outfits had a light dusting of glitter. Damn. I had to keep the truth from Cheryl. Her grandmother needed our visit to remain a secret. This was out of my comfort zone. I am the world's worst liar. Omission doesn't count as a lie, so I answered Mrs. Sanchez's question. "We're here to buy Dozer new clothes."

"What for? His clothes good to me."

Cheryl looked like she wanted to speak. Instead, she bit into her condolence food.

I hiked my messenger bag up. "The fire in Albany was where Dozer lived."

"I'm sorry to hear that." Cheryl tore off a piece of her cinnamon roll and held out. I waved it off. "If there's anything you need, just cut across the lawn and we'll take care of you."

"We appreciate the offer." I tugged on Dozer's arm.

CHAPTER 30

Several laps of the mall later, Dozer had acquired a single pair of pants, two pairs of boxers, and a set of socks. We had both switched out our sweatshirts for ADHD awareness T-shirts that didn't have tags.

I ran my hand over the extra soft material. "I still can't believe these shirts don't have tags."

"You keep raving about that." Dozer side eyed me. "I'd recommend you go for ADHD testing."

"What does my excitement over not having to cut a tag out of a shirt have to do with neurodiversity?" I asked as we rounded back by the lingerie store. "Shoe-shopping must be a nightmare for you."

"That's the ninth time you've changed topics in under a five minutes." Dozer blew out an exasperated sigh. "Also, pumps aren't my thing."

"And what is your thing?" a familiar voice called.

I stopped mid-step. Leah's opened grey trench coat showed off the electric-blue bandage dress I had seen on the mannequin. On her, the dress was breathtaking. Her hair was styled to perfection. Her faint perfume was sexy and alluring. Her shoes, on the other hand, were tacky clear plastic six-inch platform heels. Inside, colorful fake fish floated in some sort of aquamarine liquid.

"Undercover mall security guard operation?" I asked.

"No. Tonight, I'm surprising Franky." Leah licked her cherry-red lips. The rest of her makeup was more natural.

"Hold these." Dozer handed me branded paper bags containing his purchases, gave me a peck on the cheek, and ambled away.

As much as I wanted to protest his abrupt departure, I understood he's a visual person. Dozer's sexual tension had to have been on overdrive. I know mine was and I regretted not finishing what we had started. He vanished around the corner, and I sighed.

Leah gave me a coy smile. "Have the two of you hooked up?"

Her question threw me off guard.

"What?" I struggled to keep hold of Dozer's bounty.

"Come on. I see how both of you drink each other in."

"Do not." That elementary playground argument was out of my mouth and there was no way to toss it back in. "We're just..." I struggled to find the right words and fell flat.

"Romantic relationships are terrifying even when you've known the person for decades."

"My cousin doesn't deserve you."

Leah took that comment in stride. "You and I haven't gotten to know one another yet. I want you to know that the men I've dated weren't in it for love. Franky is different, and I know Henrietta was right. Dozer is in love with you. Whatever fear you have, let it go. Happiness is worth the risk."

For years, I had felt that I wasn't good enough for Dozer. Afterall his family was one of the wealthiest in the area while I was the daughter of a taxidermist artist and a family of Polish beet farmers. My prospects smelled as bad as Uncle Olaf's pile of rotting beets. My facial expression must have conveyed my confession.

Leah added, "Don't worry. There are a number of guys who are terrified of commitment. They fear love and don't want to admit they're afraid. It's part of our cultural expectations. Men are supposed to be tough, and fear doesn't sound tough. The guys you've date saw you as a safe bet. You're the girl next door who will do anything for those you care about."

This conversation wasn't what I'd expect from anyone Franky dated. All I was able to say was, "What?"

"You wear your big heart on your sleeve. That's part of why Dozer is overprotective of you. He sees your kindness and knows people think of that as a vulnerability. Why do you think you haven't been on a date in over five years?"

"Remind me to slap Franky for telling you my secrets."

"You have a lot to learn."

This coming from a woman who was taking P.I. courses from an Internet company based in the Virgin Islands. She lowered her head as if conducting an internal monologue.

"What I'm about to tell you is private. I keep this close to my heart because of how badly I've been hurt."

"I don't know if I'm the one to tell that big a secret to."

"Your cousin and I are serious. Since you are Franky's most trusted confidant, I'm trusting you with this too." She set a hand over her heart, accentuating her long fingers. What she was about to say was big.

"I'm happy the two of you are serious and I don't..." Words failed me mid-sentence.

"You two are more like siblings." She chuckled. "When I left the Marines, I was lost. It was several years before I understood the hole inside me existed because I was lying to myself about who I am. I needed to find my authentic self."

"Why do you consider that a huge secret?"

She shook her head. "A few months before I moved to this area, I transitioned."

"You were still having issues transitioning back to civilian life. That's typical for combat veterans."

"No, Talia. I was born Teo Nguyen."

"Oh." A deluge of questions race through my mind. I didn't want to sound ignorant or hurt her feelings for sharing this admission. There was only one safe question. I asked, "Isn't 'Teo' Vietnamese for Tom, as in short for Thomas."

"Yes. My mother fought in the Vietnam war, which makes my father a war husband."

From what I'd seen on TV shows, these types of revelations were eased into, not announced in the middle of a busy shopping mall after having met a person a few times. It was an honor to know Leah felt I was trustworthy. The proverbial brick wall fell on me. This was my cousin's first serious relationship.

Leah continued, "Franky is the first guy to accept me for who I am. Just like Dozer accepts you for who you are. Don't ruin what you have by running away."

It was nice to know my cousin was open-minded and that this strong woman accepted him for the questionable individual he is. A man bumped my arm. He was followed by the mall security guy in the ball cap.

"That's Martin," Leah cooed. "He was a bouncer until the place he worked at burned down earlier this year."

The image of a man disco dancing like he was in death's throng ran through my mind. I cringe as his horrible singing cut.

"Wasn't he the one who promoted Franky's bar?"

"Yes," Leah said. "Martin has brains, a good at his jobs, and is married to a wonderful man who does drag shows dressed as Cher."

I was on information overload. Outside of myself, Leah, and Henrietta all the patrons at Franky's opening night were men. My cousin had unintentionally opened a gay bar.

As fast as the entertainment hit me, it was washed away by an uneasiness. Months back, another bar had been burned down the night of a Cher impersonator drag competition and a Cher impersonator attended The Bar's grand opening.

"Franky was targeted!"

Considering his past, that shouldn't have been a surprise.

Leah's facial expression shifted to revulsion. "I hope not."

A man ran by us and rounded a corner of the calendar kiosk. Dozer came into view. The runner plowed into his chest, bounced off, and landed on a display of chapsticks. Pretzels held high in the air, Dozer stared down at the man slip-sliding on products as a uniformed Guilderland police officer caught up.

"Don't get me wrong," Leah lowered her voice. "It's obvious Dozer has his relationship scars. Once the two of you work through your issues, you'll have a strong, enviable relationship. Enjoy," she said and sashayed away.

Dozer waved a pretzel.

"Thanks." I grabbed the warm, carb-filled pastry nestled in a thin, brown paper napkin. I bit into the soft, fresh-baked, salt-covered dough and moaned. Dozer gave a low whistle as he produced a covered plastic cup of dipping mustard. This is the remarkable relationship I've yearned for, and I want more.

CHAPTER 31

"We need to take care of this couch." Dozer set his paper shopping bags on the monstrosity. "How are you handling your new shirt?"

Certain fabrics and I don't get along, like polyester. That one makes me feel like there are microscopic bugs crawling all over my body. These ADHD awareness shirts, that Dozer had gotten the both of us, were the right degree of soft. The new tag-free, elastic banded, cotton pants were also amazing. The blue jeans Dozer had bough and switched into were also a nice fit.

"The shirt is feels like it was made for me. As for the couch, it needs to be curb checked. If we do that though we'll have to share a bed." The words came out faster than my brain was firing.

Dozer spun around. The last time he his face shone like that was the day he received his divorce papers. "Is that an offer?"

"Um…" I scurried to my bedroom.

That wasn't want I had meant to say and yet I had. Dad had always said that mom and I had virtually no internal filters. Why did those filters have to malfunction on this one?

"Talia." Dozer was inches behind me. "You know as well as I do that this discussion needs to happen."

"Um…" I was buying time to formulate a coherent sentence.

Instead, my mind trailed off to the Ezkiel and my mom's engagement ring. The ring, I was supposed to inherit.

Mom's five-feet high knickknack covered dresser was directly in front of me. I wasn't as astute has I thought I had been since it appeared to me that not one item on top had been touched.

"How did that woman get Mom's engagement ring?" I asked.

"Dunno. We're off topic, again."

I barely registered his words. The robbery was on replay, and I couldn't force my mind to focus on anything else. "I watched the robbers from under the bed and didn't see either of them touch the dresser. How did this happen?"

Dozer released a low groan. "When you're in a better headspace, we need to have this talk." He moved to my side. His voice shifted to a soothing tone. "Let's try a different topic. Since we have conformation that your mother had ADHD, my sisters' mental health care provider…" He paused. "You haven't blinked in several seconds. Hyperfocus is… I'm going to drop this conversation. When you're ready let me know."

Emotionally drained, I ran a hand over a wooden jewelry box. "Why hasn't this been brought up to me before?"

"Oh Talia." Dozer leaned an arm on the dresser's edge. "Over the decades, we've had similar discussions. Since there wasn't definitive proof that ADHD is in your family, it made it difficult for you to get you tested."

My outstretched hand trembled. "Ezekiel's appearance has me rattled. I was frenzied when the police asked me if anything was missing."

I opened my maternal grandmother's antique jewelry box. The faint soothing scent of cedar reminded me of playing dress up. Swimming in a vintage dress, I clomped around the house in an oversized pair of Mom's old shoes. All the layers of necklaces wrapped around my neck made me feel like a princess.

"This empty box was purchased by my grandmother, in 1946, to commemorate our family's arrival in America. She thought Grandpa would one day make enough money to fill it. Growing up, it was full of jewelry mom got garage sales. Even they're gone."

I caressed the smooth, darkened image of hunters on horseback chasing a fox through a lush forest. In that moment, I was a bloodhound on the faint scent of a sneaky, wiry animal. Instead of a cunning fox I had a chance of catching, I had a nefarious human who had connections and gobs of money.

"I'm inept." I sat on the floor and fought back tears. Crying is a normal part of being human. At that point, I felt like crying was more about my being an utter failure, and I needed my strength to fight.

"Don't blame yourself." Dozer crouched next to me. The warmth of his hand penetrated my ADHD awareness T-shirt. He rubbed my back.

"No sleuths misses an empty jewelry box. I'm a failure."

"All detectives have their start somewhere. You need to persevere, make viable contacts, and learn—"

"What a minute." I cut him off. "When did a man who bakes for a living become an expert on this topic?"

Dozer's breath tickled my face as he dusted kisses across the side of my head. "Around the time that beast mauled my tushy."

He kissed me again. The movement was enough for me to notice an odd shadow cast by an overhead light. At the dresser's base, a piece of wood jutted out. I pulled one of the carved flowers until a hidden drawer slid open. Three one-hundred-dollar bills lay on top of white jewelry boxes. Dozer snatched up a ring box and flipped it open.

"Whoa!"

I leaned in to see what had him excited. "Is it one of dad's taxidermy cockroaches?"

Dozer spun the box to face me. A high-end jewelry store's gold logo stood out against the stark white satin lining on the inside lid. Nestled in the box was a ring I'd seen in advertisements when I was a child. The white gold ring's center stone was a one-karat, heart-shaped, chocolate diamond surrounded by four sapphires.

"What is going on? Dad never had the money to buy even a silver nose stud from this place."

"You did say that one of the robbers commented about having found an items on their list." Dozer set the ring box on the floor.

"What does an armadillo and a diamond ring have in common?"

"That riddle is worse than the raven and the writing desk."

I felt like Alice in Wonderland as I opened an elongated box. Inside was a ruby diamond bracelet.

"'Off with her head' said the Queen of Hearts."

"Happy to see you're getting back to yourself." Dozer opened another box containing a necklace.

We went through fifteen boxes of varying shapes and sizes. There were rings, necklaces, bracelets, earrings, and a few broaches.

"The beetle pin he made for Mom is missing. That hurts the worst."

"Did he use any of Franky's fleas as accents?"

"My dad wasn't a monster." I gripped the material on the left side of my chest as I feigned a heart attack. "Our pets always had proper burials, even the fleas."

Dozer felt around the back of drawer. "There's something back there." He pulled out a fragile paper. It threatened to tear as he peeled it open.

"What is it?"

He held up the document for me to see. It was a receipt for a safety deposit box rental.

I snatched the paper out of his hands and made my way across the house. "We have the information. Now, we need to the find the keys and figure out how Ezekiel fits in. First, I need to stick this to the fridge."

"If the house gets broken into, again, the robbers will have easy access to the information."

"It's where I put all the important things I don't want to lose. Mom taught me that." I grabbed a bumblebee magnet and stuck the receipt on the refrigerator at eye level. "Besides, they gave up."

I knew Dozer's worry was warranted. Light from overhead fixtures made it easy to see a fair about of clutters had been removed from my house. Unfortunately, I had multiple dumpsters worth of stuff to go.

Among the chaos lay precious memories and pieces of a strange scavenger hunt for me to follow once Mom was gone. It was up to me to find all the clues that lead to an unknown prize.

"The fridge!"

"What?" Dozer asked.

I began riffling through the junk drawer. "The day we interned mom I tossed everything that was attached to the fridge in the drawer."

"Was that library photo one of the items?"

"Yes."

I began to identify each item, in the drawer, out loud. I know it's silly to think scissors, tape, screwdrivers, wrenches, flashlights, are important, but in that moment, they were. To me, they represented a larger picture and brought me closer to my parents.

"What about the box of paperclips?" Dozer went for the muffins on the stove top.

I grunted my frustration.

"You might want to talk to a therapist."

"Logic, again." I pulled out a sturdy–five-by-seven periwinkle envelope, held it up, and set down the receipt. "Mom wants me to find all these things that lead to what she left behind."

"Gladys was an unorganized hoarder."

I held up the envelope for him to see the July postmark from Indiana. "The return address only has the last name of Knepp."

Dozer traded a muffin for the envelope. He slid the card out of the envelope. "A menorah five months before December? Your family works on a different time schedule."

Ignoring him, I slid the card from his hand and read the handwritten message:

Dear Gladys,

Our phone conversation was a shock to me. I apologize for not being as polite as possible. When you called me, I assumed you knew the truth and I thought that was the reason behind your call. As you might know, your mother's side of the family has many secrets. I am one of them.

My father Olaf had an affair that produced me. My mother hid the truth of my father as she married him right after their rumspringa. Once I discovered the Amish man I had known to be my Dat wasn't I left the Amish life.

During the pandemic, I sought out my birth father which I am conflicted about. He said you're a nut case. Regardless of his opinions on this matter I want to have a relationship and would love for you to meet my wife.

If you are interested, you already have my contact information.

> *Ezekiel*

CHAPTER 32

Day light waned into dusk while my tentativeness over solving my family's mystery had morphed into determination. The interior of my house was lit up. My coffeemaker was working overtime.

Swaddled in a cozy sweater and my housecoat, I sat at the dining room table running searches on Mom's old laptop. What scant information existed on Ezkiel was outweighed by the electronic trail left behind by Olaf.

The temperature inside the house hovered around fifty degrees. I tightened my housecoat around me and stared into the living room where Dozer stood shirtless.

"You've been adjusting that plywood for an hour." I tried to stare at the loading computer screen. That attempt was short lived at the sound of duct tape being unrolled. "What are you doing?"

"Securing the plywood."

"Placing a barrier over a hole that is larger than the hole makes the barrier secure."

"I'm not taking chances." Dozer bit off a foot of duct tape. "Any idea what happened to the other roll?"

"Franky probably absconded with it for a tractor pull." That wasn't accurate. I hid the roll and couldn't remember where I placed it.

The laptop dinged. I read over the information and groaned. Dozer gave me a pick on the cheek.

"More useless information?"

"Yup. Did you know that Olaf Kalinowski is a ninety-eight-year-old bachelor who lives in a Guilderland senior living facility? He enjoys online poker and long walks at the duck pond."

"Social media profile?" Dozer leaned over me, sending a ripple of desire down to my toes.

"You are a major distraction."

His breath brushed against my face with his soft-spoken words. "Is that the dating site your mom used?"

"Now I know the real reason you're shirtless."

He kissed the top of my head and walked into the kitchen. "Wanna answer my question?"

"Yes, it is. This is Mom's laptop from her house office."

"Anything good?"

"The senior's dating site had twenty-two possible matches that had shown up since Mom's death. If she had been serious about this mystery guy, she'd have taken her profile down."

Dozer slid a chair next to me. "What else?

"See for yourself."

I handed him the wireless mouse. He scrolled over the thumbnail image of my Mom sitting in an orange kayak and read over her profile.

"Nice and professional. At least we know Mrs. Sanchez didn't help write this one." Dozer grabbed the broom from next to the microwave and returned to the living room.

"I clicked on the username of the guy mom dated. A popup alerted me to the account's deactivation."

"That's disappointing."

I pulled out my notes scrawled on a yellow notepad. "Here's what I've got. Olaf racked up a substantial gambling debt. He's also on the verge of being kicked out of the senior home. No one visits him. A 'find anyone' search engine has him as Native American and earning four hundred thousand dollars a year. If I pay an additional $24.95, I could have a copy of his arrest warrants, liens, and employment history. It's clear Uncle Olaf is not Native American. That's why I got pizza delivery."

"Better investment." Dozer reached over me and took a slice out of the box. "Didn't that operating system become obsolete in the nineteen-seventies?"

"Ha, ha." I hit the power button, closed the laptop, disconnected the power cord, and stuffed it all into the dinosaur back into the carrying case. "Laptops weren't invented until the late eighties."

He didn't argue.

I grabbed a slice of pepperoni and bit into it. A piece of meat rolled off onto an article from the library that I used as the basis of my search.

"I gave you a plate." Dozer tossed the pepperoni aside and used a napkin to wipe sauce off the article. "That's your grandparent's fiftieth-wedding anniversary announcement. Says here the photo on the left was taken of them after they immigrated. This woman could be your twin."

"At least we know which side of the family I take after."

"Appearance isn't everything." Dozer squinted at the paper. "'Seventeen people attended the anniversary...' and it includes

Olaf's name as an absent family member. There's no mention of your Mom or you. When did they receive citizenship?"

"Mom got hers when I was in high school."

Dozer pulled out his cell phone. "For a Hail Mary pass."

"Calling Hector?"

"Better."

There was no one I knew who was better to call a Hail Mary pass from than his son. Hector was an aspiring P.I. who had been estranged from his lawyer-mother since she had been arrested for her involvement with a local amateur crime-chasing group. Yup, he had a ton of connections.

"Hello." The screen showed a close-up of Grandma Morgan's ear. "Who's there? This is the last time I accept an electronic gift from Franky."

"What are you doing?" I hush-whispered to Dozer. "She's clueless."

"Grandma, you're on Facetime," Dozer said into the phone and motioned for me to be quiet.

"Excuse you?"

"Technology." Grandma's wrinkled face came into view. "There was a time I shunned books."

Dozer pressed a thumb against his brow. "We have a few questions to ask you."

"I ain't go much time left. So, you better marry her fast."

"Not this again," I groaned.

"Grandma," Dozer's voice remained metered. "What do you know about the Polish guy you tossed your haemorrhoid donut at?"

That's when I understood what Dozer meant. My grandma and Olaf were in the same facility. I had wasted hours reading useless Internet sources. All I had to do was call my gossip loving Grandma who hated my Great-Uncle.

"That cancerous tumor doesn't shut up. Even when he's got his portable radio playing Polka music, he yammers on about the decline in accordion music and his family's lost money. If his nephew wasn't visiting from Indiana, I'd run his foot over with my wheelchair."

"Indiana?" Dozer asked.

"Yup." Grandma Morgan gave a curt nod. "That nephew is after some inheritance. Even got Olaf involved in this mess. The Amish have a saying about greedy son's of—"

"Grandma." I stopped her from a tirade. "How long ago did this person make contact?"

"A few months back." She tugged out a chin hair. "This troll blazed in here like he owned the nursing home. Even wore a facemask covered in sequins. Such a flashy display."

"You were raised Amish," I pointed out.

"If I hadn't met your grandfather, I'd have stayed. You and Dozer are what's good in my life."

"What about Franky?" I asked.

She stuck out her tongue.

"Grandma. Back to Olaf."

"He's a piece of work." She scrunched her nose. "That old windbag told us his family members might try to cash in on his inheritance. Like he's the sole heir to some lost major fortune. If his family was that wealthy, he'd be in that luxury nursing home and we'd have some quite around here."

Dozer's expression said what I was thinking: There was no family wealth. The letter Ezekiel sent mom didn't mention money either.

"What inheritance?" I asked.

Grandma's silver hair bobbed as she moved in and out of view. "The only inheritance I know of is toothpicks. Olaf said that relative should've sent him a ring that's worth a fortune. Had a chocolate diamond and emeralds. Allegedly, one of his relatives was a world traveler who sent bags of unprocessed stones to family in Guilderland. One of those relatives made them into jewelry for some high-end city store at an insane profit. Price gouging is what that is."

And there it was. Ezekiel had discovered my mom had the jewelry. He hired the two guys to break in. This didn't explain why Arny was on the list and animal-napped.

I needed to know I was headed towards catching the bad guys. "Do you know what happened to those items?"

"According to the windbag, his niece was a skilled jeweler. whose artistic talents were used to help the entire family. In 1979, the sale of one of her pieces paid for three relatives to immigrate. Instead of keeping the family's money flow going, she married a dreamer she had met at an estate sale to become a stay-at-home mom. The whole family disowned her for it, too. Tragic."

I knew my grandmother was thinking of her own family. This

161

wasn't the time to relive these painful memories. What I was hearing about my parents made far more sense to me than the story I had been told.

Mom's family wanted what was best for the family overall. Instead of continuing to make jewelry that brought money for the entire family, my mom followed her own happiness. Once she married my Dad, she devoted her life to raising me and helping her husband follow his dream. That's why Ezekiel sees my inheritance as his.

"My family is messed up."

Dozer nudged me. "She's speaking."

I was fortunate that my grandmother hadn't heard me. She already knew that I had been focused on my own loss when my Dad died. She also knew that I hadn't thought of what that did to my Mom as her identity had centered around her husband. She needed to rediscover herself and find a new path.

Grandma Morgan had been talking the entire time my mind wandered. I missed quite a bit as she ended her monologue by saying: "…and that's why Olaf thinks the Romanovs are still in power."

"He's not a reliable source," Dozer looked pained.

I was glad I missed that tirade.

Grandma Morgan spoke to someone out of view. "I'm talking about Olaf, the space cadet."

What sounded like a muffled male voice came through the speaker. Grandma Morgan responded to the off-screen man. "Heard a relative went for a walk around the duck pond."

Dozer's hot breath tickled my neck as he whispered in my ear. "He's after that jewelry."

I nudged him away.

"About time we got real entertainment." Grandma's face came into view. "Guilderland police are here. Olaf fell into the pond."

The image bounced, the screen flipped, and I was staring at the ecru pock marked ceiling tiles. After a few brief moments, Officer Anotelli's face came into view. He squinted.

"Where do I know you from?"

"Hi." I gave a bashful finger wave. "Last week, you investigated my home invasion and, my armadillo was stolen."

Anotelli managed to keep a stern face. He pointed off-camera. "How do you know this woman?"

"If you're pointing at the feisty woman in a wheelchair, she's my paternal grandmother."

Anotelli dropped out of view. When he was in view again, he held a red circular blow-up pillow. I refrained from telling him that my grandmother played that trick on the orderlies. When she wanted to check out their backsides, she'd drop her pillow to watch them pick it up. I had a clear view of the black block letters that read, "Property of Mrs. Morgan. Haemorrhoid use only."

The expression on Anotelli's face conveyed my thoughts. What had this woman done to warrant that statement?

Grandma's overly dramatic, shaky hand pulled back the pillow. She feigned a frail voice. "Thank you, kind sir."

Anotelli's stared at me. "Do you know Olaf—"

Grandma shouted over him. "I hope he drowned."

"Ignore my father's mother." I rolled my eyes. "Olaf was my mom's uncle."

Since Grandma Morgan was treating the Police Officer like he was hired entertainment, I felt it was best to clarify relationships.

Anotelli's face gave a hint of emotion while his voice remained calm. "Any connection to the man who was seen with him?"

"If he's balding, and suffers from nerves-induced flatulence, then he's Olaf's son who inherited my mom's life insurance policy. He moved here from Indiana a few months back."

I sucked in air and blurted out everything else I knew, including Ezekiel's connection to the dead women and the stolen armadillo. This was the second recap this individual received from me. After this, he'd probably ask for a raise.

Dozer tilted the screen toward himself. "Talia missed the part about her inheriting the house and a safety deposit box while the rest of the family received boxes of toothpicks."

Anotelli's struggled to keep his composure. He was probably thinking that my entire family was certifiable. If I guessed right, he kept that judgment to himself. "Toothpicks?"

I gave a dismissive wave. "It's a Polish thing."

"No." Grandma pulled the phone to her face. "Back when Gladys' family shunned her, like my Amish family did me, your mother asked me for advice."

Dozer and I exchanged worried glances.

"What advice?" I hoped she missed the part where I admitted my familial relation to Olaf.

Grandma's tone sharpened. "I told her those who cared about her would reach out to her, like my Uncle Levi. No one knew he and I kept in contact after our family shunned me. He was too scared to leave the order. That's why I inherited everything he had."

"Dad inherited it," I corrected.

"Your father ran the company until I sold him that part of my inheritance a year before he got the cancer diagnosis. If your Aunt Edna's fortune telling skills worked, I'd have held onto the company."

I was dumbstruck.

"Back to Talia's mother," Dozer interjected.

"Yes." Grandma nodded. "When they shunned her, she was enraged and asked how I handled my family. I told her I pretended they didn't exist. Then, I had my attorney make my will iron-clad by leaving all my relatives a sealed box."

"What was in the box?" I asked.

"Cow pies."

Yup. That's my Grandma Morgan in a nutshell. Never anger a passive-agressive Amish elder.

"Earlier you said Olaf's toothpick inheritance was a Polish tradition," I said.

"No." Grandma rolled her eyes. "I told you that bonehead Olaf said receiving toothpicks was a Polish insult. That jack rabbit thinks sneezing without his permission is an insult."

Anotelli's face came into view again. "We're going to need a copy of your mother's will."

I pulled out my flip phone. "Texting my attorney to meet you at the station." I hit *Send*. A moment later, I received a strange box. I tilted the phone for Dozer to see. "What's that?"

"I'm assuming a thumbs up." He groaned. "Hard to tell since your phone predates emojis."

"Pickles will be there will in hand." I flipped my phone shut.

Grandma Morgan sat ramrod straight. "My grandson, Franky, uses him, too."

"Wait." Anotelli's head oscillated between the phone and Grandma. "You're both related to Francis Calderone?"

CHAPTER 33

A thrashing thunderstorm rattled the windows. I grabbed the spare pillow to my chest and imagined it was Dozer comforting me. Despite my last-minute invitation to share my bed, he decided to sleep on the curb-ready couch.

I lay in the fetal position watching flashes of light penetrate the blinds. Through Mother Nature's anarchy, I heard the faint grumble of my coffee maker. I slid out from under the quilt and swung my legs off the bed and into cozy house slippers.

I flipped the nightstand's lamp on. Mom's sewing machine peeked out from under a mound of material. The door on Dad's side of the closet was open; Dozer was already up and I refused to greet him in a complete state of disarray.

I brushed my shoulder-length hair, and I tugged my flannel pajama top down and the bottoms up over my stomach. This was my overweight, out of shape body, and I was going to own it. I dragged myself to the other end of the house.

Overhead lights brightened the dark corners of every room. Opened curtains showed off a torrential rain pounding against the windows. Sheets of water trickled down the panes as lightning flashed. The house lights flickered.

I paused at the rum-scented recliner and stared at the hanging lamp above the dining room table. A bulb had burned out. Unfazed, Dozer sat under the fixture wearing a pair of mid-calf khaki pants and a striped polo shirt. Both hung off his frame.

"That's why my father's closet was open." I made a grab for the steaming coffee mug near Dozer's left hand.

"I hope you don't mind." He pulled it away. "Our clothes are in the dryer." He scraped his chair against the floor. "For the record, your couch is lumpy and it smells like a dead rat."

"Burrito," I corrected. "If you're going to insult my furniture, at least get the odor correct."

"No air freshener will fix that." Dozer brushed against me. "I found your second-grade journal."

"Not the Ode to Fluffy."

Dozer hesitated a long moment as if he were battling an internal argument about the wisdom of his question. He settled on asking, "What?"

Thunder rumbled. Power went out.

"Fluffy was my pet tarantula." I fumbled for the fridge. "In second grade, tucked her inside my lunchbox to bring to school for show and tell…" It was best that I let the story drop there.

The backup generator sounded like a rumbling diesel truck when it kicked in. Lights on, Dozer used the opportunity to close the gap. I braced myself for a confrontation. Instead, he gave me a peck on the cheek. "Your parents were unique."

I opened the fridge. "Where's the coffee creamer? We've got olives, jelly, beer, milk, what appears to be green soda, and hot dogs. What flavor is the green drink?"

"Leah dropped it off. She said it was healthier than what we've been drinking. I forgot to run a translation search; it's a mystery flavor." He opened the composition notebook to a bookmarked page. "As for your journal, all the entries are about that Cory kid. In the fall of 1987, you called him a 'dog breath ant eater.'"

"Mom insisted that I'd get farther in life, if I didn't swear like dad's side of the family."

"Did this kid eat ants.?"

"Franky dared him to."

"That pans out." Dozer set the journal aside. "There's quite a bit I never knew about your family. It's a learning curve."

I walked to the cluttered table. "Didn't we fill the fridge when your friend replaced it?"

"Yeah," Dozer handed me the caramel creamer. "Franky tossed most of it as we need to implement better eating habits. He's turning his life around."

"He doesn't need to turn out lives around too. Remind me to strangle him."

I poured the creamer until my coffee was tan. The world was morphing into a better place.

"It's part of this charm," Dozer said. "Since that rotting smell kept me up, I did more rummaging. That taxidermy artwork business your father ran with Cory Sr. was destined for failure from day one. Arny was the first piece your dad made when the business opened. He refused to sell it as he felt it'd bring bad luck if he did. That's when Cory Jr. destroyed Franky's flea circus. A few months later, you received Arny as a Christmas gift."

"So that brat attacked Franky's first 'multi-million-dollar get rich scheme' to get back at my dad for not selling dead animal?"

"That kid had issues."

"That's an understatement." I lowered myself into a chair at the dining room table. Mixed into the mess was Dozer's pistol, a few photos, thumb drives, and a bag of something edible.

"Candy!" I sounded like a child who was staring down a full basket of Easter goodies, instead of an adult staring at multi-colored gelatin-based goop in a softball sized package.

Dozer snatched up the cellophane bag. "Do *not* eat these."

I lunged across the table. "They're food."

Pistol in hand, Dozer backed away.

"Don't you use your gun to threaten me."

Now, I was the kid getting dragged out of the candy store after the holidays when everything was on clearance.

"It's so you don't shoot me." Dozer showed me his finger was at the side of the guard. "These are the sugar-free candies Ted gave me."

"Wait." This was more than I was able to comprehend. I sat back down. "Instead of grabbing clothes, you saved a package of fruit-flavored laxatives?"

"I keep important items in the fire-proof lockbox like my gun, extra cash, and these gummies." He shook the crinkling package. There had to be more to the story.

It wasn't a good idea to press a conversation of that magnitude before food. I splayed my hands on the table to keep from doing something stupid.

"Why the lockbox?"

"Hector is a sugar addict." Dozer inched back to his seat and set his gun on the table next to him careful to show me the safety was on. "When Ted gave me these, the first person I thought of re-gifting them to was Franky."

His answer was far more twisted than I had expected. "You saved these for my cousin."

"Yeah." The mischievous expression that flashed across his face, gave me a glimpse of his virtually unknown, playful side. "I didn't want my son to get sick, so I stashed them for safekeeping."

I had no answer. The man I had deep feelings for admitted to plotting a Franky-worthy prank on the prank master himself. It felt wrong for Dozer to mess with food. He's a kind-hearted pastry chef known to take extra care to ensure the food people ingested was safe and since these candies cause diarrhea I was torn.

Dozer shrugged. "It didn't feel right even though I knew Franky would approve of the prank."

I stifled my words of agreement by sipping my coffee. After a few satisfying sips, I glanced at a dog-eared photo. A woman who resembled his sister held a swaddled baby in a blue blanket.

"Is that you as a baby?"

Dozer handed me the faded color photo. A beaming rail thin bleach blonde woman in a 1980's, blow-out hair style wore an outfit that screamed, "I'm an extra from *Designing Women*."

"Heather is Mom's clone. The photos is from a series of pictures taken the day I was found."

"Heather's the nicest of your sisters."

I placed my hand over Dozer's hand as he had done for me many times before. "Your mother has loved you from day one."

Breathing measured, Dozer remained still. As long as I had known him, he had always avoided conversations about his possible birth family. Most adopted individuals have an agency to reach out to for a scrap of information. All Dozer has is the name of a closed convent, a cardboard box, and a soft blanket embroidered with the Spanish word for baby boy.

"She's the youngest." He reached for stained envelope. "I want to share this with you." He slid a faded crumbling newspaper articled out of the envelope and handed it to me. "That's my birth mother."

I read over the headline several time to commit it to memory. The article was a four-inch square about an unidentified Hispanic woman found dead in Amsterdam, New York.

"It was the 1970s. I never bothered to search beyond that. It's a small comfort to know wanted to give me a better life."

There was nothing more to say. We listened to rain pelt the glass unit it waned into a gentle tap before we continued to read over the documents.

On the bottom of a stack of receipts I pulled out a bunch of papers bound by a binder clip, release forms from a psychiatric facility. Dozer didn't say anything. Frantic, I pawed through medical reports, medicines, therapist referrals, my parents' wedding certificate. I stopped at Mom's Polish birth certificate and immigration documents.

"Mom's birth name was Gilah, and her father was a rabbi? Dude! I got one great-grandfather who was an Amish bishop and a grandfather who was a rabbi. All that's missing is a Catholic priest."

"Your father had a taxidermy chipmunk in priest's robes."

I cringed at the thought.

"Just so you know I rummaged through your mom's study and found a safe hidden inside what appeared to be a trundle bed tucked behind a stack of boxes."

"You are as bad as Franky."

He pointed at me. "You gave me permission to search."

I scratched my chin.

"Who's like Franky?" Dozer asked.

I sipped my coffee.

"And it's your safe that holds your mom's personal effects. Turns out, the combination is your birth date."

Jealously smacked me in the face. "I wanted to be the one who unearthed the brittle pages that prove my entire life had been a lie."

"I'll put them back so you can pretend to be the one who discovered them."

"Fine. Lay it all on me."

"I don't believe you." Dozer waved a Polaroid photo of my parents in matching jeans and T-shirts. Mom had on a wedding veil and dad wore a top hat as they stood in front of a robed judge. "Your parents eloped at the courthouse."

Written in blue ink, on the white section of the picture were the words: November 15, 1979. Guilderland Courthouse. Witnesses: Ma, Edna, Salvatore, Mr. Richardson, Cory Jackson Sr., and Albert Lauffenburger.

CHAPTER 34

The raging storm had trickled to a mild mist by time we finished examining the safe's contents. Notes, medical records, and other documents told of the Kalinowskis' heroic survival story from religious persecution to American citizenship. In comparison, I was a complete coward.

When Mom had a breakdown—one that she never recovered from. While she fought to regain her life, I abandoned her to wallow in my own sorrows. Mom was alone and vulnerable. It made sense that a con-artist was able to bypass my Mom's well-guarded demeanor.

My stomach growled... protesting I hadn't given it more food. I placed my hands against my face as if in prayer.

"Years after her initial mental health crisis, Ezekiel waltzed into Mom's life. That's when she had another downward spiral. She must have snapped after receiving that letter."

Dozer was going over the Hannukah card again. "What are we missing?"

"There's nothing to learn from a few sentences or a cartoon candelabra."

"That's what's wrong. I didn't want to sound ignorant by asking about the number of candles."

"That discount greeting card has me thinking." I grabbed my mug that bore the words: *Don't talk before caffeine,* made my way to the sink, and added my mug to the pile of dishes. "Any search engine would bring up a list of Jewish holidays and common images for each. That card shows the cluelessness of this guy."

"Leah gave us a list of this guy's victims. None of their companies had outsourced Internet sites, and the wine company was automated. How did Ezekiel pull that off?"

"Maybe his wife is his accomplice." Even I wasn't buying that scenario. I sat back down across from Dozer. "What else do we have?

Dozer handed me the papers from Mom's stint at a mental health-care facility. Rage, frustration, and relief bombarded my senses as I stared at the letters ADHD.

"We've been looking at this all wrong." I set the paper down.

"Care to share?"

"Dozer, it's been there the entire time. There are two Ezekiels. I don't know how, but there are. This guy was raised Amish. In the 1990s, he could only be reached through a Mennonite. Two of these tech savvy women died under questionable circumstances when this man didn't even own a phone."

It'd have been better if I had thought of it earlier. "Don't tell Grandma Morgan, it took me this long. She'll make certain everyone knows I was slow on the uptake."

"Deal." Dozer held up the stack of obituaries. "On the other side of your family we have five Kalinowskis whom died of heart attacks. Also, I discovered one of your uncles changed his surname to Kalvin, so you missed his obituary when you printed these up. That uncle's Obit said he had AFib. I ran that medical condition through a search engine. Turns out, AFib is an irregular heartbeat that often has no symptoms, is genetic, and frequently goes undetected just like ADHD."

"That has to be it!" I shouted. A heaviness I didn't know I was carrying was lifted off me. "We finally have answers!"

I got up and kissed Dozer on his cheek.

"You missed your calling as a motivational speaker." He was back to being flirtatious. "Got any more motivation?"

"Maybe." I flirted back. "For now, we need to figure this out. The autopsy paper gave a heart attack as a cause of death. This leads us back to ADHD. If we compare Stephanie Lauffenburger and my Mom they are nothing alike."

"The 'H' is strong in Stephanie."

I leaned against the kitchen counter. "You lost me."

"The 'H' stands for 'hyper'. Stephanie's energy level is so high she can't sit still for more than thirty seconds. Your Mom didn't have that issue. ADHD is a 'spectrum' that manifests in a different way in each individual. Also, ADHD is often accompanied by other disorders like autism, bi-polar, or schizophrenia. Those present symptoms, than can lead to a misdiagnosis."

The world was a pin-prick visible to no one else except me.

"How I did not know Mom had this? I'm her daughter."

"I think this is a matter of protective-daughter panic." Dozer was in front of me. His face full of concern. He pulled me in for a hug. "If this were the nineteen fifties when full-frontal lobotomies were considered a cure invisible disabilities, I'd understand your reaction. Today, there's a plethora of treatment options."

"This isn't panic mode." I patted his chest. "My mom hid vital health information from me, information that might be connected to events surrounding her sudden death. The medical conditions we're discussing aren't anything like foot fungus."

"You lost me on that last part." He stepped back. "Moments like this I'm convinced you have inattentive ADHD."

I glanced out the window. It was still dark. We had been up since at least two in the morning.

"Why? I don't have any of the indicators."

"Okay," Dozer said. "I understand your concerns. Let's remember that ADHD is often undiagnosed in females. Gladys was an eccentric quirky woman who enjoyed crafts, meandering conversations, struggled to follow instructions, and had a filing system unique to herself. Do you see any of this in yourself?"

I preferred to stay in denial. "Why don't we go out for food?"

"Talia. That comment supports my theory."

I whined like Franky. "This has to be learned behavior."

"Okay. Obviously, this isn't the time to have this serious discussion." Dozer glanced down at himself. "We'll go out for food as long as you don't mind this outfit."

I pointed his left breast pocket. "As long as you don't mind wearing a demonized duck in public."

Dozer pulled up his shirt to have a better view of the logo. "This isn't a dragon?"

"We'll pretend it's a dragon."

He gave a thumbs up.

I glanced at the duct tape used to secure plywood that had been placed over the hole from the attic side. I gave myself a mental head smack. Mom had taught me to keep my car keys on a separate key chain from the house keys. My mind had been preoccupied by Dozer losing his apartment to fire that I accidently left my keys in cupholder. It'd have to retrieve them from the junkyard.

"Raccoons," I muttered.

"As long as we're going out, there's a great place about thirty minutes that has free black label alcohol." Dozer called after me.

"There are two aged bottles of liquor from my college days in the cupboard. That's more than plenty."

"The tequila is halfway gone and I spilled the rum when I tripped over a pile of boxes in the dark. Your recliner needs to be steam-cleaned."

"Darkness?" I glanced at the outlets. The nightlights were gone. More stolen items that needed to be added to the list for the police. "We'll curb-check the chair alongside that couch.".

Dozer batted his long thick eyelashes. "We're sharing a bed now?"

His cell phone rang. He pressed speaker. "Hector. Talk to me."

"Is Talia there?"

"Yo," I answered as I stared out the window. A beam of light flashed outside the Sanchez house. A hunched figure bobbed out the door, down the walkway, and stopped. The beam of light washed over the Nativity scene. The front porch light flicked on, and a second figure rushed out of the house carrying what appeared to be a blanket. I tore myself away from the scene.

Dozer pulled down the shades.

"Good news," Hector said.

I asked, "You found the raccoons that hijacked my car?"

Laughter erupted from the phone. "That was your car? Oh, man. I'd have paid to see that one. A national news station picked it up and now an animal rights group is—"

"What did you find?" Dozer cut him off.

I headed to the other end of the house. I wasn't going out in my night clothes.

"Right." Hector cleared his throat. "Ezekiel was born Amish. Joined the Mennonites around 1994. He has family in the area and not much beyond that. He tends to stay off the grid."

"Duh." I entered my bedroom. The unmade bed reminded me of how bad I am at housekeeping. I tugged at the quilt. "Amish are off the grid."

Dozer rounded the other side of the bed, set the phone on the nightstand, pulled a pillow off, and whispered, "Do we really need to make the bed?"

I tossed the pillow on my side at him. He knocked it aside.

"Dad, your microphone isn't on mute." Hector's comment caught us off guard.

"Uh... Yeah..." Dozer glanced at his phone. "What have you learned?"

Hector mumbled something about us getting a room. Dozer's face flushed. Hector continued talking as if nothing had been said. "In 2003, Ezekiel inherited a business from a woman in Indiana. All of the business he inherited used antique carts. In 1999, there was a lawsuit filed against him in Cleveland, Ohio. It didn't go anywhere because his assets at the time were listed as 'tools of the trade.' Can't get much from a hammer. Oh, and Ezekiel didn't leave the Mennonite community until 2019. No cell phone is registered under his name."

Blankets in place, Dozer set the pillows against the headboard.

I adjusted them. "What was the lawsuit for?"

"Ezekiel drank too much and hurled on a woman's six-hundred-dollar purse."

I began pulling clothes out of dresser drawers. I tossed a pair of blue jeans and a white long-sleeved shirt onto the bed. "And we're back to Stephanie Lauffenburger whose father was going to hire Ezekiel in the 1990s for restoration work on one of his hose carts. Albert decided against the restoration when Stephanie told him she didn't want hers restored."

"She owns an antique hose cart!" Hector's voice sounded like a child who had been told he was going to a theme park.

"Returning to topic." Dozer's back was to me while he held up his phone. It was nice to have privacy.

"Any luck on your end?" Hector asked.

I grabbed my hairbrush. "It turns out, Ezekiel's my Great-Uncle Olaf Kalinowski's son."

"Dad, you get the best cases!" Hector said. "Olaf's connected to another case I worked earlier this year. Since he was on the fringe, I ran the basics."

"What do you have on him?" Dozer asked.

Unable to contain his excitement, Hector sped through more of what he had learned. "Olaf claims Ezekiel shoved him into the duck pond at the senior facility he lives in. The emergency response team arrived fast because a woman who was feeding the ducks pressed her alert button. A relative had jewelry that was worth millions, Olaf insists it's rightfully his; but it was willed to another relative."

I thought back to the skunk hat. "Are you sure about the dollar amount?"

"Yeah. Olaf's adamant. Also, Ezekiel got into a dark-colored four-door sedan driven by another man. Gotta go. This guy I'm sitting on is moving. Damn adultery cases." Hector hung up.

Dozer glanced at the time. "It's a few after six. We can hit the burger joint on Western for breakfast on our way to pick up liquor replacements."

He didn't need to ask me about food twice. I gave him the thumbs up. He tapped on his cell phone while I thought about what I had learned.

"Mrs. Sanchez told me that Mom's safety deposit box contained something that would have me and Franky set for life. I wonder if it's the jewelry. Do you know a jeweler who will examine the collection to estimate its value?"

"I'll take care of it." He sent off a text message, grabbed a cloth tote bag, and opened the drawer. "The burger place is a few doors down from a jeweler I know who will help us. No need for a ride share."

"Did you pull a vehicle out of thin air?"

"Yup." Dozer waved a series of text messages at me.

The last one from Cheryl read: My grandmother is singing again. Use my van as long as you bring me back a bottle of anything 80 proof.

CHAPTER 35

"Do you think Chryel knows the meaning behind that?" I pointed to an upside-down pineapple air freshener stuck to the dashboard.

"More likely Mrs. Sanchez does." Dozer eased the borrowed van into the parking lot behind the remnants of Franky's dream establishment. High beams washed over charred wood that lay in front of the dumpster. The only spot free from broken house pieces was where his SUV had been.

"Really?" I asked.

"Cheryl doesn't come across as the swinger type."

"That might not be accurate," I said. Mrs. Sanchez showed up after my house was broken into wearing an oversized dominatrix outfit."

"I'll pretend you didn't say that."

He inched up to a smattering of safety-glass shards. Neon orange letters had been scrawled on a bumper that leaned against the redbrick wall.

"Wash me." I read out loud.

"Hu." Dozer threw the van in park.

"At least there's no more skunk smell."

"Yea, I think it's a drunken hot dog. "

I followed his gaze up the building to a mangled, 1890s, wrought iron fire escape that held onto the remains of the second floor. The metal groaned. Behind the fire escape, lit by the rising sun, was an obscene spray-painted image.

I agreed. It did resemble a drunken hotdog.

Pieces of red brick crunched under my sneakers as I tentatively stepped around the mini-van. There was a faint breeze that made I was grateful that I had layers on.

The brisk air penetrated my beige sweater and blue jeans. I shuddered. Dozer was busying adjusting the rolled-up cuffs of my Dad's old khaki pants and didn't notice. I was disappointed that the demonic duck shirt was covered by a black windbreaker.

"No cones or hazard tape," I pointed out.

"They've probably been stolen." Dozer tugged on the metal plate that lay flat against the stone. The back door opened.

"That's supposed to remain locked." Dozer sent off a text message before turning on the flashlight app.

He pressed himself against the door to let me enter first.

Chivalry is nice. It'd have been nicer if I had my flashlight ready before the door had been cracked open.

"I know it's in here." I rummaged through my messenger bag. "Gum, pocketknife, nail clippers, wallet, Old English Dictionary and... Now you have me calling it a dictionary."

Dozer conked the back of his head against the painted Emergency Exit sign. "Why do you carry that thing?"

"It brings me comfort. Ha! Found it."

I pulled out a thumb-drive-sized light. The previous month, I received it as a gift at the Guilderland Fire Department's open house when I picked up an application. The beam from Dozer's flashlight app was brighter and covered a larger area than mine.

"I think it's time to upgrade your phone."

"No, I need a better flashlight." I huffed by Dozer.

It was a point of principle that I refused to vocalize that he was right; I needed to upgrade my phone. A few steps in, I gagged. Complete darkness and the stench of a doused fire greeted us.

Dozer moved past me. His light reflected off a tattered pool table its top covered in stagnant murky water. My light washed over a brown rat as it swam by me. I clicked my light off. There are things better off left to the imagination.

The Bar hadn't suffered too much visible damage. Behind the counter, bottles of colorful liquid stood resolute along the stretch of the brass mirrored wall. In the middle of the alcohol was an empty space where the cash register had been.

"Grab a couple unopened bottles from the storage." I pointed to the locked cabinet doors underneath.

Dozer slid an opened jar of cherries aside. "How long do you think it took the robbers to figure out there wasn't any cash in the register?'

"An hour. Two tops." I reached for my keys. They were gone. Fear bubbled up before I remembered I didn't have them anymore.

Dozer had his maintenance key out and unlocked the liquor cabinet door. "At least I remembered to grab these when I rushed out of the building."

"Do you want to visit your apartment?" Since we were already one level below, I thought it was logical to walk up a flight to at least see check for salvable items.

"After we finish here." He tugged on the handle. Water had caused the wood to swell shut. "Franky would've made more money having an after-fire party by charging people to smash doors to get their booze."

The door gave and slid open. I flashed the light inside and counted the bottles. "Nothing outside of the five bottles bourbon are missing." I grabbed the splintered wooden crate off the wall display. "Who filches alcohol and leaves behind a carrying case?"

"Stoners." Dozer handed me a bottle. "Payment for Cheryl?"

"Black label. Nice." I set the bottle on the counter.

Dozer's head was on a spindle as we walked back to the van. I set the bottle on the floor of the back passenger side.

"I want to know what we're missing." Dozer jangled his keys.

"Let Franky handle it." I rubbed my arms for warmth. "It's Frosty the snowman weather out here."

"There's money in the safe." Dozer went back inside the building. I closed the and locked the van.

"Really Dozer!" I shouted as I followed him back into the building.

Stagnant frigid water soaked through to my skin as I traversed a mess of fallen ceiling tiles, broken wooden chairs, and stacked empty picture frames. I stepped over a lump of clothing, entered the crammed back office, and cursed my Uncle Sal for not leveling out the floors.

Coffin-sized wooden crates lined the office. A pathway between them was large enough for single person to navigate. I shoved my light into my messenger bag.

"Didn't Franky say the order wasn't delivered?" Dozer ran a hand over the clean sealed crate.

"Yeah."

"Where'd this come from?" Dozer leaned down and inhaled. "They were added after the fire." He handed me his phone and instructed me to hold it steady.

"You figured this out from the scent?"

He pointed to the wooden pallets underneath that kept the crates from sitting in the water. "No damage."

My jeans had soaked the water up to my shins while only the pallets had been affected by the moisture.

"When this is done, you can whip this story into a best-selling novel." Dozer grabbed a crowbar and wedged it under the lid. "You'll make a fortune."

"Writer's make pennies."

He pressed down. A loud crack reminded me of a distant gunshot. The top moved upward. He clanked the metal crowbar onto the desk's oak top, denting the wood in the process.

Dozer slid the crate's top into a pool of water on the floor. "Why does your cousin have a crowbar on his desk?"

"Better than whips."

"Not going there." Dozer paused. "This scenario is too bizarre for anyone outside of your friends and family to believe it's real. You'll make a fortune."

"Do you have any idea how difficult it is to get published? And don't get me started on sales."

That was the issue I had run into almost twenty years earlier. I had received an advance of five grand and the royalty checks totaled fifty dollars. After all, anyone can write a book. Not everyone can sell one.

"My mom knows a publisher." Dozer reached into the hay-like packing strips and pulled out a forest-green bottle.

I shifted the light. Wrapped partway around the glass was a browned label. The cork was sealed in a dark wax. Even though I have no interest in wine, I was able to tell this thing had to be worth more than the special occasions three-dollar bottles I buy.

"Chateau Lafite, 1787." Dozer whistled. "One of these was believed to have been owned by Thomas Jefferson. It went at auction for over $150,000."

"Instead of buying a house, some sap spent the money on that? There's no way Franky had the money for this."

Dozer set the bottle down with the care of a parent placing a sleeping infant into a bed. "If this is real than this crate holds about a million dollars worth of wine."

"Hiding expensive items like these in a place set for demolition isn't intelligent. Franky not stupid."

I ran the flashlight beam along the numbered wooden crates and wound my way to the back. The light hovered over the word "Fragile."

Each unmarked crate was on top of a water-soaked wooden pallet. None of it made sense to me. Of all the questionable activities my cousin had been involved in, smuggling wine wasn't a venture he'd be interested in. The stakes were too high and if he was caught, Pickles wouldn't be able to find a way to skirt these charges.

I sloshed up to Dozer. "Six million dollars in vinegar."

"That's if these were stored improperly."

"What if..." More pieces fell into place. "Dozer, Was Jackson's jacket a knockoff?"

"What?"

"The jacket label you snapped a photo of and sent to your stepdad. It belonged to Jackson. Was it a knockoff?"

"Yeah." Dozer swept the light over dingy wall. A black square hole sat chest high. The safe had been emptied. "I forgot to let you know it was confirmed a counterfeit."

"They're fakes." My excitement grew as I slid more puzzle pieces into place. "Cory Jackson, Jr., is involved in counterfeiting. He's Ezekiel's partner. It all fits!" I rambled for several minutes about the winery, the cart manufacturing, and Arny's kidnapping. "That armadillo was supposed to be sold. Instead, Dad gave it to me. Cory Jr. targeted my mom to get revenge and now he's setting Franky up to take a fall for counterfeit wine. Six million carries an abysmal sentence."

Dozer pulled me close and kissed me. His lips were a warm welcome. He released me as fast as he had pulled me in. "Consider that a sneak preview of how we'll celebrate later."

I was all for that celebration.

Dozer's focus was distant.

Waving my hand in front of his face didn't get a response. "What's wrong?"

"There's something I need to tell you."

Dozer's chest expanded as he drew in air. He was preparing for a difficult conversation. After all I had been through, I wasn't ready to brace myself for more bad news. "What is it?"

He set his phone down. Placed his hands on my forearms. I internally braced myself for the bad news.

His face creased with concern, showing his age. "I'm not a maintenance guy."

All the tension left my body. "That?"

"How'd you figure that out?"

"Your tool of choice is duct tape."

"Every handyman uses duct tape." Dozer argued.

"Not on leaking pipes."

"What else did you figure out?" He headed to the bar area.

I followed. "You're probably helping your son's boss out."

"Not much gets by you."

"I haven't figured out why." That was the missing piece.

"Since I have connections and am innocuous, it was easy for me to obtain information for the private investigator he hired. That's why I moved into this building as a maintenance guy. Easier for me to get information."

"Does that mean you still own your home?"

"No. Hector does." He grabbed an unopened bottle of liquor. "I was going to tell you… Then, you were in the car accident, and your mother died. I wasn't able to be in multiple places at once. It tore me apart not telling you."

"This does hurt."

"I'm sorry. There hasn't been a decent time to have this discussion." He sloshed over to the pool table and set the bottle down with a splat. "Raphael thought the former maintenance guy had been stealing from the people in this apartment building. Raphael didn't want to take a chance of getting caught up in the illegal activities, so he left. That's what was in his note."

"That family RV trip was part of your amateur detective work?" I wanted to scream. Oh yeah, I had in fact missed that my best friend was investigating criminal activities. That was like missing a triceratops waddling through a family barbeque.

"For your safety, I'm not supposed to tell you any of this. We've known for a while that the case Hector has been working ties back to your mother. Now that you've pieced the other parts together. I refuse to hold any of the information from you."

Water dripped behind me. I stared at Dozer for several breaths. Leah's words about cultural expectations of men and fear repeated in my mind.

I leaned into to give the man I love a peck on his check. At the last second, he moved. Our lips met. The kisses were slow at first. They quickly intensified. All my trepidation melted away under the warmth of his body pressed against mine.

Franky's voice cut in. "I ain't into kink."

I leaned against Dozer. "Why are you here?"

"Your boyfriend sent me a text to get here ASAP, to facilitate activities while it's searched. You know, keep things legal. What you two were doing crosses that line."

"You said you didn't receive a shipment." I hooked a thumb to the back room.

"Right. When they saw the building was toast, they left."

I made my way to the bar. Under the counter was a sealed mason jar. I pulled it out, marched up to Franky, and handed it to him. "It's illegal to sell homemade liquor like this."

Franky stared at it as if it were a Mars rock. "I don't know anything about running a bar. After I finished the required bullshit, I didn't bother to do inventory on what I inherited from Raphael."

Dozer grabbed the jar from me. "Do you have more of these?"

"That was it. I figured it was a novelty thing like them wax candies you chew to get the liquid inside."

Dozer grimaced. "Did you swallow the wax?"

Franky shrugged. "Why not? It's food safe."

He adjusted his crutches. They swished against his navy-blue windbreaker. The top of his orthopedic sandal rested over the bottom of a paint leg. He was wearing a pair of grey slacks.

I retorted. "That wax is a few shades safer than lead paint."

"Hey. You're the one who ate those chips."

Dozer raised his voice, "Back to the topic."

Franky groaned. "When Raphael owned the joint, there were random liquors added to his supply. Most places have shrinkage. He had the opposite issue. Every weekend he'd have extra. Those sales are better than the watered-down beer."

There was a knock at the back door.

Car headlights poured over the stocky frame of an exhausted Rick Olsen dressed in tattered jeans and a winter coat. His distinctive strong baritone voice was weakened to a fragile tenor as he choked out, "Francis Calderone"

"You ratted me out to my landlord?" Franky was ramrod straight. His facial features were lost in the bar's dimness. That made it difficult to tell if he was being playful when he confronted Dozer. "I thought we were family."

CHAPTER 36

At a quarter to ten the rideshare driver dumped me off at my driveway. Winter's gentle grip on fall was a warm welcome to the thirty-eight-minute ride in a mango-scented sauna. I handed the gruff man a five dollar tip and wished him luck on his surgery. My ride away from Dozer and Franky's heated discussion about boundaries would've been pleasurable if the driver hadn't droned on about his transformation from human to lizard.

If I had used Cheryl's van, I'd have forced Dozer to ride shotgun in my cousin's truck. Knowing Franky, he piecemealed Betty back together via junk yard parts and elbow grease.

"If it were Dozer, he'd have used duct tape on the carburetor," I told Franky's house key as I slid it out of my pocket.

A therapist was going to make a fortune off of me. During my ride home, my cell phone had dinged. Unable to slip my hands in the jeans pocket without getting the attention of my driver, I chose to wait until I was home.

I checked my messages. Pickles let me know he dropped off the paperwork free of charge. I flipped my phone shut and tossed it on the table where it slid off the bag of candy onto the Guilderland Library photo.

The photo bombing, nine-year-old Cory Jackson, Jr, stared at me. That's when I knew I had the perfect novel opening. I'd make the world forget the phrase "It was a dark and stormy night" and immortalize "Police scoured a dense forest in search of Arny, a taxidermic armadillo."

Next paragraph I'd explain how Cory Jr. destroyed Franky's ambition to make it big as a flea circus ring master. Followed by my father closing the animal art business to protect my cousin and his ludicrous dream. Score one for Dad.

Most sane humans use an insect bomb to remove pests— then again, this is my family we're talking about. Sane isn't in the cards for us Morgans; a fact I had finally accepted.

Dozer was correct: I'd make a mint on a semi-autobiographical story about how Cory Jr. was a real-life hemorrhoid to our eccentric pedigree.

My brain was piecing together the novel faster than I was able to write. I needed a laptop that didn't freeze every five minutes and a printer that didn't sound like it was an active woodchipper.

I dug into my messenger bag and pulled out the wad of cash left from my mom's hidden stash. Two hundred and sixty dollars remained. Enough to buy a low-end refurbished laptop. Not enough to get a printer as well. I upturned my bag, dumping the contents on the table in search of my tip money. Lip gloss, dictionary, pocketknife, beer caps, crumpled bills, a game token, and a quarter.

Another $32.25 was added to my spending money. I was feeling rich already. It was time to make a name for myself.

The opening paragraph was the main thing I fixated on while I dried off after my shower. I shimmied my way into one of Mom's long-sleeved, white sweaters. It landed below my muffin top.

My hair was in a ponytail when I glanced at the alarm clock, a few minutes shy of noon. It was the magic lunch hour traffic, which is worse than what happened to Cinderella when the clock hit midnight. Instead of a carriage turning into a pumpkin, peaceful Carman Road was transformed into a death-defying, real-life video game.

Crossing that road to catch a bus was the motivation I needed to move fast. I raced to the kitchen table and crammed everything back into my messenger bag, set the house alarm, and hurried out the door where I was greeted by a loud, banging sound.

Next door Cheryl slammed her fist against the front door of her house. "Let me in!"

Literary gems like this don't present themselves everyday. I waded through the sea of painted-plaster lawn ornaments onto the paved driveway and up to Cheryl.

"Grandma!" She jiggled the door handle. "This is *not* funny!"

From the other side of the door, Mrs. Sanchez cackled.

"Are you okay?" I rubbed my arms to warm myself. There wasn't time for me to run home and grab another layer. This meeting had to be quick for me to stay on schedule.

"Talia." Cheryl's appearance indicated she had just rolled out of bed and her breath carried the scent of French vanilla coffee. Her bathrobe swayed to reveal her cotton-candy pink flannel pajamas. One hand held a newspaper in a blue plastic bag while the other ran through tussled dark hair.

"Is this a game?" I asked.

"Once a week we go through this."

"Have you tried hiding a key?"

"I don't know how she finds them. I wait until she's asleep to hide it. The last one remained in that for a month." She pointed to a plastic rock.

"Where else have you hidden them?"

Cheryl pointed to a loose brick under the window. "That's one place, behind the shutters, in a soup can under a potted plant, under the door mat, and even under baby Jesus."

She jabbed a thumb toward the Nativity set. Each masked statue was bundled in a wool blanket. I remembered the camera Mrs. Sanchez hid in zombie gnome and crouched to inspect the statue of Saint Francis of Assisi. The undesirable clerical cut that resembled male-patterned baldness circled his tilted head. His eyes were painted brown to match his simple robe. A blue bird rested on his shoulder while a bunny rabbit sat at his bare feet.

"Are you okay?" Cheryl asked.

"Searching for a security camera."

I glanced down the driveway to see a white Guilderland police cruiser pull in. It stopped several feet from us. Officers Anotelli and Yarwood stepped out. I waved to both men.

"Any word on my armadillo?"

The men remained stoic. I knew the emotionless thing is part of the job description; but if I were in law enforcement and had to investigate a stolen, dead, hard-shell rodent, I'd be on the hunt for a new career.

Cheryl used her slipper-clad foot to nudge a lawn gnome into the skeletal rhododendrons. "What was that about putting my grandmother in an elderly home?"

Mrs. Sanchez shouted from the other side of the door. "Over my dead body!"

Anotelli joined Cheryl on the porch. Since three's a crowd, I stepped backward, tripped on a plastic pig, and bashed into a lucky cat statue. It smashed into pieces on the asphalt. I hoped that wasn't the equivalent of breaking a mirror.

Yarwood glanced down while my gaze was fixed on an unnatural gap in the horizontal beige metal blinds. The gap widened. A figure stood in shadows, careful to avoid detection. Mrs. Sanchez had to have been a hide-n-seek champion as a child. Cheryl checked her breath at the base of the steps behind Anotelli.

He spoke in a commanding voice, "Ma'am, I need you to open this door."

"Not it!" Mrs. Sanchez yelled.

Inside lights shut off. Blinds zipped shut. Rustling noises came from the other side.

"She's barricading herself in, again." Cheryl groaned. "The last time she did this she used the couch."

"Good luck." I was down the driveway in record time.

When I closed in on Carman Road. I glanced at the telephone pole I had hit. Propped against the base was a wooden sign: This pole owned by Talia Morgan. Guilderland's 100th resident to replace it. Power was out for a mere four hours.

I kicked the sign over as a yellow sports car whizzed by me. Some viewed speed limits as a suggestion. Flashing red lights followed. A few years earlier, it was safe to walk these roads. That luxury is a part of our past thanks to apartment complexes and pop-up developments. A rare break in traffic allowed me to cross to the street. I was at the bus stop less than five minutes when a burgundy pick-up truck pulled up next to me. The passenger window opened.

"Stop dillydallying and get in!" Mrs. Sanchez shouted.

I pretended not to hear her. I preferred to think she was locked away in the split-level ranch.

Again, I heard Mrs. Sanchez's voice, "Come on, I ain't got all day. Get in!"

The distinctive smell of bacon wafted up to me. I peered through the open window to the thinning white hair sticking out like porcupine quills.

"I'm incognito," Mrs. Sanchez gave an over-dramatic stage wink. "Come on Talia. Traffic won't wait much longer."

I glanced back at a line of cars forming behind her. Not a bus in sight. I had forgotten to check the bus schedule. I clamored into the vehicle. Once we were on Western Avenue Mrs. Sanchez threaded the one-ton pickup through traffic on two wheels.

"When I was in my twenties, I got hired as a stunt car driver for that folded movie company." When the truck was on all four again, Mrs. Sanchez patted the dashboard. "Haven't lost my touch."

To keep my stomach from revolting, I stared at one of Cheryl's burgundy wrinkled business suits, draped on Mrs. Sanchez like a child playing dress-up.

"How's my hair? We're out of hair gel, so I used lard."

Maybe Franky was correct: Aliens had been listening in, replaced a number of humans, and I was on my way to meet their leader.

"You do know that's not kosher."

"I'm Catholic." Mrs. Sanchez turned down a side street and parked on the edge of a sloped manicured lawn. She pulled a hand sanitizer wipe out of her pocket. "We've gotta clean our prints off. This thing it's hot."

That admission was impossible to ignore.

"How'd you get this?" I used the tips of two fingers to take a wipe from her and opened it.

She didn't answer. Instead, she wiped down her side of the vehicle and climbed out. I followed suit. Once we were both in front of the truck, Mrs. Sanchez spoke.

"Mr. Ramirez doesn't believe in automatic starters. He left the keys inside the truck while it warmed up."

"What is going on?" I asked.

"Follow me."

"No," I protested.

"I'll tell you on the way," Mrs. Sanchez tugged on a twine belt. "Had to use this to keep my pants from falling off when I move."

I planted my feet firm on the concrete sidewalk. I wasn't moving until I had answers.

"This here is one of those top-of-the-line materials that resembles polyester." Mrs. Sanchez ran the suede-like sleeve down the side of my cheek. "See?"

"You're avoiding the topic."

"Darn right I am. We're in a race against time and you're more concerned about this truck I borrowed."

This behavior is too familiar. I used the same tone on her that Mom had used on Franky. "When you take an object that doesn't belong to you and don't ask for permission, it's called stealing."

"The truck's unharmed and the keys inside. That's as good as returned."

Mrs. Sanchez sounded like my Aunt Edna. It dawned on me: this woman was safe and familiar to my mom. As scary as it sounded, her quirks were what helped Mom heal.

The short-lived comfort washed away as the information converged. I was, aiding and abetting an escaped elderly woman whose facilities were questionable. In my defense, it wasn't my fault. She was the one who snuck out of her home, commandeered a truck, and told me to get in. That sounded like a lame excuse used by a seasoned kidnapper. I prayed we didn't get caught.

Mrs. Sanchez's eccentric appearance gained honks from passing cars. She was going to get me killed. My death attire: a white sweater, a black bra, and faded blue jeans.

I tightened my grip on the strap of my messenger bag in an attempt to comfort myself. We were in Guilderland after all, a relatively safe area known for fewer finger flips than Albany.

Three distinctive yellow Guilderland fire trucks raced by, followed by an ambulance and a magenta Porsche whose plate read, "Pickles."

My legal savior was a certified ambulance chaser. He was going into my novel. I had to figure out how to avoid liable especially when I addressed the bullet hole.

"If I hadn't talked your mom into that dating site, she'd be alive." Mrs. Sanchez placed a frail arthritic hand on my arm. "That's why I need to make some right in this world."

I peered down at at her. She blinked. A tear trickled down her wrinkled cheek and caught on a chin hair.

This woman's intentions had been good. It was impossible for me to be mad at her when a stranger had taken advantage of my mom. I gave Mrs. Sanchez's hand a firm squeeze. "There was no way to know she had an underlining heart issue. Her death was most likely an innocent mix-up and all the rest was happenstance."

I wasn't certain who that statement was meant to comfort. In all honesty, it wasn't working on me.

"Your mom confided in me. It's not like she loved this guy. He was a means to break up the monotony. When you hit sixty, there's a lot of monotony."

I decided to tell her what I had learned. Mid-explanation my words stuck in a cloudy haze. There was more I had missed. It was a low hanging branch I wasn't able to reach, and I was distracted by a distant low hum. Dozer's words about ADHD rolled through my thoughts. "ADHD is a spectrum."

Mrs. Sanchez patted my arm. Shaking me out of my thoughts.

"Your mother's emotions were hidden deep," she said. "And I thought... Well, it doesn't matter what I thought." She paused for what seemed like hours before she spoke again. "You know, you remind me of my late daughter."

That wasn't where I had expected the conversation to go. This woman was struggling in ways I'd never understand. When she motioned for me to follow, I did.

Exhaust fumes filled the pre-wintery air as we passed idled vehicles waiting at the red light. Wisps of baby-fine hair fell against Mrs. Sanchez's forehead. We continued down the clean sidewalk for several blocks until we were next to a stopped public transit bus. I stared at the advertisement on the side.

Hector stood next to a plump balding man in a tweed suit. The man's rosy cheeks invoked images of gingerbread houses, but Hector's stern face and leather jacket screamed mug shot.

Mrs. Sanchez stared at the image. "Is that an advertisement for indigestion medications?"

I stood back to read the large letters.

"Men's Clothing." I pointed to Hector. "That's Dozer's son. They have acting and modeling connections. I'm guessing he needed cash quick."

"That man of yours has good genes and Hector reminds me a little of my late husband. Did you know I met my husband during harvest time?" She giggled. "We were pulling gourds that day. I threw a bad one at a troublemaker. Instead, I hit Carlos in his chest. My aim's never been good."

That was a bit more information than I needed to know.

"We're a quarter mile away from a computer store." I guided Mrs. Sanchez away from the bus. We hustled to the corner. I was knocked backwards by a kid on a skateboard.

I raised a fist in the air. "Sidewalks are for walking!"

The kid flipped me the bird as he sped toward a distant cloud of black smoke.

"These kids today want to be the next Internet sensation." Mrs. Sanchez rocked back on her heels. "In my day, we were content minding our own business. You know, my husband's sister immigrated to this area around forty years ago. She was pregnant at the time and the baby's father was stuck in Mexico. It's a shame. She lost the baby in her third trimester. It would've been nice for my daughter to have a cousin her age like you and Franky."

"Oh God. I'm old enough to be a grandmother!"

"Yup. My daughter was seventeen when she had Cheryl. Died a few months later of a drug overdose."

Her story choked me up.

"I think the safety pins won't hold my cuffs up much longer." She held up a foot. Varying-sized safety pins held a section of material ankle-high above a pair of thick soled brown medical shoes. She pointed up at the street sign. "That leads to Ezekiel's house! Come on, your mom told me the address."

She motioned for me to follow.

I protested, "We don't have any evidence that connects him to anything and if he was involved in my mom's death, there's nothing stopping him from killing us."

"We're just looking."

A chill, that had nothing to do with the weather, ran the length of me. Hector hadn't mentioned Ezekiel owning property in Guilderland. I was correct: there were two Ezekiels.

The prospect of losing my mom's friend drove me to go against my better judgment. I hurried to catch up.

Mrs. Sanchez was in the lead. "Fourteen of my twenty-seven trail cams caught Ezekiel driving the van the night your house was broken into. I tried to follow him. By the time, I rolled the emergency ladder out the window they were gone. Turns out, Cheryl saw the lights, too, and called the cops. She spoils all my fun."

I did a face palm. This elderly woman found entertainment in sneaking out of windows and chasing criminals. I was thankful Cheryl attempted to keep her grounded.

"Why didn't you tell me?" I asked.

"And risk you telling my granddaughter how I escape?"

"Ezekiel wants the lost safety deposit keys."

"Did you try your dishwasher?"

I knew I'd regret asking, "Why would I put them there?"

"That's where I found my dentures the last time I lost them."

"I can assure you they aren't in any appliance."

"Vacuum cleaner? Wait, you have a central-vac system." Mrs. Sanchez pulled herself up to full height. Her spiked hair slashed my vision. "You know, a man as hot as Ezikiel has to have a long list of victims in his wake."

"You need glasses. That man is not hot."

"He didn't make you swoon?"

I was correct, there were two Ezekiels identity. "The guy who got mom's insurance money is about my height and a bad combover."

"That's not Ezekiel. He stands about six feet tall, dark hair and resembles one of those guys you see on the cover of a romance novel. Except his complexion screams, 'I overuse a tanning bed.'"

CHAPTER 37

The few remaining safety pins held one of Mrs. Sanchez's pants cuffs in place. The darkened edges of the other cuff dragged on the asphalt. Lard held a few spikes up as she shuffled along whistling like a cockatoo.

She fist pumped the air. "Toot toot!"

We wound around post-Korean War, cookie-cutter homes. Each one sat behind a yard fit for *Leave it to Beaver*. The two distinguishing features of each were the house color and lawn ornaments. These all reflected the owner's personalities. One yard had a silhouette of Darth Vader watering a plastic butterfly garden.

I pulled my flip phone out of my jeans' back pocket and pressed the side button. The minuscule screen flashed blue. No way of knowing how long we had wandered.

"Talia," Mrs. Sanchez kicked a rock off the road. "Even I have a smartphone. Granted mine is for emergencies."

I had a severe detainment for technology. Even worse, I hated spending money. It was 2021 and I didn't have a social media account. If it were up to me, I'd be living on a hundred-acre farm. My nearest neighbors would be livestock.

My cell phone buzzed. Caller ID was shot. I answered, "Talia speaking."

"Cops are at your home searching for you and—" Dozer was cut off by Mrs. Sanchez shouting.

"Zombie flamingos."

She pointed to an asymmetrical, white lattice archway where a pink flamingo lawn ornament stood.

"I'll let Cheryl know…" The phone crackled, then went silent.

The screen resembled a 1980s malfunctioning video game. I flipped it shut shoved it into my messenger bag.

"We're heading home."

"Why? We're almost to Ezekiel's house."

"Your granddaughter's worried and my phone's dead. Not the kind of deceased that can be revived by a charge. It's the kind that involves a clergy member."

Mrs. Sanchez's face flashed horror.

A sharp pain hit my neck. A zing permeated my body and all went black.

CHAPTER 38

Surrounded by darkness, I tried to move out of the fetal position. A hard object pressed against my back while a duffle bag that reeked of day-old gym socks pressed against my face.

An intermittent rattling overshadowed the buzz of tires on asphalt. Muffled voices carried through the solid carpeted barrier.

"Using a taser on a defenseless woman, and cramming her in the trunk of a car is illegal," the feisty Mrs. Sanchez argued. "Get your hands off me! Help! Elder abuse! Help!"

The car bounced. I was slammed against the lid of the trunk and crashed down on to the dummy tire. At least I knew where we were on Western Avenue.

Mrs. Sanchez's voice came to me again. "Didn't your mother teach you that it's rude to rummage through a woman's purse."

Several minutes later, the car lurched to a stop. The trunk popped opened. Sudden sunlight blinded me. I reached up to block it out. Strong hands yanked me upward by my wrist.

When my vision adjusted, I had a full view of our kidnapper. Locks of dyed brown hair flanked surgically-created, high cheek bones and unrealistic thick lips that looked like they had been stung by a bee. His fake tan screamed, "My trips to the beach happen via green screen."

His mouth barely moved when he said, "Peekaboo."

Even as a child, I found that game revolting. I struggled against his grip. "Screw you!"

Next to me, Mrs. Sanchez grunted. She wiggled out of another man's grasp. "Cheap sweatsuits and knockoff watches are cliched."

She kicked at him and got air.

"Remember me?" The man in front of me asked.

I soaked in every purchased detail. "You're the felon who broke into Dozer's house."

"Duh. You always thought you were better than me." The man adjusted his striped silk tie. "Your stupid cousin's French Revolution reenactment is nothing compared to what I'm going to do to you."

Horror bubbled up inside. I needed to escape. I tried to wiggle my arm free. "Let me go, Cory Jackson, Jr."

"Scumbag!" Mrs. Sanchez spat at him.

Cory Jr. focused on her. "You think you're any better?"

She bought me a few precious seconds. Terrified, I glanced around for an escape route. The condemned X rested in the center of the white garage door. Cracks marred the slender asphalt driveway that trailed down to a desolate road. An unkept postage stamp-sized front lawn sat at the edge of thick woods. That described several developments in the Town of Guilderland.

I was shaken back to reality by Cory Jr. His near bone breaking grip made me wince.

His voice a low rumble in quiet. "My partner transposed the house numbers and I wound up in the house belonging to the man I waited decades to kill. Instead, Stuart had enough time to grab his gun and chase us. We hopped fences and ran through yards to shake him. If he hadn't shot our guard dog, no one would've known we had been squatting."

Mrs. Sanchez went dead weight. The thick-necked man in maroon sweatsuit bent down to pick her up. She kicked him in the balls. His face matched his attire. He crumpled to the ground.

"Serves you right!" Mrs. Sanchez reached for his sidearm.

A third man man drew his gun and pointed it at my neighbor. He pulled the hammer back. "One more word and I'll kill you."

"You destroyed my life," the crazed man said as he shook me.

I pushed back. "What are you talking about?"

He pulled me close. "Your friend tackled me."

"Still not helping." I didn't want to tell him that Dozer protected me by tackling several men when I was in college. They were inappropriate and three of them served time for assault. "Be a more specific."

He leaned dangerously close. His breath reminded me of fruit snacks. I stared at a set of shaking black saucers edged by a thin line of hazel in a sea of pink.

"I spent eighteen months in jail because of you."

This doped-up mess had a vendetta against us for his own misdeeds. My mind went back to the night Dozer and I met. The man he tackled had plead guilty to avoid a lengthy trial. That man's name was named Ezekiel Knepp.

The lunatic wrapped duct tape around my wrists destroying several options, including throat punches. "You're pathetic."

He dragged me to the backyard. My sneakers went from uneven asphalt to matted down grass. A squirrel chittered from the edge of the black water inside a large hot tub.

"If we kiss a squirrel, will it become a prince?" Mrs. Sanchez sounded optimistic as if she believed it was a possibility. "That'd be great! Mine needs to be able to cook. I always burn the rice."

"Move!" Cory Jr. yanked me forward.

A cold trickle rushed through me. I eyeballed the area for a weapon. The quarter-acre of dried grass was enclosed by a moss covered planked privacy fence. A worn path led to a fenced in area where a Snoopy-inspired dog house sat. Across the top, a shaky hand had scrawled the word "Killer."

Wind whipped the odor of bacon from Mrs. Sanchez's hair. She hesitated at the wooden steps. The shorter henchman pressed his gun into her back.

"It's these orthopedic shoes." Mrs. Sanchez gripped a metal railing. "Getting old ain't easy."

She stepped onto the narrow porch. Rotted wood held on to a ripped screen — its cross bar rested on the porch. A loose latch was attached to the side of the house and kept the screen door in place. Mrs. Sanchez's exaggerated hunched back bobbed up as she stepped through the open door on to linoleum.

I was a heartbeat behind. Cory Jr. pressed a hard object into my lower back.

"Keep moving." His softly spoken words a near threatening whisper had the opposite effect. I wanted to stand my ground. He shoved me. "I said move!"

Mrs. Sanchez led the way through an unkept, 1960s kitchen. Aged, crusted food caked the edges of pots. An unlit sterno sat under a frying pan containing what appeared to be dried up beans. It was hard to tell through the overpowering stench of mildew.

She whistled. I followed her gaze to a black spot on the stucco ceiling. The 1980s had a hand in this design as did a bad water leak.

A door creaked shut behind us, followed by a click. We were locked in by a door my attic raccoons could easily knock down. Indents on thick, dark, plush, carpet remained vestiges of long-gone living room furniture. Cream-colored squares dotted beige walls, an indication that photos had once hung there and the previous owners had been long-time smokers. Rays of hopeful light broke through slender slits between newspapers on the front picture window. Green camping lanterns lined the floor, one of them lit up a taxidermized armadillo.

I shouted, "Arny! You're okay!"

I was jerked sideways. Mrs. Sanchez hissed. My messenger bag tossed aside. I was knocked down. The rug squished, my knees ached. I stared at a crack that ran across the ceiling. An argument erupted between the three men in another language.

Mrs. Sanchez shouted a retort in Spanish. The room went silent.

The larger henchman bent in half to face Mrs. Sanchez. "You speak Spanish."

"Of course, you moron. I'm from Puerto Rico. Whoever taught you two Spanish should be shot. You suck at conjugations and that guy picked up your bad habits."

The shortest of the three men pointed to himself. "Portugues is my native language."

Cory Jr. placed the tip of his gun to Mrs. Sanchez's temple. To my surprise she held an expression that screamed "pissed off mother bear." I was impressed. If it were me on the receiving end, I'd have soiled my pants.

Cory Jr. lowered his voice. "I scored ninety on my Spanish Regents."

"Liar." Mrs. Sanchez huffed. "I am not a potato and you used the masculine when I clearly denote the feminine. Now, be a good boy and release us."

She held up her bound hands.

"Enough!" Cory Jr. shouted.

I hoped the elderly woman next to me was buying time. If she wasn't, we were going to be killed.

The overpriced man leaned over me. "Where is the deed?"

"What deed?"

"Don't play dumb. You got the keys to the safety deposit box, so you've got the deed to the company."

"No. I don't." I was even more confused. "If you're referring to my father's company, it sold years ago."

"No." Cory Jr. pinched the bridge of his nose. "Your mother sold the company itself. The building, the land, and the farmhouse are in her name. The Yoders maintain everything in lieu of rent. That's two hundred acres of prime land waiting to be developed."

"You stole Arny for a deed?"

"Arny?" Cory Jr. asked.

"The stuffed armadillo next to the lantern, his name is Arny."

"They are daft." Mrs. Sanchez tsked.

The men exchanged glances that were best described as a child caught sneaking in the fridge foraging for a midnight snack.

The man in the maroon jumpsuit shifted his stance. "Who keeps a creepy thing like that on display?"

"Arny's not creepy. He holds Christmas stockings." There I was, facing possible death, arguing over a dead decorative animal.

"You dress it up in an Elf costume, don't you?"

I nodded.

"Enough!" Cory Jr. shouted. "It took my father years to find your grandmother's illegitimate daughter and gain her trust in order for us to earn back what is ours. Since my father is dead, I get everything."

"There's nothing that's yours." I tried to make myself appear menacing.

"It's all mine." Cory Jr. adjusted his suit jacket. "That woman had learned of her birth mother when she was doing that Amish running around thing. She even tried to find her mom. That's how she wound up meeting that Olaf guy. Their son, is Ezekiel."

My mind played a chorus of *I'm My Own Grandpa*.

The psychopath was on a roll. "Stealing her son's identity was cakewalk. Ezekiel is as easy to manipulate as his mother."

This unhinged piece of excrement was proud of screwing over pacifists. Hell has a special place for this guy.

"None of them saw it coming and neither did your mother."

I shouted, "Beowulf would eat you!"

Cory Jr. stared at me, unblinking. "What?"

Mrs. Sanchez said, "I think the jolt you gave Taila scrambled her brains."

"Never mind." Cory Jr. waved his gun. "Your dad backed out of the business deal he and my dad signed. My family lost everything. That's why I used Ezekiel's identity. He had a clean record, it made it easier earn people's trust. Those women begged me to take their homes, diamonds, cars…"

He pointed to his lips. "These were free from that hairdresser in Stuart's building. She's a former plastic surgeon. While I was there, I switched out her plants' water for something a bit more combustible. No one know that I'd start that fire."

Mrs. Sanchez coughed into her hand. "Loser."

Cory Jr. ignored her. "Once I have the cart business, I will combine all of what I've acquired into a well-oiled, self-sustaining machine, leave car warrantee sales behind me, and retire to a tropical island."

Mrs. Sanchez gave an overexaggerated eyeroll. "What a lousy plan. You'd do better playing the lottery."

"We're here, aren't we?" Cory Jr. raised his arms indicating our drab holding area. Behind him was a furnished dining room. To his right was another door. "Killing your mom was easy."

The room became a pinprick of color. This man admitted to murdering my mother.

"Out of all the women I murdered," Cory Jr. leaned in. "Your mother was the the biggest challenge. Untrusting, and closed off. If it weren't for that Lauffenburger woman and her Save the Pine Bush movie project poking around for interviews, your mom would've been gone months ago."

The tall muscular guy held out a crinkling bag. "Want some?"

Cory Jr. grabbed a handful. "All those others were just a warmup. It was fun posing as your cousin, until that crime app group got involved." He devoured the food.

Mrs. Sanchez whispered to me, "Keep him talking." She stuck out her chest.

Taking her cue, I announced, "Mrs. Sanchez is having a heart attack."

"Am not."

"She has dementia."

"Ignore Talia." Mrs. Sanchez leaned forward. "I was wondering what the Lauffenburger woman's project was about. And where are we located? This is a nice boarded up house. Not many of them in Guilderland."

Cory Jr. crouched in front of us. Beads of sweat had gathered on his wrinkle-free brow. "She and her activist friends are trying to stop another developer from eliminating more of the Pine Bush. They want to save this ugly dime-sized butterfly and return this town to its former glory."

Mrs. Sanchez piped up, "You say 'activists' that like it's a swear word."

Cory Jr. ignored her. He was on a roll. "In order to get what was mine, I used Ezekiel Knepp's identity. That computer savvy wife of his found his birth family. I had been smart though. In case he showed up I made sure to convince your mother that I was a former Amish friend of her cousin who happened to have the same name. Not a complete lie. When you mother started questioning me about the real Ezekiel, I was forced to slip a little something extra into her coffee and instant heart attack."

I wanted to leap off the floor and pummel this guy

"You're insane!" I shouted.

"Your opinion doesn't matter."

Cory Jr. pulled a handkerchief out of his pocket and wiped at his brow. The taller henchman used the sleeve of his sweatshirt to do the same.

"I lost the company and the life insurance money." Cory Jr. unbuttoned the top of his white dress shirt.

The men were having some sort of medical issue. I had to take Mrs. Sanchez's lead. Our chances of living increased if we kept this guy talking. "How'd you figure out who my uncle was?"

"You know *Six Degrees of Kevin Bacon* has nothing on this area and your Aunt Edna loves to talk."

"Aunt Edna's superpower is misinformation."

"No." Cory Jr. put the gun to my forehead and pulled back the gun's hammer. "That's a lie."

Mrs. Sanchez glared at him. "Believe it, numbskull."

Cory Jr. pulled the trigger. The gun clicked. He shook it. Tried again. Nothing. He held it out to the smaller henchman. "You got me a broken gun."

The shortest henchman grabbed the gun and stared down the silencer's barrel. "I swear it's good."

I recognized the voice of the guy holding the gun. He was one of the men who broke into my home. I looked down at their sneakers. The taller man was wearing knock off brand high-top sneakers--the guy who answered his cell phone.

"We can take 'em." Mrs. Sanchez leaned in and whispered. "Safety's on."

The men were full-grown toddlers using the gun to play Hot Potato. One of them, hit the trigger. A sound that reminded me of fire erupting in a gas grill startled the men.

Mrs. Sanchez giggled. "They hit something."

She pointed to a squirrel on the floor. A hole was in the center mass of his lederhosen.

Cory Jr. picked up Franky's taxidermy friend and tossed him into a garbage bin. His tiny plastic knockwurst bounced onto the floor.

"We broke into your cousin's house thinking you'd have passed the key to him. That squirrel was the right size to hold it."

I used one of my newly learned Yiddish insults on him.

Through clenched teeth Cory Jr. spoke each syllable with menace. "Speak English."

Mrs. Sanchez released a string of Spanish words then followed up in English, "It's not our fault you're not as educated as us."

Score one for Cheryl's grandma.

Cory Jr. led the other two guys into the side room. He stood next to the door while the others shuffled past. "My condolences on the loss of your uncle. I heard he drowned in a duck pond. All I had to do was convince Olaf I'd give him half of the inheritance and he was mine to control. Once I have the deed, I'm set for life."

He entered the side room and closed the door behind him. I needed to stay calm and formulate a plan before we were killed. All I had for possible weapons were batter operated lanterns and the contents of my messenger bag that were strewn across the rug.

"Why are the contents of my bag on the floor?"

"The thick neck T-rex man dumped it." Mrs. Sanchez set her restraints on the dingy rug. "When we get home, I'm adding these guys to that stupid criminal website."

"How did you get free?"

"I flexed my muscles when they taped over the jacket. It gave me wiggle room. The ones on your ankles don't want to move."

"Get the knife in my messenger bag."

Mrs. Sanchez riffled through the pile. "Your knife isn't in there. Neither are your keys." She used nail clippers to cut the tape. "How were you planning on getting back into your home?"

I nearly shouted my epiphany, "The safety deposit keys are on my keyring in the junkyard!"

"When you were in the trunk, they said they planned on killing Dozer. I told them he'd take them all down."

A golden horizontal light shone out from under the closed hollow door. Hushed voices argued. Their sound reminded me of a youth orchestra duet. One man's screech was another child's violin bow, scraping across taut strings.

I ripped the tape off and was on my feet when Cory Jr. yelled, "After we kill them, we'll search her home for that deed."

A lantern flickered. I tried the front door. It didn't budge. Several nails had been wedged into the gap between the door and the jam. I tugged at one of the nails. It didn't move.

Incoherent shouts intensified. Cory Jr. yelled, "Keep your voice down. The neighbors might hear you."

I pushed Mrs. Sanchez toward the kitchen. "That way."

The side room door flung open. The shorter henchman rushed out. My heart pounded as he rushed past groaning in pain. Another door slammed shut.

Mrs. Sanchez whispered to me. "If he hadn't eaten that bag of candy so fast, he'd be in better shape."

"Did they eat all of the candy?"

"Yup." She pointed to the empty cellophane bag.

In a moment of shocked disbelief, I yelled, "They ate Dozer's bears?!"

Cory Jr. stepped back into the room. "Knowing they were his makes them even tastier."

His stomach gurgled loud enough we heard it from twenty feet away. He pointed his drooping gun at us. "In the room."

Mrs. Sanchez shook her head. "Yup, stupid criminals."

"No." Cory Jr. used both of his shaking hands to raise the gun.

Unimpressed, Mrs. Sanchez gave him the finger. Cory tripped over a lantern, hit my dictionary, slid for several feet, and landed on his rump.

"Run!" I shoved Mrs. Sanchez aside.

She hurried out of the room. I bolted through the kitchen door. My sneakers hit the linoleum. Pain went down my back. I landed hard on my stomach. Air left my lungs. I fought to catch my breathe. Cory Jr. grabbed my feet.

My pulse, a thunderous beat inside my ears, blocked out all noise. Pressure around my left ankle intensified. I was yanked backward. I clawed at the stained faded images of stars.

"No!" I shrieked and kicked.

A sickening crack overshadowed all sound as my foot connected. Cory Jr. yelped like an injured dog and released his grip. I scrambled to my feet. In the doorway Mrs. Sanchez held a wooden cross bar like a baseball bat.

I ducked.

She swung the piece of wood over me, lost her grip, and the weapon flew across the room. There was a clank. Mrs. Sanchez gasped and motioned for me to hurry.

"You idiots!" Cory Jr. shouted.

I launched myself out the backdoor.

Mrs. Sanchez struggled to keep her pants up as we ran around the house. She yelled, "Beans everywhere."

Swearing came from behind me. The zip of a bullet sounded by my right ear. Mrs. Sanchez vanished around the garage. I darted down the driveway.

A male voice yelled, "Freeze!"

I raised my hands in the air and began to cry. This was it. They were going to kill me. I shouted. "I'm too young to die!"

"Weee!" Mrs. Sanchez yelled.

Near-freezing water hit my face. I collapsed onto the cracked asphalt.

Mrs. Sanchez yelled, "I see why people join the Fire Department!"

"Ma'am. Hand over the hose." A gentle male voice came over the cacophony of sounds. The water stopped. I opened my eyes. A gaggle of body shields crept up the lawn. Mrs. Sanchez stood next to a Private Well sign.

Running water rushed onto the brown grass as Mrs. Sanchez dropped the hose.

"Party pooper." She reached into her oversized blouse and pulled out her cell phone. "I had 911 on speaker phone."

CHAPTER 39

Franky drove his burned rubber-scented, death trap truck a few miles below the speed limit while I sat in the passenger seat attempting to reel in my brain. The emergency room professionals had treated me for minor injuries and the police interviewed me.

"I can't believe those guys thought Mrs. Sanchez's mind shot." Franky broke the silence. "They drove in circles to confuse her, in case she somehow managed to escape and the whole time, she 911 on speaker."

"Not the frail old lady they anticipated." I clutched the borrowed sweater. "Thank your mom for lending me clean clothes. Those wet ones are going into the dumpster."

"You're getting a dumpster?"

"It's time to clean the house. Wanna help?" I asked.

"As long as you're okay with Leah's assistance."

"You know, she's perfect for you."

Franky's smile reached his eyes. He turned onto the street that led to mine. The truck's high beams washed over the darkened area revealing cars parked in driveways. Leafless bushes swayed in a breeze, and a black cat darted through evergreen hedges. As much as I wanted to follow the bedazzled collared feline, I wanted my own bed and Dozer even more.

Franky stopped at the intersection to let a coydog cross the road. "Dozer tracked down the guys involved in the stolen goods shipments. Please don't be mad."

"Why?"

"I figured since Dozer wasn't all there for you during your grieving, you'd write him off. And I don't want you to do that. He's good for you."

"We're fine." I rubbed the crook of my arm. The blood-draw cotton ball was still taped in place.

I thought back to the moans from the kidnappers as they were carted off to their hospital rooms. They had been treated for a couple fractures and dehydration from explosive diarrhea. That last part made me happy.

"Now that I've got Leah, I know what it feels like to be accepted. That made me see how important Dozer is for you. Don't screw this up."

The clock on the truck's radio read 12:47 a.m. There was more behind what my cousin was saying. I tapped my hand against the passenger window.

"Get to the point."

He crept the truck around the corner. "The insurance paid out. I'm thinking of taking Leah on a trip to Tahiti. She deserves it."

"Franky."

"Sorry."

We passed a row of well-manicured lawns. He was stalling.

I lowered my voice, "Franky, spit it out."

"The crates were part of a counterfeit scam Cory's running. Turns out, he used all the companies he acquired from the women he killed to create an elaborate scheme. Raphael was the one who figured it out and got out of the area until things cleared up. For once, I worked on the right side of the law."

"I'm proud of you."

That compliment was genuine. My sleaze ball cousin was turning his life around.

"You won't believe this." Franky spoke louder than necessary. "Pickles finished going over the original will. The farm, the land, and the building the company occupies were all left in trust to us. Your mom handled the estate and we're to inherit it all upon our signing legal documents and that insurance policy is all yours on account of it having been changed too close to your mom's death."

"I'd rather have mom."

He patted my hand. My cousin was providing comfort.

"Don't screw things up with Leah," I said.

"I don't plan on it." Franky tapped the steering wheel. "Depending on our spending habits, we're set for another twenty-plus years. That's why Aunt Gladys did the toothpick thing, to keep people from trying to get their hands on our money. All we need to do is find the deed, which must be in safety deposit number fifteen."

My aching body suddenly felt warm. It was as if my mom was hugging me. It pained me that our relationship had been strained.

"Our last conversation was an argument over the appearance of a job interviewer."

"Was he attractive?"

"He wore a leather pants, and I swear his father was Fabio."

"Leather pants to an interview." Franky whistled. "Even I don't stoop that low." The truck's headlights reflected off of Mrs.

Sanchez's tacky lawn ornaments as we turned into my driveway. "Once we find those keys we're set."

"Not quite," I said.

"Oh?"

"We still have to find Grandma Morgan's daughter who happens to be Ezekiel's mom."

"Shit." Franky slapped the steering wheel. "Excuse my language."

I was stuck on the irony. "Did you apologize for swearing?"

Franky pointed to the air freshener hanging off the rearview mirror. A small square containing Leah's face was taped to both sides.

"She's not a fan of cussing. That's why I'm quitting."

I wanted to let him know how proud I was of him. If I did, it'd to his head. "Here I thought the jewelry was the hot ticket item."

"Nah. Your mom switched out the stones to pay for your schooling. It's all worth a whole $72.35."

Dozer was on the porch waiting for me.

"He's the best thing that ever happened to you." Franky nudged me into the bitter cold.

I slammed the truck door shut. Franky pointed behind me. He mouthed the word "Go."

During the course of a month, much of what I had known had been proven to be a pile of lies. There were many questions I yearned to have answered. Even so, the most important quandaries had been laid to rest. I inched up the walkway to my new life. Dozer descended the steps. I quickened my pace and launched myself into his arms.

Into my ear, he whispered, "You smell like something my mom's Pomeranian barfed up."

"Not the romantic welcome-home party I expected."

Dozer tucked a of cluster of my hair behind an ear. "After you hung up. I kept calling until a guy answered and told me you were his. I was terrified that I'd never be able to tell you that I love you."

We were about to kiss when a male voice shouted, "About time you told her how you feel."

I spun around. Crutches at his side, Franky dressed in a 1970s leisure suit leaned against his truck's front end. Neon orange spray paint ran the length of the dented passenger side door.

Dozer shouted back, "Stay out of this!"

"I can't. Our family's a package deal!" Franky nestled his crutches under his arms. "I've been telling him since the ink was dry on his divorce papers to get off the pot and marry you."

Dozer yelled, "That wasn't a marriage proposal!"

"Better put a ring on that finger."

I faced Dozer. "Did that conversation really happen?"

The steady glow of the lamppost light rounded off his features. Flecks of grey whispered his age. Fear flashed in his dark eyes as he prepared himself to speak.

"Yes."

The rumbling muffler of the idle truck almost blocked out the faint word. His tense body relaxed as he said, "After the papers were signed, Franky wanted me to have a party. He even bought a sign that read: 'Talia, I'm Divorced. Marry me.'"

I reminded myself of how lucky I was when I brushed my lips against Dozer's.

"Yo ma," Franky's voice cut into our moment.

Dozer and I broke apart.

I shouted. "Your timing is worse than the raccoons!"

Franky had his cell phone to his ear as he stood next to his truck. "I'm there now. Get out the chart, see who won. Dozer finally told Talia he loves her and she didn't slap him!"

EPILOGUE

It felt natural to have Dozer's arm draped over me. As did his breath tickling my neck, the scent of him, and a tangled flannel sheet twisted between us.

He pulled me closer. I reached my hand over his muscular arm and squeezed as he kissed my cheek. I was a melted bowl of cookie dough ice cream on a hot summer's day and had no desire to slide out of the warm bed into a darkened room for any reason.

"Later today, we're sheet shopping," Doze kissed the top of my head.

"What do you have against flannel?"

"They're not Egyptian cotton."

Two weeks had flown by since I had confirmation that my mom had been murdered and the news station had cashed in on the video of my mother's death. Phone calls from news reporters had dwindled to a handful. Most of the time, you hear that crowds of people stalk a person in situations like mine. They lack a brazen woman like Mrs. Sanchez on their side.

I aspired to have her tenacity and spunk when I reach her age. Honestly, I didn't have the nerve to wear a pink wig to chase after news van screaming, "Demons be gone!"

Dozer's weight lifted as he shifted to sit on his side of the bed. He flipped the nightstand light on and faced me. There was a long pause. It was as if the silence spoke for us.

"Death is the most difficult part of life and you've had to navigate murder, kidnapping, moving into a new home, and Franky's broken foot."

"Franky's foot was the worst."

The doorbell rang again. A series of rapid knocks at the door followed.

Dozer pulled away, clicked the light on, and slid into his boxers. "It's 6:02 a.m. Someone had better be dead." He held up his pistol. "I might have to amend that statement."

Annoyed, I slid out from the sheets and pulled on my bathrobe. "I'll grab a shovel."

Gun held at the ready, Dozer crouch-walked to the entrance while I shuffled behind him. He used the barrel of the gun to pull back the window curtain.

"At this hour?"

Dozer groaned as he punched the alarm system key code. The disembodied voice announced that the alarm had been disarmed.

Dozer flung the door open.

"I wasn't expecting to see your hotty." Mrs. Sanchez winked.

He asked me, "Does the no shooting rule still apply?"

Mrs. Sanchez held up my keys. "I got 'em for ya."

Flabbergasted, I slid between the two and pulled the keys from her hand. "How did you get them?"

She leaned in and whispered, "I borrowed my granddaughter's van and snuck into the junkyard to get them." She straightened herself up. "It wasn't easy on account of my arthritis, but I knew I had to get those for you." She gave Dozer a full body scan. "If anyone asks about the Greulich's cow, it's not at my place."

She scurried off.

"I'll pretend I didn't hear that part," I said.

"Me, too." Dozer shut the door.

I flipped through the keys. When I came across two, I didn't recognize I held them up. "Got 'em."

Dozer pulled me close. "Ready to solve the mystery?"

"Yes." I wrapped my arms around his neck and kissed him.

ABOUT THE AUTHOR

Stacie Ann Leininger is on multiple spectrums including Autism and ADHD. She also has PTSD and Dyslexia. She has been writing since childhood. Her first published piece appeared in a magazine when she was nine. In 2002, she earned a B.A. in English from the College of St. Rose where she was introduced to several members of the International Women's Writing Guild (IWWG).

Stacie has attended IWWG's Upstate New York conferences where she met and studied under brilliant award-winning writers. Stacie has won several literary awards, through the decades, including Iliad Press Presidential Award for Literary Excellence, awarded when she was seventeen.

Most of Stacie's works have been under pseudonyms. These include, but are not limited to, poems, flash fiction, and short stories.

In 2019, she was published in *Dark Yonder: Tales & Tabs,* a crime anthology. In 2021, she released Book 1 in her all-ages series *Gleothane* titled *Gleothane: A Call for Warriors* under her pseudonym Cora B. Edwin. In 2022, she released *To Overcome is to Be: A Collection of Poems Written Between Ages 13 and 22,* followed by *They Labeled Me Crazy: A Collection of Poems Written Between Ages 15 and 23,* and *Guilderland Crime App.* All of these works are available on Amazon.

Currently, Stacie is working on several pieces that include the world of Gleothane, urban fantasy, and poetry books. Above all, she desires to use her literary talents to be an inspiration to others who have invisible disabilities and struggle with mental health issues.

You can follow her on Instagram: Stacie_Ann_Leininger.

Made in the USA
Middletown, DE
24 February 2024